Before I Burn

GAUTE HEIVOLL

Before I Burn

Translated by Don Bartlett

Atlantic Books
LONDON

First published with the title *Før jeg brenner ned* in 2010 by Tiden Norsk Forlag, Oslo.
First published in Great Britain in 2013 by Atlantic Books, an imprint of Atlantic Books Ltd.

This translation has been published with the financial support of NORLA.

9 8 7 6 5 4 3 2 1

A CIP catalogue record for this book is available from the British Library.

Trade Paperback ISBN: 978 085789 216 4
E-book ISBN: 978 085789 218 8

Set in 11.75/15pt Minion
Designed by Nicky Barneby @ Barneby Ltd
Printed in Great Britain by the MPG Books Group

Atlantic Books
An Imprint of Atlantic Books Ltd
Ormond House
26–27 Boswell Street
London
WC1N 3JZ

www.atlantic-books.co.uk

Most things are so meaningless.
But then something unparalleled occurs,
which rises in the sky
like a flaming cloud

and consumes everything.
Then everything is changed
and you yourself are changed
and what you thought had value before
has no longer any value for you at all.
And you walk through the ash of everything
And you yourself are ash.

PÄR LAGERKVIST (1953)

A STORY CAME UP IN CONVERSATION while I was visiting Alfred. At first I didn't consider that it had anything to do with the fires. I hadn't heard this story before, it is absolutely heart-rending, though at the same time full of, well, what could you call it?

Love?

It happened a little over a hundred years ago in the region where I was born and bred. A man committed suicide by blowing himself up. He was thirty-five years old. He used dynamite. Afterwards, it was said, his mother went around gathering the fragments in her apron. A few days later, after a brief ceremony, his remains were laid in grave number 35. According to the cemetery records, under 'Other Remarks' was added *insane.*

I don't know if this story is true. However, it is something you can understand. If you sit down and reflect, you do slowly understand. Ultimately, it is clear it was the only right thing to do. It is what you do. You have no choice. You walk around gathering all the fragments in your apron.

1

I.

A FEW MINUTES PAST MIDNIGHT on the morning of Monday, 5 June 1978, Johanna Vatneli switched off the kitchen light and carefully closed the door. She took the four steps through the cold hall, opened the door to the bedroom a fraction, causing a strip of light to fall across the grey woollen rug they had spread over the bed, even though it was summer. Inside, in the darkness, Olav, her husband, lay asleep. She stood for some seconds on the threshold listening to his heavy breathing, then went into the small bathroom, where she let the tap run quietly, as she always did. She stood bent over, washing her face, for a long time. It was cold in there; she was standing barefoot on the rag mat and could feel the hard floor beneath her feet. For a moment she looked herself in the eye. This wasn't something she usually did. She leaned forwards and stared into the black pupils. Then she tidied her hair and drank a glass of water from the tap. Finally, she changed her knickers. They were covered in blood. She folded them and put them in a bowl of water to soak overnight. She pulled a nightie over her head, and at that moment, in her abdomen, she felt a stabbing pain, the one that was always there but had worsened recently, particularly if she stretched or lifted something heavy. It was like a knife.

Before switching off the light she removed her teeth and dropped them with a plop into the glass of water on the vanity shelf under the mirror, beside Olav's.

Then she heard a car.

It was dark in the living room, but the windows, strangely shiny and black, gleamed as though from a dim light outside in the garden. She walked to the window and peered out. The moon had risen above the treetops to the south, she saw the cherry tree, which was still in blossom, and had it not been for the mist she would have been able to see right down to Lake Livannet in the west.

A car with no lights on drove past the house and continued at a slow pace along the road towards the collection of homesteads known as Mæsel. The car was black, or perhaps red; she couldn't tell. Not moving at any great speed, it finally rounded the bend and was gone. She stood by the window waiting for one, two, perhaps three minutes. Then she went into the bedroom.

'Olav,' she whispered. 'Olav.'

No answer. He was in his usual deep sleep. She hurried back into the living room, knocked into the chair arm, hurting her thigh, and reached the window in time to see the dark car returning. It was coming out of the bend, and continued slowly past the living room wall. It must have turned around by the Knutsens' house, but no one was living there, they had travelled back to town the night before, she had seen them leaving herself. Outside, she heard the crunch of tyres. The low purr of the engine. The sound of a radio. Then the car ground to a halt. She heard a door open, then silence. Her heart was in her mouth. She went back into the bedroom, put on the light and shook her husband. This time he woke, but he didn't get up until they both heard a loud bang and a tinkle of breaking glass from the kitchen.

As soon as she entered the hall she smelt the pervasive stench of petrol. She yanked open the kitchen door and was met by a wall of flames. The whole room was ablaze. It must have taken a matter of seconds. The floor, the walls, the ceiling; the flames were licking upwards and wailing like a large, wounded animal. She stood in the doorway paralysed with shock. Deep within the wails she recognised – even though she had never heard it before – the sound of glass cracking. She lingered there until the heat became too intense. It was as though her face was being detached, dragged down from her forehead and over her eyes; her cheeks, her nose and mouth.

That was when she saw him. She caught no more than a glimpse lasting two or three seconds. He was a black shadow outside the window, on the other side of the sea of flames. He was rooted to the spot. As she was. Then he tore himself away and was gone.

The hall was already filled with smoke; it seeped through the wall from the kitchen and lay under the ceiling like thick fog. She groped her way to the telephone, lifted the receiver and dialled Ingemann's number at Skinnsnes, the number, after the events of recent days, she had written in black felt pen on a notelet. As her finger turned the dial she considered what to say. *This is Johanna Vatneli. Our house is on fire.*

The telephone was dead.

At that moment the electricity short-circuited, there was an explosion in the fuse box, sparks flew from the socket by the mirror, the light went out and everything went black. She grabbed Olav's hand, and they had to fumble their way across the floor until they reached the front door. The cool night air was sucked in at once, and in no time at all the fire had a better grip; they heard several dull thuds and then a roar as the flames broke through the ceiling into the upper storey and were soon licking at the inside of the windows.

In my mind's eye, I have seen this fire so many times. It was as if the flames had been waiting for this moment, for this night, for these minutes. They wanted to burst into the darkness, stretch skywards, illuminate, be free. And then they really *were* free. Several panes cracked at once, glass tinkled and the flames were unleashed, they reached outwards and upwards, into the air, and immediately bedecked the garden in an unreal, yellow light. No one has been in a position to describe the fire to me because no one was there apart from Olav and Johanna, but I have seen everything in my head. I have seen the nearest trees edging even nearer in this light, seeming to collect and glide silently and imperceptibly to the centre of the garden. I have seen Johanna dragging Olav down the five steps, into the long grass, beneath the old cherry tree that seemed cast in stone, with thick grey moss up the trunk, through the garden and out onto the road where she considered them safe. There they stood staring at the house they had occupied since 1950. They didn't say a word, there was nothing to say. After perhaps a minute she tore herself away while Olav remained where he was, dressed only in a nightshirt. In the flickering light he resembled a small child. His jaw hung open and his lips moved as though struggling to form a word that did not exist. Johanna dashed back through the garden, past the fruit bushes and apple trees that had only come into bloom a few days ago. Dew had fallen on the grass, and the hem of her nightie was wet around her ankles. Standing on the steps, she could feel the intense, billowing heat from the kitchen and the whole of the east-facing floor.

Then she went in.

Some of the smoke inside the hall had dispersed, so it was possible to see the kitchen door, which was still closed, and the living room door, which was wide open. She ventured a few cautious steps across the floor. On all sides she was surrounded by roaring and cracking, but it was upstairs that she was heading. Every forward movement was accompanied by a stab in her lower abdomen. The knife was wrenched out and thrust in. She grabbed the banister and hauled herself up until she was on the landing between the rooms on the first floor. She opened the door to what had been Kåre's room, and inside, everything was as before. There was his bed, white and neatly made, the way it had been for all the years since he died. There was his wardrobe, the chair on which he had rested his crutches, the picture of the two children playing by the waterfall and the angel of the Lord hovering above them, they were all there. Her bag, too, the one containing three thousand kroner. It was in the top drawer of the dresser, which was still full of Kåre's clothes, and the moment she caught sight of one of his old shirts – it was the one with a little tear above the chest – she felt she no longer had the strength to make her way back down. It was as if she suddenly gave up everything at the mere sight of the shirt. She dropped the bag on the floor with a thud and sat down gently on the bed. She sensed the mattress springs and the old, familiar, comforting creaks beneath her. The smoke was rising through the cracks in the floor, collecting and advancing to the ceiling. In front of her eyes a serene figure of smoke appeared to be slowly taking shape. It had arms, hands, feet and a hazy face. She lowered her head and mouthed a silent prayer with no beginning and no end, a couple of sentences, nothing more. But then there was a loud, sharp report from directly behind her, and it was enough for her to forget all else, jump up and beat a hasty retreat. She was back inside herself, the smoke wraith had gone, the room was totally befogged and it was hard to breathe. She snatched the bag and ran onto the landing. Hurried down the stairs and descended into a thick, acrid blanket of smoke that stung every part of her face. She realised it was coming from all their clothes in the bedroom, which were smouldering and on the point of catching fire. Her throat tightened, she felt nauseous, her eyes streamed, but she knew exactly where to go to reach the door. For the last few metres she fumbled blindly, but of course she had been this way so many times before and she found the door with ease. Once on the steps outside she felt the heat seeming to press her from behind and push her several paces from the house. She filled her lungs with pure, fresh night air and sank to her knees. I have seen her in my mind's eye, kneeling in the grass surrounded by light that changed from yellow to almost white, to orange and almost red. She knelt with her face in the grass as she gradually recovered her breath. At length, she dragged herself to her feet, but by then neither Olav nor anyone else was anywhere to be seen. She scrambled up the slope to her neighbour's house, which was now fully illuminated by the fire. Her neighbour came charging out before she had time to knock. It was Odd Syvertsen. He had been woken by the light. She grabbed his arm, either holding him tight or supporting herself so as not to fall. All she could manage was a whisper, but he heard every word.

'I can't find Olav.'

Odd Syvertsen moved first, leaping for the phone while Johanna rushed down the slope and back onto the road. The house was now fully ablaze. Loud crackles and bangs were still echoing around Lake Livannet and into the mountain ridges westwards. It sounded as if the sky itself was being torn apart. The flames were like large wild birds twisting around one another, above one another, into one another, they wanted to break free, but could not. In the space of minutes the fire had grown tall and powerful. Yet all around her there was this strange silence. I have seen all of this.

A house is burning at night. It is the first few minutes, before people have been alerted. All around there is silence. There is only the fire. The house stands there alone and no one can save it. It has been left to its fate, to its destruction. The flames and the smoke are being sucked up into the sky, or so it seems; there are creaks and groans, like distant responses. It is frightening, it is terrible and it is beyond comprehension.

And it is almost beautiful.

Johanna called Olav's name. First once, then twice, then four times. It was eerie to hear your own voice alongside the sound of the flames. The trees seemed to have moved even closer to the house. They were extending their branches. Curious, panic-stricken. With stabbing pains in the pit of her stomach she ran around to the outbuilding. To her it felt as if a huge abscess inside had been lanced and hot blood was escaping.

He was standing between the house and the barn, caught in the intense light. His nightshirt flapped around his body, although there wasn't a breath of wind and he stood without moving. Coming closer, she discovered that the wind was issuing from the fire itself, a gust that boded ill, a gust that was both ice cold and voraciously hot. She pulled him away and they ran back up to the road, where they stood, huddled together, as Odd Syvertsen came bounding down the incline. He was flurried and out of breath as he joined the elderly couple. He tried to move them away from the overpowering heat, but it was impossible. They wanted to watch their house burn to the ground. Neither was able to utter a single word. Olav stood like stone, though the nightshirt softened his appearance with the cool white fabric wrapped around his shoulders and arms. Their faces were lit up, clear, pure, as if age had been erased. Then the fire suddenly took hold of the old cherry tree outside the kitchen window. The one that always flowered so early and that Kåre had always climbed. In late summer it was laden with fruit, I have been told, and the largest and sweetest cherries always hung on the branches furthest from reach. Now it was alight. The fire swept through the blossom and branches, and then seared the entire crown of the tree with a distinctive crackle. Afterwards a high-pitched voice was heard, but it was impossible to tell whether it belonged to either Johanna or Olav: *Lord God Almighty. Lord God Almighty.*

I have seen it all in my mind's eye. It was the eighth fire, it was a little after half past twelve, early on the morning of 5 June 1978.

Then the fire engine arrived.

They heard the sirens from as far afield as Fjeldsgårdsletta, or perhaps even further away, perhaps right up by the chapel at Brandsvoll, perhaps they heard the fire alarm wailing in Skinnsnes, too? It is not inconceivable, since you can hear it from the church. But, anyway, they heard the fire engine. The sirens grew louder, shriller, more piercing, and soon they could discern the blue lights racing past the old sand-casting works at the end of Lake Livannet, past the slaughterhouse, the Shell petrol station and the priest's house with the balcony, past the old schoolhouse in Kilen and Kaddeberg's shop, before the fire engine slowed as it climbed the hill to the few houses at Vatneli.

It stopped and a young man jumped out and came running towards them. 'Anyone inside?' he yelled.

'They got out,' Odd Syvertsen said, but the man didn't seem to hear. He ran back to the fire engine, unhitched several coiled hoses and threw them out in no particular order. They rolled down the road like wheels and toppled over. Then he opened some sliding doors, tossed a couple of axes onto the ground, and a solitary helmet, which rocked to and fro on the gravel. He stood for a few seconds gazing at the flames, his arms hanging limply by his sides. For a few seconds he stood beside Olav, Johanna and Odd Syvertsen, and they had the appearance of a group, observing the incomprehensible event that was taking place.

Four cars arrived at great speed. They each parked some way behind the fire engine, turned off their lights, and four men dressed in black came running over.

'There may be people inside,' the young man shouted. He was wearing a thin, white shirt that fluttered around his lean chest. He uncoupled two of the hoses from the powerful water pump at the front of the fire engine while two other men stood waiting for the water to issue forth. At that moment there was such a huge explosion within the blaze that the ground shook and everyone doubled up as if they had been hit in the stomach by a shell. Someone burst into laughter, it was impossible to see who, and Odd Syvertsen put an arm around Olav and Johanna, and shepherded them away with an affectionate but firm pull, leading them up the slope to his house. This time they obeyed without a word. He got them inside and dialled Knut Karlsen's number. He and his wife came at once – they had been awoken by the sirens and the vivid mass of flames – and in the ensuing hours it was decided that Olav and Johanna could move into their cellar until things had eased.

The flames billowed across the sky, but Olav and Johanna didn't see them. The light changed from white to rust-red, then purple and orange. What a sight it was. A shower of sparks was sent flying into the air as the frame of the house collapsed, it hovered weightlessly for a few moments, then died. The leaves on the trees crinkled. The wild birds were gone; they had finally broken free of one another. Now the fire burned quietly with tall, vertical flames. More cars arrived. People got out, left the doors open, wrapped their jackets tightly around them and slowly approached the fire. Among these was my father. In my mind's eye he came in the blue Datsun, stopped some distance away and got out like the others, but I have never been able to see his face properly. He was there, I know he was there outside Olav and Johanna's burning house on that night, but I don't know what he was thinking or who he spoke to, and I can't see his face.

Ash lay all over the garden; large, lazy flakes floated through the air, then fluttered over the trees and covered the parked vehicles as quietly as snow. A motorbike started up and left, ridden by two young men. One with a helmet, one without.

There was nothing you could do. Olav and Johanna Vatneli's house was razed to the ground.

In the end all that remained was the chimney. By then it was almost morning and most of the vehicles had gone. Only the smoke hung like a thin, transparent haze over the garden and between the closest trees. The two people in Knut Karlsen's cellar had no clothes apart from the nightwear in which they stood. And the bag. Containing three thousand kroner.

At four o'clock it was so light that the birds began to sing. Theirs was a strangely intense song, a steady exultation that mingled with the drone of the water pumps. A huge amount of water had been needed, so the hoses had been rolled down the rough slope to Lake Livannet, and the water pumped up thirty metres.

Three journalists and a number of photographers circled the site of the blaze. First of all, they talked to the rural police chief, Lensmann Knut Koland, then they walked up the slope and knocked on the cellar door. They were allowed to talk to Johanna; Olav was lying on the divan with a rug over him and staring up at the ceiling, in a different world. Johanna answered with controlled composure, giving identical answers to all the questions. She spoke slowly, so they had plenty of time to take notes. Then photographs of her were taken. Several, from various angles, but only those showing her despondent face appeared that same day in the local newspapers: *Fædrelandsvennen*, *Sørlandet* and *Lindesnes.* She had singed eyebrows, soot on one cheek and a cut to her forehead, and she looked like a survivor of a mining accident.

By and large, she was composed.

After they had all gone, it occurred to her that she didn't have her teeth, they were in the glass beside Olav's on the vanity shelf, but then she remembered there was no longer any shelf, nor any glass, nor any teeth; neither her teeth nor Olav's existed any longer. In my mind's eye I have seen this, the strangely lucid, chilling instant when she realised she had lost absolutely everything, even her teeth, and only then did tears start to trickle quietly down her cheeks.

II.

EVER SINCE EARLY CHILDHOOD I have been told the story of the fires. At the beginning it was my parents who told me, but it wasn't until I grew up and heard it from others that I realised that in fact it was all true. For long periods the story has seemed to disappear, only to crop up unexpectedly in a conversation, a newspaper article or simply in my consciousness. It has pursued me for thirty years although I have never known exactly what happened or indeed what it was all about. As a child I remember sitting in the back seat of a blue Datsun going to my grandparents' at Heivollen, and on the way there we would pass the house where the pyromaniac lived. It was as though I could feel a waft of something outlandish and alluring as we drove past. Immediately afterwards we passed the house belonging to Sløgedal, the composer and organist at Kristiansand Cathedral, and my father used to point to the old barn bridge which didn't meet the new barn that had been erected. *It burned down when you were christened*, he said, and so it went on until in some way or other I connected the fires with myself. Yet there was so much I didn't know, which was why I had never thought of writing about the fires. It was too big a subject, too far-reaching and too close to home.

The story had been there like a shadow until the moment I decided to write it down. This happened suddenly, in the early summer of 2009, after I moved back home. It came about in the following way:

A few weeks earlier, in April, I was sitting on my own up in the old loft of Lauvslandsmoen School rummaging through boxes of old text books, yellowing exercise books and miscellaneous papers. I remember this loft from my schooldays as being extremely messy and full of jumble. We used to hide up there sometimes, that was when we had a woodwork class in the cellar, and we would tiptoe up all the steps, past the music room, up the final, darkened staircase and sit in the freezing cold loft, as quiet as mice, waiting for someone to notice that we had absented ourselves.

The books were cold and my fingers left marks on the damp papers, which must have been up there for twenty or thirty years. After a while I stumbled on a pile of black and white photographs wrapped in plastic, and with a vague sense of anticipation I began to flick through them. I recognised the faces straightaway but was unable to place them. Most of the photos were of children, but among them was one of a group of adults. Gradually it dawned on me that the photos were of my own time at the school. They were of kids from my class, there were a few older children, a few younger ones too, pictures of the school playground or inside the classrooms, and there were a number in which my teachers appeared. There was also a photo of a small boy singing on a stage. His hair had recently been cut and he was wearing a knitted jumper with a shirt that barely protruded over the top. The occasion must have been some kind of Christmas celebration because I could make out a decorated Christmas tree and paper chains in the background. More people were there with him, and everyone was holding a lit candle. It took me four, maybe five seconds. Then it clicked: That's me!

That was when it all started, with the sight of this boy innocently standing there and singing. I looked at myself, stared at my own face for several seconds without seeing who it was. It is difficult to explain why, but the experience had such an impact on me. It was as though I understood yet didn't understand that it was me. And that it made no difference. Why I don't know. But that was when the story of the fires made its re-appearance, as a kind of extension of this discovery. It was this picture of me, with a thin, steady flame rising from my hand, as it were, that led, a few weeks later, to my realisation one evening at the beginning of June that I would attempt to write the story of the fires. It was like taking a deep breath.

And so.

III.

WHEN THE FIRST BUILDING was set alight in the region of Finsland in Southern Norway at the beginning of May 1978, I was not yet two months old. A few days after my birth, my father collected Mamma and me from the maternity ward in Kongens gate in Kristiansand. I was laid in a dark blue travel bag and driven the forty kilometres home to Finsland, and when I was taken from the car to our Kleveland homestead for the first time it was in a tremendous snowstorm, which didn't abate until two days later. Thereafter it was sunshine and silence, white winter days, until the wind turned southwest and spring arrived. At the end of April there was still snow lying where the sun didn't reach, but the warmer temperatures had well and truly arrived, and on 6 May, the day it all began, the forest was already perilously dry.

A month later, just before midnight on 5 June, it was all over. There had been ten fires, and it was the day after my christening, which was held on the third Sunday after Whitsun. It had been hot and sultry for weeks, and that Sunday was the hottest day yet. The heat shimmered and quivered above the rooftops and made the tarmac bulge at the end of the plain in Lauvslandsmoen and Brandsvoll. In the afternoon there was an enormous deluge and all of a sudden the world felt fresh and new. The weather cleared, insects whirred through the air and the evening was warm and still.

It was the evening before the worst night of all.

In fact, the story of the fires is closely entwined with the very first months of my life and culminates the night after my christening. However, it was far from certain that there would be any christening on that Sunday. Early that morning, at seven minutes past twelve, a dark car had been observed travelling at great speed towards the church. By that point panic had set in. The car was advancing on the church, as I said, climbing, but then it disappeared from sight, and no one knew where it had gone. Events were monitored hour by hour. Minute by minute. The worst was feared. So long as the church is spared, people thought. So long as the church is spared. It wasn't said out loud; however, everyone was thinking it. The worst of all would be if the church burned down. That was why they kept watch. Not just near the church but throughout the entire region. People sat on their doorsteps, listening. My father sat outside our brown house on Kleveland farm while I lay asleep indoors. He had a gun with him, Grandad's rifle, which I would see him use later, but on this night he hadn't been able to obtain ammunition for it. Nonetheless, it was a gun, ammunition or no ammunition. The bottom line was that you kept watch. No one had the remotest idea who the arsonist was. Or who might suddenly emerge from the darkness. Nothing like this had been experienced since the war. Indeed, during those weeks there was an atmosphere in the region that was reminiscent of war. Even those who were too young to have lived through the war also thought about it in those terms. That is what everyone has told me. War had returned.

On Monday night it was all over, barely twenty-four hours after Olav and Johanna's house had been set alight. It was still 5 June, just before midnight, after interviews lasting three hours. Before that, Alfred had conveyed the sad message to Lensmann Knut Koland, who, along with detective colleagues from Kristiansand and KRIPOS from Oslo, had set up a base in the old council room in Brandsvoll Community Centre. The sad and liberating message. Alfred had to do it, not Ingemann, even though the latter had probably put two and two together a long time ago. When the evidence came to light, however, he couldn't do it himself. Neither Ingemann nor Alma could – Alma, who at that time was lying in bed, unable to move.

An arrest soon followed, and then the quiet avalanche of events.

During the final thirty minutes before midnight, cars drove from house to house around the whole district. There were four police patrol cars, plus a number of private vehicles. There was no need to knock: generally there was someone sitting on the front steps keeping watch. The vehicle would stop, or drive by slowly, as someone shouted through the window:

He's been arrested.

The news spread. People walked in the darkness, over the night dew, across fields to neighbours', identified themselves and passed on the message that he had been arrested. They said the name, and then all went quiet for a few seconds until the listeners could collect themselves.

Him?

Everyone was notified, including Sløgedal, the cathedral organist, who sat in hiding a short distance from his homestead at Nerbø, waiting with a loaded gun. Later he told me about that night. How light and celestial it had been, how dark and earthbound and unreal, all at once. The police knew Sløgedal had taken up this position; they were the ones who gave him the gun, so they drove up with the news. At last he was able to get to his feet, return the rifle and ask:

Who is it?

John dropped by Kleveland. He stood on the lawn outside my parents' bedroom, whispering until my mother woke. He kept whispering her name until she dressed and came to the door so that he, too, could say the four magic words that were passed from mouth to mouth that night:

He has been arrested.

And so it spread like wildfire. It even got onto NRK's late-night news bulletin. The police had notified the Norwegian News Agency and asked them to circulate the information as quickly as possible to allay fears. But by the time it was read out from Marienlyst in Oslo, the whole region knew.

He had been arrested.

Everyone could go to bed, lights were switched off one by one, but doors were still locked, after all, you could never be certain. From now on, no one would ever be certain.

Household after household in the region eventually settled

down. At last you could sleep, and next morning you would wake up believing it had all been a dream.

This had been no dream, though.

Fædrelandsvennen published a total of three front-page spreads in four days, the first on the morning of Saturday 3 June when the region woke to news of four more torched buildings. In addition, there was a front page in *Verdens Gang* and in *Dagbladet*, both of them national newspapers. Two in *Sørlandet*. Two in *Lindesnes* as well. A front page and one inside page in *Aftenposten,* also a national paper. On this same Saturday there was also an interview with Ingemann on page three of *Lindesnes*; that was the one where he was pictured standing next to the fire engine with a hand on the water pump and an inscrutable expression on his face.

Apart from this, there were a variety of minor mentions in regional newspapers and NRK's daily radio updates. As well as a four-minute slot on the main TV news broadcast on Monday evening when in fact it was all over, but panic still hung in the air everywhere like fog. The news item showed a distant shot of Anders and Agnes Fjeldsgård's house, the maple trees on either side of the front entrance where the windows had been smashed and petrol poured over the floor. The two maples are still there, and I was surprised to see that they hadn't grown in more than thirty years. The clip showed the restless shadows of leaves flapping above the walls of the house while first the reporter, and then Lensmann Koland, described the sequence of events. Next, the cameras focused on the scene in Vatneli: the smoking ruins and the chimney that towered in the air like a huge tree bereft of its branches. That was all that was left of Olav and Johanna Vatneli's house. Two firemen walked past on the road. They were both bare-headed. One was holding what looked like an ice axe, as though he were a glacier hiker on his way into the frozen wastes. The other was empty-handed, and I didn't recognise either of the men. Towards the end of the item there was footage of the smoking heap of rubble, which was all that remained of the Sløgedals' barn at Nerbø. That was fire number ten. A solitary man stood there hosing down the debris as if there were something planted in the heap of ashes that needed watering. Thousands of litres of water. It was Alfred. I recognised him even though he was more than thirty years younger and, what was more, had his back to the camera.

IV.

IT WAS SUMMER. Everything had turned green, leaves had appeared on the trees, the lilacs were in flower and throughout June I sat on the first floor of the ex-bank in Kilen trying to work out how all the pieces fitted together. I had rented the room for a spell in the hope that the silence and the view would bring me closer to myself and my writing. I sat alone in the room, which had been stripped bare of almost everything, with only the sky, the forest and a view of Lake Livannet in front of me. I had a basic chair, a rickety table and an old-fashioned, red office lamp that had been left in one of the storerooms, the kind that seems to stoop over your work like a curious onlooker. I settled myself and saw the birch tree swaying in the wind directly outside the window. I was sitting in the midst of the countryside in which I had grown up, in the midst of everything that had marked and shaped me and in some way made me who I was. I saw leaves fluttering and shaking and shadows darkening tree trunks, I saw the road and scattered houses leading up to Vatneli, I saw the sun glistening on an open window and continuing to glisten when the window was closed. I saw the sky and clouds drifting slowly in off the sea from the south-west, I saw them change form as I gazed, I saw the birds, which had long been busy in the short, hectic summer, I saw the winter-pale chicks splashing at the water's edge on the other side, just below the garden belonging to what had been Syvert Mæsel's house and last of all I saw the lake, and the wind that caused the surface to ripple all day and sparkle, even in the shadows where the water was usually black and still.

The next day I was there again. Staring out. Didn't write a thing. All of a sudden it felt impossible. The third day I became aware of a large bird by the shore. It was balancing on one leg with its head and a long, pointed beak lowered. It was a heron. I waited for it to take off, or to dive into the water, or at least to change legs. But it did none of those things. It stood there, unmoving, until I got up and went home.

And so the days passed. I sat for a few hours with Lake Livannet in front of me. Tried to make things happen, without any success. Afterwards I let myself out, went down the steep staircase that had been erected on the outside of the building especially for me, and drove the few hundred metres to the shop to buy some things. I wandered around in the bright, congenial atmosphere, picked up some milk, bread and coffee. It was good to stroll around like this, picking up something solid and simple and putting it in the shopping trolley. In the aisles I bumped into people I knew, people who had known me all my life, who had known my parents and my father's parents, who had seen me as a child, who had seen me grow up and move away, who had seen me become a writer, and who now said they were pleased I had moved back, even though I always emphasised that it was only for a shortish period. I hadn't come back to stay, I said, but now, right now, I'm here.

When summer was over I still hadn't got down to writing about the fires. There was something creating a mental block, but I couldn't say exactly what it was. However, I had gained an overview of the events that occurred, although I hadn't yet spoken to anyone involved. I had worked through the extant newspapers and interviews and seen the item that had been shown on the main news. NRK had put it on a DVD and sent it to me from Oslo. I played it again and again. When I was about to watch it for the first time I was very tense, nervous even. At home, alone in the house at Kleveland, I inserted the disc into the machine and watched it disappear. This was the first time I would see living pictures of the countryside where I had been born, of Finsland in the summer of 1978, the countryside which the whole of Norway had seen that night more than thirty years ago when the news item was broadcast. It took a few seconds, then the picture appeared and I pressed play. I recognised the location at once, even though there was something slightly alien and unfamiliar about it all. Something had changed, but I couldn't put my finger on what. Was it the forest? Was it the houses? Was it the roads? I don't know. There was something distant, bygone about the images, yet I could still see that this was home. There is the village of Kilen, it struck me, no doubt about that, and there's sparkling Lake Livannet, almost the same as today, and there are the long plains of Brandsvoll, the power lines that spread like a scar through the area, and Anders and Agnes Fjeldsgård's house as good as unchanged. Everything was there, and everything was almost as I knew it. All the TV coverage was characterised by a kind of paradoxical serenity. The camera work was slow, the reporter gave a very full commentary as the pictures glided in a leisurely manner across the screen, and this slowness and the long-winded reporting meant the item lacked drama. You saw the billowing forests, the tall sky, the clouds as light as flecks of froth, birds sitting motionless on the telephone lines, a gentle breeze wafting through the leaves on the trees. You saw houses, you saw cars and you saw clothes drying in the wind. It was like any peaceful summer day in 1978, or it could have been ten years earlier or ten years later. It was timeless countryside, yet it was in precisely this countryside where I was later to become an adult, and which in some ways I would never leave. It seemed a long time ago; however, I felt that at any moment I could take my eyes off the TV, look outside and there it would all be, unchanged. The black, smoking ruins, the few onlookers standing around in untidy groups. They were still there. There were mothers with children in their arms. There were children on bikes, hanging over their handlebars. Older people huddled together as if supporting one another, preventing each other from falling, and there was a man with a hat who looked at first glance like Reinert Sløgedal, the old sexton and schoolteacher, and father of Bjarne Sløgedal, the organist at Kristiansand Cathedral.

Finally, there was Alfred, hosing down Sløgedal's ravaged barn. That, too, was an image of simplicity and composure: one solitary, bare-headed man. The sky above. A razed building. Thin, white smoke slowly rising, being borne away on the wind. The jet of water sluicing the wall and the scorched earth, splashing against the distorted sheets of roofing.

It must have been just a few hours before he delivered the news.

Then the item was over and the screen went black.

I watched the DVD a second time. And once more. It was as if I couldn't have enough of it, as if I hoped to catch a glimpse of myself, or my father. Or anyone else I knew. After all, that wasn't completely beyond the realms of possibility. I knew, of course, that my father had been outside the house in Vatneli on the night it was reduced to ashes, and I knew for certain that I had myself been to the devastated farm belonging to Olga Dynestøl on the Sunday, straight after the christening, even though I had been fast asleep in the travel bag the whole time.

V.

IN SEPTEMBER I set my writing aside and went to Italy, to the northern Italian town of Mantua, to take part in the sizeable literary festival there. As always when I am on my travels, I was quite tense, but I didn't know then, nor do I know now, exactly what caused this tension.

It was a hot evening in Mantua with a fierce gusting wind that had apparently come all the way from the Sahara, and I was due to do a reading from one of my books in Piazza San Leonardo, a small square in the centre of town. I walked from my hotel, which was situated close by Piazza Don Leoni. It was half past eight on a Saturday evening with lots of smiling people about. There was laughter and music in the narrow, crowded streets, but I felt quite alone. I followed Corso V. Emanuele to Piazza Cavallotti. There, I bore left across a car park with a long line of parked and abandoned scooters. I continued down a few cramped alleyways with no names, at any rate, I didn't see any signs, up Via Arrivabene, and then it was straight ahead to the square beside the stone church.

By then I was already soaked in sweat. Quite an audience had assembled, because several writers were going to do readings, before and after me. I was nervous, as I always am before I mount a stage. I greeted my interpreter, a woman in her fifties who had lived in Stockholm over thirty years ago, but who nevertheless spoke almost fluent Swedish. When at length it was my turn the audience was in darkness, while up on stage a strong white light shone into my face. It was still suffocatingly hot, and the wind was so strong that it howled like thunder in the microphone. I don't know whether it was the heat or the dry desert wind, or whether it was something I had eaten or drunk, or perhaps the intense light, but standing in front of the microphone, I suddenly felt unwell. Within a few seconds all my strength seemed to ebb out of me. My arms went slowly numb and my knees were giving way beneath me. I felt as if I was going to faint. The sea of faces began to heave. A mist veiled my eyes. It was like a bitterly cold afternoon a long time ago when I fell and hit my head on the ice of Lake Bordvannet, and my senses switched off one by one. Lying supine, I had felt the cold, hard ice against my head and shoulders and thought I was dying. So this was how I would die, I had time to think, on my back, ten years old, on my own in the middle of the lake. First my eyesight shut down, it slowly lost all colour, the forest disappeared, the pale sky above me, everything went, until I lay there completely blind. Next all the sounds faded and then I was gone, as the snow continued to fall quietly on my face. Now the same was about to happen to me here, watched by several hundred curious Italians. Or almost the same. For that was when I caught sight of some familiar faces down in the crowd. At first I didn't know exactly who they were, but I was aware I knew them, and I couldn't fathom why no one had come over to me before I went on stage, because surely it is natural enough for old acquaintances so far from home to say hello to one another? I was unable to place them, either, but then I spotted Lars Timenes, whom I remembered from when he lived in the former telephone exchange in Kilen. I clung to him, as it were, as he stood there, small and down at heel, while I called to mind how he used to sit in a chair in the middle of the sitting room, mercilessly illuminated by the constant flicker from the television. Straight afterwards I spotted Nils, my neighbour at home, standing in front of the stage as well, Nils, of whom I have no more than a fleeting memory, a friendly back as he walked away. There was Nils, and there was Emma, who used to sit staring at me from the corridor in the rest home when I went to visit my father, and there was her daughter Ragnhild, who was a grown-up yet still a child and who lived in another part of the country, but came home every summer and talked like a stranger. There was Ragnhild, and there was Tor, who one night left a party, went behind the house and shot himself, and there was Stig, next to whom I stood in the youth choir and with whom I sang beneath three Roman arches in a church, or in the chapel beneath a picture of a man with a hoe, or at the rest home in Nodeland. Stig, who went swimming and vanished from sight, who sank deeper and deeper and wasn't rescued until it was too late, Stig who just managed to make it to voice-breaking age, he was there in the audience, too. And there were more. Teresa was there. Teresa, who taught me piano for a whole winter. Who always stood over my shoulder with a slight stoop, waiting, now she was there with all the others, watching. And there were more. Jon was there, who taught my father, who was always called Teacher Jon to distinguish him from other Jons in the area. I remembered Teacher Jon from the elk hunts because he used to set off before all the others. He set off while it was still dark and sat ready and waiting for several hours before the hunt began. Now he was waiting in front of me. Ester was there, too. Ester, who always played the elf when we celebrated Christmas at my grandmother's. Ester laughed in a way that made everything inside you melt. Ester was there. And Tønnes was there, a little to the back. Tønnes died only a few days after my grandmother, as though it was inconceivable that he should be the only neighbour left alive. And there were even more. There were many I recognised, whom I had seen at one time or another, perhaps at the post office counter, or in front of the postcard stand at Kaddeberg's, or at the Christmas party in the chapel when the chairs were pushed back against the walls so that there was room for four concentric circles of people, each alternate circle rotating in the opposite direction around the Christmas tree while the snow swirled against the windows, and everyone's cheeks were flushed as they sang. It was as though I knew them without knowing who they were. Even those I had never seen before. For all I knew, Johanna was there as well, and Olav, and maybe Kåre had made an appearance on his crutches at the fringes where the darkness made it impossible to see. Perhaps Ingemann and Alma were there, too. Perhaps Alma was there, too, with both legs intact, closing her eyes and leaning her head back. And who knows, perhaps Dag was there as well? Perhaps he was standing there with his arms crossed, right at the back of the church steps where I couldn't see him.

I have no idea where they came from, but they stood there, silent, serious, pale and reserved, waiting for me to begin.

They had come to listen to me.

Somehow I managed to collect myself enough to get through the three or four pages I had chosen. I read a story about a father who falls off a ladder and a son who knows he cannot carry him indoors to the sofa.

When I finished there was a burst of applause. I wasn't prepared for it. After all, I had read the passage in Norwegian, and no one, apart from my interpreter, would have understood a word. Nonetheless, the applause was resounding and sincere. Like a storm around me, the clapping merged with the wind, and the moment I raised my eyes I saw Pappa. He was right at the back, at the top of the church steps, with the massive door behind him. I had seen him once before, a few years earlier. On that occasion we had both been sitting in our respective cars. It was night. I had been driving in the deserted, well-lit tunnel beneath Baneheia, the Nature Park in Kristiansand. Then a car came towards me. I could see from quite some distance it was him. Yet only after he had passed by did it strike me that neither of us had waved. And so it was this time, too. Neither of us waved. Not long afterwards I saw Grandma standing there as well, with Grandad directly behind her. They stood to the right of Pappa. I don't know whether they were smiling. I don't know what they were thinking. But I saw them. And they saw me.

The next day I took a taxi to Bologna airport. I was behind schedule, and we sped off at a 170 kilometres an hour on a motorway called the A1, which went straight to Rome. I just made it to the airport in time, boarded the KLM flight and found my seat by a window on the right, at the front. I sat down and, full of a kind of expectation, watched all the others who would be traversing Europe, all the way to Schiphol, Amsterdam. But I was unable to recognise any of those who entered and took their seats. All the dead had remained with the crowd in the darkened square in Mantua. Somehow I was reassured, and as the plane roared up the runway and lifted into the air I fell into a doze. We made a wide arc over the Po Plain; I saw the river winding like a snake, the tin roofs of the houses shining with a matt gleam, not a sign of life. Just flat, rust-red countryside. After a while the plane straightened and before long I could see the Alps rising beneath us. With a strange serenity, bordering on happiness, I thought of all the newspaper cuttings lying at home waiting for me, how I always feel before a job which, from a distance, appears both alluring and intimidating, and as we passed over Lake Constance I saw a ripple extending outwards in the water like a feather.

So, I had to go to a little square in Mantua to begin my story about the fires, that was how it felt at any rate as I sat high above Germany flicking through my black notebook, the one in which I had written nothing while at home staring across Lake Livannet.

There, at a height of 8,000 feet, I began to write about the eighth fire, the one that began early in the morning of 5 June 1978, the one that broke out in the kitchen and culminated with Olav and Johanna Vatneli's house in ruins. Every so often I peered out of the window and looked down on the continent gliding peacefully by beneath me. Lake Constance slipped slowly behind us and was gone, and I turned back to my notebook. Across Europe, high above Stuttgart, Mannheim, Bonn and Maastricht, until we descended towards Amsterdam I wrote about these two people I had never met but whom I soon felt I knew. And it wasn't until we had taken off again, from Schiphol on course for Kristiansand, that I managed to get the fire out of my head. As we flew over the North Sea I was at ease, clear in my mind, and I stared out of the window, through my reflection, into the blackness and down at the sea I knew was beneath me.

VI.

THE FOLLOWING NIGHT I knuckled down, and ever since sitting in the darkness over the North Sea I had known where I was going to start.

I set off from home in the dusk, turned left at the crossing outside the library in Lauvslandsmoen and continued northwards. The drive took only four or five minutes and I left the car by a high granite wall. It was a quiet September evening, no one was around, only the cows in the fields. A gentle wind from the west. A storm was approaching, heading in from the sea. I am always so at peace when a storm is on the way. I don't know why, but that was how it was this evening as well; I felt like sitting on a bench, lying down, stretching out, sleeping.

I didn't see any swallows even though I stood very still for a long time. Perhaps they had migrated south, or perhaps it is only in my dreams that they have nests in the church tower?

Earlier that day I had been to see the church verger in Nodeland, and had been allowed to see the cemetery records, a leather-bound book with the number 5531 on the title page. I was given permission to take it home. It contained 616 names. Minus the stillborn babies, that is; they were merely given a number, but they were still included. All were allocated a row and a grave number. Everything was ordered and well organised. This was the closest I could get to a map of the cemetery.

However, it transpired that I didn't need a map. Now, I walked straight to the grave. It was the second one on the right after entering the gate. I hadn't known beforehand that was where it would be. It was almost frightening. But there they were, Olav and Johanna, the woman who had gone into the burning house and up to the first floor for her bag. The man who had been in shock at that point, standing outside gawping like a child, and who later that morning, when the sun was rising, lay on a sofa in Knut Karlsen's house, screaming.

As I stood by the grave I remembered the interview that was carried out a few days afterwards. Once everything was over and Olav was back to his normal self. I remembered almost verbatim what he had said: *I am so soft like that. Johanna is quite different. She's so calm, she is.*

That was what he said, the old stonemason. He was so soft. She was so calm.

I stayed in the cemetery until I felt the first raindrops on my hair. At length I found Ingemann and Alma thirty paces away, and beside them, Dag. They were separated by a two-metre-wide wall of earth. He had been given a black headstone, a bit smaller than the others, with room for only one name.

Before getting into my car I walked over to Pappa, whose last wish had been to be buried in the same grave as Great-Great-Grandfather Jens Sommundsen. And so it came to be. His wish was fulfilled. It was – according to the records – grave number 102. Jens, who had faced so many ordeals in his life and had become so gentle as a consequence. He lost two wives. And two children. He was the type of man people sought out if they needed to unburden themselves. I think Pappa had a desire to be like him, and that was why he wished to be buried in the same grave.

I didn't find Kåre. According to the ledger he should have been in grave number 19, but that wasn't much use. Grave number 19 no longer existed.

VII.

A FEW DAYS LATER I RANG ALFRED. Briefly I explained the reason for my call. As always when I am nervous, I struggled to find the words. He answered in a voice that was measured and distant and close all at the same time.

'I remember everything as if it were yesterday,' he said.

We spoke for two, perhaps three, minutes about the fires. Then I told him about the TV news item in which he had been standing with his back to the camera, hosing down Sløgedal's ravaged barn. He hadn't seen the item himself, he told me; it had been shown on the evening of 5 June, when he had been in quite a different place. He said, 'I wasn't aware of anyone filming me.'

I went to visit him and his wife Else that same evening. I took my black notebook with me, nothing else. It was a mild night, and I set off from home at a little after six. The trees had begun to bud, and this had happened almost without my noticing; some leaves were lemon-yellow, others were orange, akin to a flaming red, and then there were those the wind had blown off, which lay on the tarmac, brown and shrivelled. In the gardens forgotten apples hung from the branches, and wild rose bushes blossomed with blood-red hips which we always used to prise open with our teeth. I remembered the smooth skin, the taste on my lips and the sight of the furry seeds huddled together like tiny sleeping children.

When I arrived the sun was still high in the sky.

In some way or other, Alfred was a part of my childhood. I remember him from the time Finsland Sparebank had offices in Brandsvoll Community Centre, right at the end facing the road. I went there with Pappa. It was down a long corridor and then to the right. I often had my piggy bank with me, which had to be cut open to disgorge the money. This opening of the piggy bank was always a matter of great sorrow. Alfred was the bank manager and a cashier at Finsland Sparebank, and he generally sat with a serious expression in an office on the other side of the counter, isolated as it were from the world around him. He never had anything to do with my paltry savings, his head was filled with great and weighty thoughts, or so it seemed. That is why I remember him. Likewise the postman. That was Rolf. I remember him from Kilen Post Office, which has gone now. He would stand there sorting mail without looking up from his work. I can also remember him arriving in a post van, getting out, distributing newspapers and letters to the mailboxes on the old milk ramp by the road as though he was only doing it this once, and never again.

Alfred was a member of the voluntary fire service in 1978. There must have been around twenty members in all, and they lived within a radius of a few kilometres from the alarm, which was attached to a post next to the fire station at Skinnsnes. All you had to do was place a compass point on the station and draw a circle. No one was allowed to live beyond hearing distance of the alarm. Apart from that there were no special requirements for joining the voluntary service. Actually, yes, there was: you had to have a car. The fire engine had space for only two men.

The fire station lay at the geographical centre of the region, just a few hundred metres from the large house where Alfred had made his home and started a family, to the west of the chapel and the old co-op building which had been converted into stables. I suppose it is a trifle misleading to call it a fire station; in reality it was a fairly ample concrete garage with a metal shutter, an adjacent door and an outside lamp. That was all. Only the fire chief lived closer. That was Ingemann, who was married to Alma. Ingemann was sixty-four years old in the summer of 1978. In addition to his job as fire chief he had his own workshop in an outbuilding across the drive. The post of fire chief in Finsland was, strictly speaking, not a job. There were never any fires. You were talking maybe a couple of call-outs a year, and then as a rule it would be to minor forest fires. Nonetheless, he had a suit that hung in the workshop and that he donned whenever the alarm went off, which was why they called it the *fire suit.* Ingemann and Alma had only one son. They had had him late in life, when Ingemann was over forty. His name was Dag; he was born at the height of the summer in 1957 and had been very much wanted. There was Dag, Ingemann and Alma. All three of them lived within the magic circle.

I sat talking to Else and Alfred for a long time. They were so calm and level-headed; I didn't need to give any further explanations as to why I had come, why I wished to write about the fires. It appeared to be obvious to them. They had read my earlier books and seemed to have complete confidence in my ability to write about the fires as well, and to believe that I would do it in a proper, dignified manner. I took as good as no notes, so engrossed was I in what they told me. They spoke in hushed tones, as everyone did when conversation turned to the fires. They lowered their voices and told their story slowly, dwelling on precise details. It struck me that in a way they were afraid of being seen with me.

'It's quite some time ago now, you know,' Else said, as if suddenly giving up. 'It's over thirty years ago, it is. That's a human lifespan, isn't it.' Then she pointed at me.

'Yes . . . and you,' she said, 'you'd just been born.' She added, with a strange gleam in her eyes: 'And look at you now.'

Then Alfred told the whole story. He had set aside time to remember before I came, and now he told me everything as he recalled it. He spoke quietly and in a businesslike fashion, just as an old bank man would. Now and then, however, he drew a deep breath.

And so.

When he had finished there was a second's silence. Alfred sat staring at a point to the left of me, out of the window from which you could see the whole road down to the community centre.

Afterwards Alfred told the story of the man who blew himself up, and the mother who subsequently walked around collecting the fragments in her apron. I don't know how we got onto this, strictly speaking it had nothing to do with the fires, but somehow it was appropriate. Once again Alfred adopted the same sober narrative style, and that made the story even more shocking. I didn't need to take notes; the story is unforgettable.

As I was about to go we broached the subject of the letter. There was a letter. Else and I sat in the living room while Alfred went to look for it. While he was away she said absent-mindedly, almost to herself: 'Such a good boy. The best boy in the world.'

I believe Alfred knew exactly where the letter was because he was back within an instant and I took it while Else and Alfred quietly awaited my reaction. It was a thin piece of A5 paper, written on both sides. The handwriting sloped gently; there was a rather childlike quality about it. I began to read with a mixture of reverence and immense curiosity. Once I had finished, I said:

'He must have been . . . intelligent.'

'He was,' Alfred said. 'He was a smart lad.'

That was all. Then I re-read the letter, as if there were something I had overlooked or misunderstood.

'You can take it with you,' Alfred said as I folded it for a second time. 'I don't need it. Just take it with you.'

At first I hesitated, but then I dropped it into my inside pocket. I was unsure whether I should thank him or Alfred should thank me, and the situation ended with neither of us saying anything. I stood up and cast a glance through the window. I saw the fields outside and the lights by the road. Before going into the hallway I looked at the picture on the wall above the TV. It was all black apart from some letters in gold: *By God's Grace.*

Alfred accompanied me to the front door, and out into the cold night air. It was as though he didn't want me to go, or he felt there was something he had forgotten to say. A detail from the story, or a crucial recollection, something he had omitted but which might appear from nowhere and cast everything in a new light. The forest around us was by now completely black; it seemed to have crept closer in the few hours we had been together. It was like a dark, impenetrable wall, but the sky was still clear and light with long, sleigh-shaped clouds. We went down the steps and Alfred walked with me to the car. All that could be heard was the sound of our footsteps. We exhaled transparent, frozen breath from our mouths as we spoke. Then Alfred said: 'You're so like your father, you are. We liked him a lot, all of us. He was a fine man. It's such a shame he's no longer with us.'

2

I.

HE WAS VERY MUCH WANTED, and when he did finally arrive, it was as if a miracle had taken place. A perfectly formed boy. And as an only child, he didn't have to share their love with anyone. He was on his own a lot and liked to sit at the kitchen table drawing while Alma cooked. He learned to read early. Even before he started school he had sounded his way through several of the popular books displayed on the first floor of the community centre. He used to cycle there, and return home with a full carrier bag of books hanging from the handlebars. Later he became the best in his class at reading, and writing. He wrote long stories, all with a violent, and often bloody, end. These dramatic, harrowing tales seemed out of character. He was so quiet, and rather shy. Good-natured to a fault. Not to mention how polite he was. No one bowed as deeply or thanked as emphatically as he did. No one was as helpful or as considerate as he was. If anyone asked, they never received no for an answer. He often helped the elderly, checking if there was any snow-shovelling, wood-carrying or house-painting to be done. Ingemann and

Alma lit up when the conversation turned to Dag. Sometimes people asked how they had got such a wonderfully well-behaved boy. They had no answer, but their faces were radiant. It was as if all the love they had given him ever since he was an infant was blossoming in the boy, and he passed it on to those he met. That had to be the explanation, their unrestrained love. Indeed, he was loved by everyone. And he knew that himself; he cast down his gaze when anyone spoke to him.

Twice he had seen a house burn to the ground. That was before he was ten years old. Both times he had been utterly silent, and afterwards he hadn't mentioned the fires.

Of course, the alarm didn't go off very often, but when it did he was allowed to go with Ingemann in the fire engine.

It would start with the telephone ringing in the hall. Ingemann picked up. *Yes?* he said. Alma came through the kitchen door, drying her hands on her apron. It was quiet for a few seconds. Then came Ingemann's voice: *Fire, fire.* It was like a magic formula. Everything else was put on hold. Now all that mattered was the fire. Ingemann, who was usually a calm, sober-minded man, suddenly became agitated. But even in the midst of the ensuing chaos he always remembered Dag. Dag followed him out of the door to the post outside the workshop. There, his father lifted him up so that he could reach the large, black handle that activated the fire alarm. It was as much as he could do to turn it. But he managed. Then the alarm went off like a cascading torrent from the heavens. He followed his father to the workshop and watched Ingemann put on the fire suit, then followed him round the corner to the fire station while holding his hands over his ears. That was how it was. He had to cover his ears until they reached the fire station. Then he clambered into the fire engine, slammed the door and they drove off. They barrelled along, his father switched on the sirens, and Dag's blood seemed to solidify in his veins, at first it solidified, then it throbbed ferociously, then he glanced over at his father and he could feel how proud Ingemann was of him. He had to cling on tight, and as they approached the fire he was told to keep a good distance from the flames, to stay in the background, not to touch anything, not to get in the way, not to be a nuisance. Just watch. And he obeyed. He stood watching a house being transformed. At first smoke poured out of the windows and up between the roof tiles. The whole house steamed as though it were being subjected to enormous pressure. Then the flames broke through the roof and a coal-black column soared to the sky. The smoke was sucked up into the air. Then it eased, floated across the sky like ink and began to drift with the wind. Next came the lament, or the tone, or the song, or whatever one might call it. A loud, high-pitched, singing tone that did not exist anywhere else but in the middle of a burning house. He asked his father what it was, but Ingemann just gave him a strange, uncomprehending look. Nevertheless, he was sure about the tone. He had heard it. The wailing. The song. The first time he heard it he was seven years old. That was the time with the dog. He had climbed up a tree some distance from the fire engine and the house and the flames. Up in the branches, he sat staring, as quiet as a mouse. He was the only person who had heard the desperate barking and whimpering inside the smoke-filled kitchen, but he didn't climb down and tell someone. He just sat tight, exactly as his father had stressed he should. He stared down at the men rolling out the hoses and dashing to and fro across the yard. He felt the immense heat that billowed towards the tree in great, chilling waves. He saw the jets of water rise, gather momentum and become swallowed up by the smoke. There was the sound of tinkling glass, there were cracks and creaks, as if the whole house were a ship on its way to open sea. Then flames burst through one first-floor window and licked up the wall. It was as if something had finally broken loose. By then the kitchen had gone quiet.

Afterwards he climbed down and ambled towards his father. He stood beside him until Ingemann lifted him into his arms, and he was sitting on his father's arm as the house collapsed.

At the time he didn't tell anyone about the dog, but it came out during the trial. He said that in prison he had started dreaming about the dog. He would wake suddenly in the night, not knowing where he was, and lie beneath the duvet without moving, frozen with terror, feeling the weight of the dog on his feet.

He was so very much wanted. And when he did finally arrive he was loved above all else. He grew up and was liked by everyone. But he cast down his eyes when he spoke to people.

Ingemann taught him how to use a gun. First of all, a small-bore gun, then a rifle. The two of them used to rig up a target at the end of a field – a white disc with a much smaller black circle in the centre – and they lay down beside each other on an empty sack, aimed and fired. When the shots had fallen silent, they got up and strolled down the field to inspect the targets. It turned out that he had talent. He concentrated his shots closer and closer together inside the black circle. His father took him to shooting meets in Finsland and surrounding areas. They put the gun on the rear seat and drove off while Alma stayed in the kitchen and had food ready for when they returned. He won cups, usually first prize. On the rare occasion he was beaten there was always an excuse: either the wind had suddenly changed direction or the sights had been set incorrectly or the mat was slippery or he was tired or he had eaten too much or too little before they set off. There was always an explanation, apart from when he won, no explanation was necessary then of course, that was the norm. He was the best. He carried the cups home and placed them on the living room table, where they were allowed to stay for a day or two so that Alma and Ingemann could admire them, and then they were moved to the shelf above the piano. Every fortnight or so Alma removed them, placed them on the table, dusted the shelf and put them all back. The cups were like a victory for all three of them.

That was the way it felt: a victory for all three of them.

Every day he cycled to the crossroads by the disused shop, and then headed along the road to Lauvslandsmoen School. He was happy there. School was like a game. What was his best subject? Norwegian? History? Maths? He was equally good at all of them. He was the best student in the class. It was almost the same as with shooting, no one could compete with him; he was right at the top, and he was on his own.

And that was what he wanted to be. He was beginning to target that. It became a necessity. He was not going to be overtaken by anyone, so he started competing with himself. Still, there were occasions when he made mistakes. A test didn't go as well as he had anticipated. Tiny slips crept in, or bigger errors, or he had quite simply made a huge howler. He had taken the corners a little too fast. Sometimes he got a B, even a weak B. And then he went silent and broody and glared daggers at the teacher, it was Reinert Sløgedal, who had been a teacher in the region since the war. Dag sat there for a long time just glaring, and if anyone asked how the test had gone, they would see something in his eyes they didn't understand, something alien, something stubborn and intransigent and ice cold. They left him alone until the alienness was gone, and they never asked again about the test result because they only wanted Dag to be himself once more.

One winter he went to the priest. That was in 1971. He knelt in front of the altarpiece with the others, and prayers were said for each and every one of them.

He started *gymnas*, upper secondary, in Kristiansand. That was in 1973, at Cathedral School. He had to get up early to catch the bus, which stopped outside the chapel in Brandsvoll. He was happy in the town, but it was always good to get back home. When winter came he left for school in darkness and didn't arrive home before nightfall. Alma had his meal ready. She and Ingemann always waited for him, they had an extra portion for him warm in the oven and saw the lights of the bus as it approached over the plain, and when he finally entered he had red cheeks and snowflakes in his blond hair and his eyes were full of all the things he had seen and experienced that day. He hung his jacket on the hook in the hall, went to wash his hands while Alma drained the water off the potatoes, and then they could all sit down to eat.

He felt how good it was to come home.

He went from being the class's undisputed number one to merging more into the background. That is, he still got good grades, sometimes excellent, but he was no longer the best. He became more anonymous. From the outside he seemed to be coping with this well. However, his new classmates learned to leave him in peace when they were given back their tests or other work. They, too, saw the ice-cold eyes and the strangely stiff face. And they also only wanted him to be himself. Everyone just wanted him to be himself.

Everything was fine so long as he was left alone.

He was coming to the end of school. It was the spring of 1976. The birch trees broke into leaf. There was an explosion of green. The school-leavers' magazine said of Dag: *Apart from school and shooting, his main interest is the local fire service. A burned child dreads the fire, as they say, but this doesn't apply to Dag. Over the years he has prevented a lot of valuable property from falling prey to flames, but that's mostly because he loves to drive a fire engine.*

That was indeed true. He did love driving the fire engine, but emergencies were few and far between.

At the end of May he took the written exam in Norwegian. One of the essay titles ran as follows: *What does it mean to be an adult, according to the prevailing rules in our society? Give an assessment of these rules from your perception of what characterises an adult. Heading: Adulthood.*

That was the one he chose. He described the main features of adulthood, and was awarded a grade B. He had taken the exam and passed it with flying colours. His average was B. Everything had gone well. Not top grades, but nonetheless he was eligible to enter university. No one in the family had achieved that before him. Alma was proud and Ingemann whistled to himself in his workshop. Now the way was open. Dag had become an adult, he was still good-natured, he had his life and his future ahead of him and he had taught himself that he didn't have to be top dog.

Later that summer he was called up to do military service. He had chosen the infantry, and was posted to Porsanger Garrison, in Finnmark. It was a journey of more than two thousand kilometres. And that was for someone who had never been further afield than Hirtshals, in Northern Jutland.

As he was leaving, Alma bounded down the stairs and across the yard. There was something she had forgotten to give him, a little envelope, which he wasn't allowed to open until he was on the train to Fornebu Airport. She hugged him, and all of a sudden it felt strange and unnatural. He pressed her lean body against his as he scanned the plain towards Breivoll feeling that he didn't want to travel at all. Alma went into the house wringing her hands in the pocket of her apron while Ingemann accompanied him to the crossroads by the shop and helped him to stow the suitcase in the bus luggage compartment. There were people on board they knew, so it was just a brief, everyday farewell from his father. When the bus set off, Ingemann stood at the crossroads alone, not really knowing where to go.

He was on his way, the long journey had begun. He broke his promise and opened the envelope when the bus was passing Kaddeberg's shop. There was five hundred kroner in the envelope and she had written on the enclosed slip of paper: *Fancy that, our lad is going out into the big, wide world. Don't forget Mamma and Pappa.*

II.

I WRITE FOR A FEW HOURS EVERY DAY. Autumn is drawing in from the south-west. The heavens open, and the rain glistens over Lake Livannet. After a night of howling gales all the leaves have been blown off the trees. So we are back to long, quiet days. It is getting colder. One morning there is hoar frost on the grass. The lake is like liquid glass and reveals a perfect reflection of the sky. On such days, writing comes to a halt. I get up, walk to the window, place my hands on it and lean my face against it. Not a bird in sight.

A few days after my visit to Alfred I rang Karin. I have known Karin all my life. I remember her from the library. She was the person I sought when I wanted to borrow books; she sat behind the counter and stamped the back of the book once, then the brown slip and put it into the card index tray. That was how it was. Two stamps and I could take the book home. The library opened in new rooms when I was four years old. I can just remember the room on the first floor of the community centre from when I was there with my father, but since 1982 it has been in the same place, in the middle of

Lauvslandsmoen, by the crossroads where the road splits into four: one road to Dynestøl, the second north to the church, the third to Brandsvoll and Kilen and the last westwards, up past our house. I cycled down to the library in the evening, and returned with cold books after the ride. When the wind came from the north-west the library door used to blow open. The wind pushed it ajar and that happened several times while I walked down the aisles between the shelves. I remember the distinctive sound through the door, it howled and moaned, and I will never forget it. Whenever the wind picks up, my thoughts turn to books.

Karin was the daughter of Teresa, who had so much music in her, who played the old church organ and held the Christmas concert with Bjarne Sløgedal on 23 December 1945, when he was a mere eighteen years old. I found the programme in the loft at Lauvslandsmoen School, and I was surprised to see what the two of them had devised. The stoves were stoked up high while they played 'Weihnachten' by Wenzel, Schumann's 'Abendlied' and finally Charles Gounod's version of 'Ave Maria', before everyone wrapped up warmly and went out into the winter's night.

Anyway.

Teresa was Alma and Ingemann's closest neighbour. She almost lived inside the magic circle. They were only separated by the road and the small, clear river that flowed placidly through the fields. As I've said, Teresa also extends into my life. I went to see her for a whole winter to learn to play the piano. She can't have been far off eighty then. She stood behind me, watching my fingers; I remember her regular breathing somewhere above and behind me. The little coughs and the twitches, if I made a mistake. She took children and adults from the whole region, everyone who wanted to play an instrument. She had done so all her life. I sat on the tall stool in her lovely and warm living room with her standing behind me following my every movement. I went there on Wednesdays, with frozen fingers, and played the same part of 'Amazing Grace' over and over again. She had to drum it into me before it stuck. I don't recall any other tunes; however, I can still play 'Amazing Grace' with relatively little effort. I don't know if I was a good pupil, but at least I did what I was told. I always did. I remember she said that I had to relax my fingers over the keys and let them practically move of their own accord. And I did as she said, I let my fingers relax over the keys and tried to let them move of their own accord.

I met Karin one Friday afternoon in late September. Sitting in her living room I could see right over to the house where Alma, Dag and Ingemann had lived. It had been painted brown since then, while in my childhood it had always been white. Otherwise there were no great changes: the workshop was still there, and between the trees I could glimpse the garage where the fire engine was housed.

We sat chatting about this and that until the conversation turned to the fires.

It transpired that Teresa had received two letters from prison. In addition, she had made daily entries in her diary. Karin had found all of this in a drawer after Teresa died. She passed me the letters and I read with the same mixture of feelings that I had experienced at Alfred's. From one letter I gathered that Teresa had given him a guitar. However, it was unclear whether she had sent it by post or she had turned up at Kristiansand Courthouse and delivered it in person. At any rate, he wrote to her thanking her for teaching him to play the piano when he was a child, and at the same time told her he had already taught himself to play the guitar. And that music was becoming more and more important to him.

So he had gone to Teresa to learn to play an instrument, too.

The second letter was very incoherent, something about Our Lord God and several named individuals from the region. It is difficult to summarise. Altogether very disjointed.

So there were now three letters, including the letter to Alfred. Furthermore, there were Teresa's diaries. A whole boxful of them, the same editions every year: the small, green books published by the Norwegian Farmers' Union. There were short remarks about the weather, about pupils she'd had. I flicked back quickly. As far as I could see, my name wasn't mentioned. However, there was quite a bit about Dag, especially around the time of the fires and afterwards. The last pages, the undated ones entitled *Notes*, were covered with her slightly forward-sloping handwriting. These last pages were in the form of a letter, but I doubt if she ever transferred them to notepaper and sent it. If, contrary to expectation, I should be mistaken, the question is: To whom?

Apart from the three letters I have seen, there were said to be more. From what I could glean, they poured out from the prison in the first months. Mention was also made of this during the trial; it was referred to as *enormous correspondence.*

That was in the weeks after the arrest, when he was alone and the dream about the dog surfaced. And he started writing. It was as if something was forcing its way out. All the letters were stamped *The Courthouse, Box 1D*.

He wrote to all his victims, but I don't know how many answered. I have tried to find out who received a letter, what was in it and whether they replied. But it has been impossible. As a rule I was met with the same response: *I don't remember. I threw it away. He was out of his mind, wasn't he?*

III.

SHE HAD BEEN looking forward to seeing him again. He had written to them all autumn. Every week she waited expectantly for the small, brown envelopes postmarked Porsanger Garrison, with the Norwegian lion in the middle. At first he had written long, detailed letters that Ingemann read aloud at the kitchen table. Afterwards, she quietly re-read them on her own, and Dag seemed to come even closer. He talked about his life in the garrison, about the other soldiers, who were, he said, either odd, hard work or likeable and who came from all over the country; he wrote about the food, which was monotonous and bore no comparison with Alma's home cooking and he wrote about the exercises they went on by the Russian border. She tried to visualise everything, this strange, frozen world, and Dag right in the middle of it.

In December they received a letter in which he said he hadn't been given any Christmas leave. Someone had to stay in the camp, so there was a lottery and he was one of the unlucky ones. Ingemann and Alma had taken the news with composure. On the morning of Christmas Eve he phoned. It was a short conversation because the coins were racing through the machine. He spoke to Ingemann first, then had a few words with Alma. She thought his voice sounded strange, but it probably wasn't that surprising; after all, he was more than two thousand kilometres away.

In the New Year, a letter was a long time in coming. However, in February they received a postcard. It showed a watchtower on the border between Norway and the Soviet Union. On the back they read: *The soldier in the tower is me.* At first they were excited. Just imagine! There couldn't be many parents whose son's photograph was on a postcard. Then the excitement faded. It was Ingemann who spoke first – the person in the picture could not possibly be Dag. He bore absolutely no resemblance to their son. Alma noticed that too, but she didn't comment. She dried her hands on a tea towel and pinned the postcard to the window frame after Ingemann had gone to the workshop, and never mentioned it again. The card hung there for a few days, although neither of them said another word about it. Then one morning she unpinned the card and rested it against one of his trophies on the shelf above the piano.

They didn't hear any more until well into March. There was a card saying he was coming home. Nothing else. Not even his name. Just: *Coming home on 14th.* He had signed it *The soldier.* It was Ingemann's opinion that he had been given leave. After all, that wouldn't be unusual. Alma wasn't sure. There was something about the signature. It wasn't like Dag. She didn't understand it. She wished she had a telephone number to call him on, but there wasn't one, or at least that was what Dag had told them in one of his first letters.

Late in the afternoon of the next day, as Alma was washing up, she caught sight of a man on the road from Brandsvoll. He was walking without any apparent haste and she could see there was something familiar about him. It took a few seconds. Then she clicked.

It was him.

All of a sudden he was there, in the yard, it was the thirteenth, in other words, the day before he was due to arrive. He was wearing the uniform soldiers wore on leave, his long blond hair was gone, now you could see his bare skull.

'Is that you?' she asked.

He just stood there with the March sun at his back and smiled. She approached slowly and then embraced him.

'You've been so far away,' she said.

'But now I'm home, Mamma,' he said. 'I'll never go away again.'

He stated that as a fact. It seemed a little odd, but Alma didn't pay it any further attention, she was just happy to see him. Happy and surprised and slightly apprehensive.

'How have you been?' she asked.

'Fine,' he replied.

'I'm glad,' she said. Then they just dilly-dallied in the yard as the roofs dripped. They heard the workshop door open, and there was Ingemann in the doorway.

'Is it you?' he asked.

'Looks like it,' Dag said.

Ingemann wiped his hands on a filthy rag, and went over and shook his son's hand.

'I hardly recognised you,' he said with a strained chuckle. All three of them stood there in the low March sun. Their shadows were long and lean and stretched all the way to the house. They didn't talk about the postcard or the signature or why he had suddenly come home.

'I've got to get some shut-eye,' he said, and no wonder after travelling for almost twenty-four hours.

That night, after she had gone to bed, Alma lay awake for a long time. She stared up at the ceiling listening to Ingemann's regular breathing. She lay there feeling strangely empty, as though she had talked and talked all day and now she didn't have a single word left.

The following day he didn't tell them anything. He was still worn out after the journey, he said. He needed to rest and sleep. They ate in palpable silence, then he went up to his room and back to bed.

He had a long lie-in every morning. April came. The snow melted, the fields lay dark and bare, a gentle breeze soughed through the forest. He stayed at home all spring. Long lie-ins became a habit. Occasionally he didn't get up until after twelve o'clock, and then he hardly had the energy to go downstairs. Everything seemed to be very heavy; every day was suddenly full of insuperable obstacles. And under these circumstances it was best of course to stay in bed. Alma said nothing. She cooked food she knew he liked, took it to his room and put the plate on his bedside table without a word.

Concern was mounting in a visible frown between her eyes. Like a gash.

Then things brightened up.

After a few weeks it was almost as before. He no longer lay in bed all morning. He got up, had a shower and seemed happier than he had been for ages. It had been a fleeting transition and had passed on its own. One evening he went into the kitchen while Alma was baking a cake. He tiptoed up behind her and gently placed his hands over her eyes. She was bewildered; this was the first time he had done anything of the kind. It felt strange, but at the same time quite nice.

'Who is it?' she asked, teasing.

He didn't answer.

'I think I know who it is,' she continued.

Still he didn't answer.

'You'll have to let go now,' she said at length. And then she laughed as she struggled to get free, she laughed and laughed as he held on. He was holding her tight and she twisted from side to side. Then he let go.

He was himself again, the good boy she knew so well. She smiled and said: 'Now you'll have to let your hair grow.'

The weeks passed. Dag and Ingemann were in the habit of shooting at a target every Saturday morning, just like in the old days, while she was alone in the kitchen baking bread. They fired a round of five shots each, then they got up and walked down the field to study the black circle, Dag first, Ingemann following with his hands in his pockets, and when they returned they ate the hot bread that steamed as Alma sliced it.

It was midsummer. The heat came. It came in waves from the end of the plain towards Breivoll. He turned twenty. The swallows circled high in the sky. In the evenings he drove to Lake Homevannet to go swimming. She didn't know that he went alone. Or that he swam alone to the underwater rocks about thirty metres from the bathing area.

His hair grew. It wasn't long before his skull was covered. She was glad to have him back. She felt it in her stomach whenever she looked at him. It wasn't that. Of course she was glad. She smiled, and she hadn't done that for quite a while. Yet there was still a gash between her eyes. It wouldn't go.

He spent the whole of the summer upstairs in his room. He had a radio and an old record player, and music blared out every evening and night. He didn't tell them anything about his stint by the Russian border, only that he had once seen a wolf. During the initial days she had attempted to be cheerful, and both she and Ingemann had asked questions and prodded him about all sorts of things. But his eyes had seemed to darken at every question, something happened to his face, it stiffened, and a strange, oppressive atmosphere spread around the table. From then on, questions from either of them became rarer and rarer. Then they stopped, neither she nor Ingemann asked anything. It was best to let sleeping dogs lie, and carry on as before. All they had was the story of the wolf. It went as follows:

One night he was sitting alone in the watchtower with the temperature registering minus forty degrees centigrade. Suddenly the animal trotted across the snow; he had been tracking it through his binoculars. Every so often the wolf stopped and listened, then it went on. The snow was crusted, the moon shone and the animal left no paw marks. Then it crossed the border.

That was the story of the wolf; otherwise nothing.

Through the autumn he began to increase the volume of the music. Alma lay awake listening. At times she thought she could hear his voice, singing or talking. For long periods there was total silence. Then the music blasted out and she thought she heard someone laughing.

In October, Alma started cleaning for people, as she had done in years past. By choice, for neighbours, people who lived within walking distance. She didn't like cycling, she preferred to walk. She walked to Omdal, to Breivoll and to Djupesland. She washed the hall and kitchen floor of the chapel in Brandsvoll, and she cleaned for Agnes and Anders Fjeldsgård in the big, white house by the Solås road.

In December the first snow came. One morning the whole world was white and pure. Alma baked seven kinds of Christmas biscuit, exactly as she used to, and Dag came into the kitchen and was allowed to taste them while they were still warm. Warily, she asked what he had considered doing when Christmas was over. He said that he hadn't thought that far ahead.

'But surely you're going to do something, aren't you?' she asked.

'Oh, yes,' he answered. 'I'll find something.'

'You could start some course or other, with your school-leaving grades and all that.'

'Yes,' he said. 'We'll see.'

That was the end of the conversation about the future. Christmas came. All three of them were in church on

Christmas Eve. They sat among neighbours and acquaintances from the region, all with a singular gleam in their eyes they never usually had. Alfred and Else and their children were there, Anders and Agnes Fjeldsgård, Syvert Mæsel, Olga Dynestøl, and many, many others. Everyone was there, Teresa was perched in front of the organ, high up, and glanced in the console mirror as she approached the end of 'Deilig er jorden'. My father was there, too. He sat in a front pew beside his mother and father and Mamma, and she had a growing child in her stomach, and that child was me. There was something quite special about sitting stiffly, dressed up and solemn, among all those you knew so well, it was as though everyone was showing themselves from a new and unfamiliar side, it was wonderful and a little strange, and Alma could feel the Yuletide peace settling over her and she was almost calm.

The New Year came. The year was 1978.

January arrived with short, bitterly cold days. Dag was outside in the workshop with Ingemann. Helping to keep it tidy, clearing away any junk that had accumulated during autumn. He swept the floor, burned old rubbish and splashed diesel on it to make it light. Then there was nothing else to do. He took to lying in again. He dug up all his old comics. Donald Duck, Silver Arrow and The Phantom. In the evenings he went somewhere in the car. The car Ingemann had bought for a song and done up in time for Dag's eighteenth birthday, the summer almost three years ago. He could be out for hours on end. Alma had no idea where he was. She used to wake up in the darkness, not knowing whether he had come home. What was the time? One? Three?

Six? She lay listening, cold and tense. But he always came home eventually. Nothing ever happened.

February came. With a metre of snow. Power cuts came and went. In March, mild weather swept in from the south-west, trees dripped, roofs ran and roads were as slippery as soap. Then it veered back to the south-east and they were in deepest winter again. For three days snow came down like a carpet, and when at last it stopped, there were mild, sunny days when the world seemed to stand still. Slowly, spring came. April arrived with long, bright days. The river flowed quietly. The ice vanished, the water glittered. At night there was a smell of raw, damp earth. His hair was almost as long as when he went into the army.

One evening when he was about to drive off, Alma asked where he was intending to go.

'Out,' he said pithily.

'Where?' she asked.

'That anything to do with you?' he snapped, then slammed the door and drove away. She didn't react, but afterwards she couldn't shake his words out of her head. They sank inside her, lay still and ached. She lay awake in bed that night as Ingemann slept soundly beside her. *That anything to do with you? That anything to do with you?* She could hear his voice. It was Dag, yet she wasn't sure. Good, kind Dag. She thought she heard him laugh. She dozed off, woke up with a start. She had dreamed that she was standing by a cradle, that he was a baby, but he wasn't there. The cradle was empty, but it was still rocking. She got up, crept barefoot to his door. Knocked, and opened it wide. He was lying awake on top of the duvet, fully dressed, a Donald Duck comic open on his stomach. At first he appeared frightened, as though for a few seconds he thought something terrible had happened. Then he was calm. Then he smiled.

'Mamma,' he whispered. 'Is that you?'

IV.

6 MAY, 1978. The flames by the roadside grew, caught hold of the grass, moved into the heather, the juniper bushes, then spread quickly into the forest. Spring had indeed been dry, unusually dry. All it needed was a spark. A cigarette tossed from a window, a moment's thoughtlessness.

The alarm went off.

It wailed across the region until people realised what it was. It had hardly been heard before. People stopped and exchanged looks.

That was the fire alarm, wasn't it?

Then the fire engine came down from the station with sirens blaring. Down round the tight bend, past the house, over the tiny bridge. It turned left, sped up and continued past the disused co-op with the balcony and the flagpole above the road. It raced down the hill past the chapel and the community centre and on to Kilen.

Dag was driving while Ingemann sat beside him clinging onto the handle above the door.

The fire engine was quite new, no more than five years old. It was an International with room for a thousand litres of water in the tank and equipped with a twenty-five-kilo pump at the front. The vehicle held the road well, and Dag drove quickly and efficiently. They met a couple of cars, which slowed down, swerved onto the verge and let them pass. In Kilen the sirens had been heard approaching, and there was a little crowd standing outside Kaddeberg's waiting to see what was going on. By the shop Dag had to jump on the brakes and sling the fire engine to the left, into the road to Øvland, making the water in the tank slop around and the whole vehicle roll from side to side.

They were the first to arrive at the scene of the fire. Immediately, however, a man came running out of the forest. It was Sjur Lunde, the owner of the land. He had rung the station. While waiting for the fire engine he had been trying to get the blaze under control on his own.

Within a quarter of an hour all the firemen were there. They parked in a line behind the tender. Alfred was there. Jens was there. Arnold. Salve. Knut. Peder. Everyone was there. From a distance the line of vehicles looked like a long train with the red tender as the locomotive pulling the blue, white and brown carriages after it. A relatively limited area was ablaze. There was no wind. And a little lake was close by. The fire was a formality. The pump was lifted down from the vehicle. It took four of them to carry it, but it shot the water out at a decent rate. For a while Ingemann gave a hand, but then the others took over and he stood back and watched. He was getting tiny intermittent stabs in his chest – it felt like his heart – but they went as soon as he quietened down.

Dag was holding the hose when the water came through. The pressure was good and he directed the jet straight at the flames. For a good while he knelt and sprayed the flames while the others stood behind him watching. Then he turned and shouted for someone else to take over. At once one of the men grabbed the hose from his hands, and Dag strolled back to the fire engine and joined his father. Dag's face was red, and a cut to his hand was bleeding. He was out of breath, yet collected and somehow at peace. He seemed happy.

'You did a fine job,' Ingemann said, so low that no one else could hear.

V.

MAY 1978. I slept during the first weeks; later Mamma took me in the pram to and from the school in Lauvslandsmoen. It was no more than a kilometre and I slept on the way.

One fire isn't a topic of conversation. It is soon forgotten. It passes.

But a second?

It came a mere ten days after the first. It took hold of the Tønnes' old hay barn, the one at the bottom of the Leipsland ridge, just a few hundred metres from my grandmother's house. I remember the four cornerstones that remained standing in a perfect square for all of my childhood, but neither my grandmother nor my grandfather nor anyone else told me what had happened there.

The barn was ablaze when the fire engine arrived; all you saw was the building's framework like an intensely burning cobweb at the centre of the fire. Water was quickly pumped into the hoses, but nothing could be saved. The alarm had gone off too late. It was a controlled burn-out.

Bit by bit, a crowd had gathered and they stood facing the raging flames. The news spread, even though it was the middle of the night. More and more cars stopped along the road. People got out and approached in silence. They were so close they felt the heat on their faces and hardly spoke; all they did was stare. It was quite dark, and the sight was both frightening and almost enticing. After twenty minutes the framework collapsed, a shower of sparks rose like fireflies into the sky and fierce flames burst into life again. Someone laughed. It was dark and impossible to see who it had been.

Two fires in ten days. What could you say?

The following day was 17 May, Norway's Constitution Day. As usual, it started with a service in the church, which on this occasion was as full as ever it was. The sun shone through the window above the altarpiece of Jesus's last supper, making the dust in the room sparkle. Two birch twigs had been bound to the Roman arches, and fresh birch leaves wreathed the lectern. Omland was conducting the service. He wore a black cassock and spoke about a log branded with the owner's mark floating in the river. In backwaters, where it cannot reach its destination, it still carries the mark, and even from there it can find its way into the correct channel and be what it was originally intended to be.

Nothing about the fires. Of course not. These were the days before anyone had an inkling of what was to come.

Then there was food for everyone in the cramped cellar beneath the community centre, where the ceiling was so low that almost everyone had to stoop when they entered. The procession then departed from Brandsvoll and marched for three kilometres past Knut Frigstad's house, past the old doctor's surgery on the bend, past Anders and Agnes Fjeldgård's house, to continue alongside glittering Lake Bordvannet, where birch trees stood with their thin foliage, and culminated at Lauvslandsmoen School, where the flag was hoisted and all the old people sat waiting in the sun.

My parents were there, too, and I lay asleep in a deep pram. The procession was coming over the Lauvslandsmoen Plain, headed by the flag-bearer, then the band in their red uniforms and cylindrical hats, and I woke and Mamma lifted me out so that I could see where the music was coming from.

In the evening there was a party in the Brandsvoll Community Centre. Grandma and Grandad were in the hall. As were Ingemann and Alma. Aasta was there with her husband Sigurd. Olga Dynestøl sat on her own, right at the back next to the wood-burning stove. My parents, however, were not there. They needed to sleep, which was quite understandable, given they had a two-month-old child.

Syvert Mæsel read the opening address in a firm voice, as he always did. He stood alone on the small podium with the woven tapestry hanging behind him. Everyone sat still with a solemn expression because what he said always had gravitas and substance. Perhaps the audience thought about everything he had seen and heard during his three years in Sachsenhausen concentration camp. Afterwards they sang 'Finsland, My Homeland'.

Soon shines the sun over snow-white dell,
The evening sun blazes through cloud so well,
Finsland, she sleeps under winter's fell,
Lies there so frozen and hard.

Five verses. Teresa sat at the piano, which was situated beneath the podium.

In the interval, several people went over to Ingemann to enquire about the fires. Two fires in such a short time. What was going on? Ingemann shrugged. They looked at him, and he looked at them with an indefinable expression. He had no answer. He cast down his eyes.

Then there was food and coffee and entertainment, and before everyone went home they got up and sang the national anthem.

That night all was still.

The new fire engine had really been put through its paces. After each emergency the equipment had to be cleaned. The hoses had to be unfurled to dry in the sun, then rolled up and attached to the vehicle. The pumps had to be lubricated, checked and given a round with the grease gun. All this was Ingemann's responsibility. He rolled the hoses out on the tarmac outside the fire station and left them there for a few hours before painstakingly rolling them up again. This was a job that took the whole morning, and he couldn't go at it too hard because as soon as he did he felt stabbing pains in his chest. At twelve o'clock he went in to eat. Dag was still in his bedroom asleep, so Ingemann and Alma ate alone, and in silence.

When they had finished, Alma cleared the table while Ingemann lay down on the sofa in the living room with the newspaper on his chest. After a brief nap, he returned to the fire station and resumed his work.

He had painted some of the equipment white. It was so

easy to lose things in the dark. That was why he had painted all the fire service's petrol cans. They were the so-called jerrycans that were used by the Germans during the First World War. Hence the name. Their special feature was the handles, which meant two men could carry them. That made them quicker and easier to move, which suited the fire service down to the ground. He picked up the paint pot again and stirred its contents. After placing the cans in a row outside the fire station, he knelt down and with a slim black brush painted on each one *FB*, for Finsland Brannvesenet, Finsland Fire Service.

While he was engaged in this task he heard footsteps on the gravel. It was Dag coming up the path, and he stopped in front of Ingemann, blocking the sun.

'Well, if it isn't old sleepyhead,' Ingemann said with a bright chuckle.

Dag didn't answer; he just watched his father's hand and the brush slowly and fastidiously painting the black letters. When Ingemann had finished, Dag helped him to carry the jerrycans back to where they had been, after which the fire engine had to be reversed into the station. Dag did this while his father made sure the vehicle was backed as far as it could go. He stood in the darkness, inside the garage, as the fire engine slowly reversed towards him. It was so tight that he would be crushed against the wall if it didn't stop in time. He waited, unperturbed, as the vehicle inched closer and the room was filled with exhaust fumes. Then it came to a halt with a metre's clearance from the wall.

'Perfect!' he shouted.

Afterwards they ambled the short distance back to the

house, chatting in low voices. They, too, had begun to speak in low voices.

'Let's hope that was the last fire,' Ingemann said.

'Yes, let's hope so,' Dag replied.

'I'm getting too old to be putting out fires,' Ingemann said.

'Too old?' Dag pulled up and studied his father. 'You're not too old. I'm sure you'll be with us next time as well.'

The latter took Ingemann aback, but he said nothing. Instead he shook his head and smiled at his son, and by then they were home, and on entering the hall they could smell Alma's rissoles and forgot everything else.

The following night, all was still.

People went to bed. Lights were extinguished, doors locked, cool sheets parted.

Only the outside lamps were on. The white domes, the moths and all the nameless insects fluttering towards the light in fear.

VI.

THE AIR IS CLEARER, SHARPER. Three degrees centigrade. The birds seem confused, they are zigzagging across the sky as though no longer sure where south and north are. The water is black, smooth, like oil. The reflection of the closest houses is nigh on perfect. Sometimes I wish I had never left this region. I should never have gone to Oslo, should never have started studying, should never have started to write. I should have stayed here, right here, in the midst of this serene landscape, in the peaceful woods with all the shining pools and lakes, among the white houses and red barns and the placid cows in the summer. I should never have left all this that I love so deeply. I should have stayed here and lived a different life.

Every now and then I have the feeling that I am living two parallel lives. One is secure, simple, a life without so many words. The other is apparently real life, with me in the middle of it, at my desk writing every day. The first life can disappear for lengthy periods, but makes an occasional appearance, it is as though I am suddenly close to stepping inside it, I am on the verge and I have a sense that at any moment I will catch sight of the person who perhaps really is me.

After a while it becomes too cold to sit by the window. I have turned up the heat, but it doesn't help. In the end, I fetch my jacket and wrap it around me. From the window I can see up to where Olav and Johanna's house used to be, and some way down, by the old post office, is the house they rented for the last months before she fell ill and was accommodated in the rest home in Nodeland. The fire must have been reflected in the lake. That must have been a sight.

I read Dag's letter several times, slowly, assiduously, as though I might get closer to him if I just read carefully enough. As though the mystery around him lies in the words themselves.

I write a sentence in my notebook: *Who is it we see when we see ourselves?*

That is the question.

I remember one episode. I must have been in the first class, in which case I would have been seven or eight years old. I was standing in front of the class and telling a story. I don't remember what the story was about, but I know it was very exciting because it had me and everyone else in its thrall. I remember thinking: Hold your horses now, you mustn't exaggerate, you mustn't tell any more lies, soon you'll have gone too far, soon they won't believe you any more, soon they'll see through you, soon they'll see that you're lying, soon they'll all get up and walk away and you'll be left all alone.

But they believed me. It worked. They didn't rumble me. It was as quiet as the grave until the story was finished, and for a few seconds afterwards. Then I heard: *More!*

However, what happened next was very important. When the bell rang and everyone made a beeline for the door, our teacher held me back. Her name was Ruth; I liked her a lot. She crouched down in front of me with a hand on each of my shoulders, as though I had hurt my face or done something wrong. I remember her face, her eyes, her expression. *Where did you get that story?* she asked. She seemed concerned, and so as not to worry her further I shrugged and cast down my eyes. I didn't dare say that I had made it up. That it had all come to me on the spur of the moment. That it was a fabrication from beginning to end. I wanted to free myself from her grip, but I didn't know what to say. She continued to stare at me with those concerned eyes of hers, and I promised myself that I would never tell a story like that again. For the first time, I had done something illicit. Me, who was always so well behaved, who always did what was right. Now I didn't know what lay in store for me. *You're a writer, that's what you are*, Ruth said, looking at me with a strange smile. *I'll n-never do it again*, I stuttered, feeling a vague sense of shame force its way up from my stomach to my chest and face. Then she let go of me and I charged out to join the others, but her words didn't let go of me, they were impossible to escape. Ruth had planted them, and quietly, oh so quietly, they began to grow. I was not like the others. I was a writer. I felt it could be seen all over me. It was written on my face, or in my eyes, or on my forehead. I had promised I would never tell stories again, I would just behave myself and do what was right, and I hoped for a long time that all of this would pass of its own accord.

VII.

AT A FEW MINUTES PAST 1 A.M. she got dressed and went down to the kitchen. She put the kettle on the stove and waited for the water to boil. When the coffee was ready she took a clean cup from the cupboard and sat down in Dag's seat at the kitchen table, from where she could see across the plain towards Breivoll. There was something light inside her, something that was totally weightless and never rested, which made it impossible to sleep. It was like this almost every night; she lay beside Ingemann staring for ages at the ceiling. She heard the music in Dag's room, and whenever it went quiet she pricked up her ears. She could hear him getting out of bed and mumbling something, but she couldn't make out the words. Then she dropped off and snatched a couple of hours' sleep at around midnight. She slept lightly, as though hovering just under the surface. Fragments of dreams drifted by, but everything was distorted and unrecognisable as if it belonged to someone else.

Then she was awoken by someone descending the stairs. Keys jangled as he threw on his jacket. The lock clicked. Silence in the house after the sound of the car faded.

After a while she got up.

She sat listening to the clock's regular tick above the refrigerator. Steam rose from her cup like long, ragged flags fluttering in the wind and dissipating.

Much later, she saw a car approaching from across the plain at great speed. It was still dark outside. The headlights shook. The car slowed down as it came to the crossroads, then turned left, and the headlights cut like a knife through the white, transparent mist hanging over the field.

It was him.

The car drew to a halt outside the kitchen. She heard the car radio blaring for a few seconds before it went quiet, she heard the door opening, his steps on the gravel. She heard him talking to himself in the yard. She was almost used to it now. He would suddenly ask himself a question. Or reprimand himself. She had heard that on several occasions, but had said nothing about it to Ingemann. Initially it had happened while the music was playing, later also when there was complete silence. At first this had frightened her. She had been sitting alone in the living room with some sewing when she heard Dag talking upstairs. She had the impression there was someone with him. A second person. Someone from his old class? She had gone upstairs and knocked on his door, and when he opened it only he was there. His face had frozen into a strange grimace, and it was this expression that had frightened her. But then his whole face softened, everything melted, the bizarrely distorted face seemed to slide away, and she saw it was him.

She got up now, went to the door and stood listening with the steaming cup in her hand. The yard had gone quiet. Then he came in.

'What are you doing up?' he asked.

'Would you like some coffee?' she said.

'Coffee in the middle of the night?'

'Why not?'

She filled a large, white cup and put it down on the other side of the kitchen table, in what was actually Ingemann's place.

'Are you hungry?' she asked. 'We've got some fresh bread, you know.'

He sat down at the table while she took some bread from the cupboard and cut three white slices that fell to the side one after the other. He said nothing. He smelt of spring nights and exhaust fumes.

'Have you been gadding about?' she asked.

'You could say that,' he replied.

She put out some jam that had been in the freezer since the previous summer, some clove cheese and Prim spread. All of this she served in a semi-circle around him. She got out some milk, too, and poured it into a glass.

'Come on, eat,' she said.

'You don't need to wait up for me,' he blurted, raising his eyes.

'I couldn't sleep,' she said with a little smile, flicking the hair off her forehead.

'You couldn't sleep?'

'No. I suppose I'm just like you,' she said. 'You don't sleep either, do you.'

He didn't respond, just looked at her and smiled. They didn't say anything for a long while. It felt good. There was quite some time before morning broke, before Ingemann got up and the day began. Only the two of them now. It was good, somewhat unaccustomed, crystal clear, and she wished it could go on and on. He ate greedily; she sliced more bread and placed it on the edge of his plate while essaying a smile. It was wonderful to see him showing a healthy appetite. That was how it had always been: the more he ate, the better she felt.

'It's cold out tonight,' he said, chewing and looking out of the window pensively.

'Are you cold?' she asked. 'Shall I get you a jumper?'

He shook his head, drained his glass of milk and stood up, ready to go. She knew at once it was over.

'I suppose it was cold in Porsanger, too, wasn't it?' she asked out of the blue.

'Minus forty,' he answered, without looking at her.

She got up.

'Couldn't you tell me a bit about it, Dag?' she asked, feeling her face go hot and flustered. 'Surely you can tell me . . . Pappa and I know next to nothing.'

Dag relaxed, and his movements slowed.

'What would you like me to tell you?' he asked.

'What really happened.'

His gaze lingered on her, then he shook his head almost imperceptibly.

'What really happened?'

'Yes,' she said with an even voice. 'What happened to you.'

'To me? What do you mean?'

She moved closer while Dag stood rooted to the floor. She went up to him, and now she could smell the smoke.

'You're so . . . You've become . . . Can't you tell me, Dag? Please. Just tell me everything.'

They were standing in the middle of the kitchen floor. The light from the ceiling lamp engulfed them and made his hair gleam greasily. She sent him an imploring look, then dropped her gaze, saw his open shirt, hands, brown cord trousers, socks.

'Are you crying, Mamma?'

She didn't answer. She was standing very close to him, with eyes closed now.

'Do you want me to tell you?' he continued nonchalantly.

'Yes, Dag, it would make me so happy.'

She heard him take a deep breath. She swallowed and felt her heart thump out of control. She looked up at him, and now he had that same stiff face she had first seen upstairs in his room. And at that moment she froze with fear.

'Dag,' she whispered.

'Mamma,' he said in a low, thick voice.

'Don't you want to tell me?'

'It's . . . Mamma, it's . . .'

He shook his head sadly.

'Come on, Dag,' she prompted. 'Let's go and sit in the living room.'

She went ahead, and he followed hesitantly, then stopped in the doorway.

'Don't you want to?' she asked again.

'Mamma, I . . .'

'Couldn't you play something first?' she asked hastily.

'Now?'

'Not too loud, though. Then we can have a chat afterwards.'

He vacillated, watching her, then smiled, and a warm flush surged through her.

They had bought the piano for his sake. That was after he had started going to Teresa on a regular basis. He needed to be able to practise at home. And so they had ensured he could. Ingemann had acquired the piano at a house clearance sale; he had lashed it to the small trailer belonging to the fire service, and then he and Dag had driven it home. They had managed to transport it indoors with the help of Alfred and several other neighbours. She could remember the day so well. It was *the day the piano came*, they said later, as though they were talking about a child. It was only when she saw them carrying it that she realised how heavy it was, and when they had finally got it into position by the window, she said, loud enough for everyone to hear, that this piano would never be moved again.

He sat down on the piano stool, looking up at her expectantly.

'What shall I play then?'

'You decide,' she replied. 'Anything you like.'

'Anything?'

He flexed his fingers like a concert pianist. Then he played. Very softly so that only the two of them could hear. She noticed that he was rusty, he hit a false note now and then, but nevertheless. It was slowly coming back. He was playing.

She stood a little way behind him, studying his back, neck, head, the hair that had grown quite long, almost as it had been before. She looked up at the postcard that still leaned against the cups, she saw the picture of the soldier in the watchtower, she saw the endless snow-covered plains and the Russian border, like a white, treeless road leading past the tower and beyond into infinity.

When he had finished he sat with bowed head staring at the keys.

'That was lovely,' she said in a hushed voice.

'Would you like to hear more?' he asked.

She nodded.

Then he played 'Nearer, My God, to Thee', for he knew this was the one she really wanted to hear. She sat on the edge of the table and closed her eyes. The tears began to flow, she couldn't hold them back, the ground gave way inside her, and he played simply and crisply, without a single false note. She was sitting like this when he sprang to his feet and slammed the lid with a crash and a doleful echo.

'Now you can tell me,' she whispered.

'Yes,' he said.

'Tell me everything, Dag,' she said, rising to her feet as well.

Then the telephone rang.

She stared at him in horror for a second. There was no time for more, because he was already in the hall picking up the telephone and speaking in a low voice. She went to the door and watched him making notes on a pad.

Then he called Ingemann.

Fire! Fire!

She hastily prepared two packed lunches, slicing more

bread and spreading it with Prim and some cheese, and then she poured the rest of the coffee into the thermos. At just that moment the alarm went off in the half-light. It was Dag who had been outside to sound it; he must have run because he came back in almost straightaway, sweating and panting. The sound was so ear-splitting that the elegant glasses in the cupboard jangled. Ingemann came down the stairs doing up the last of the buttons on his shirt. He was groggy with sleep, his eyes swimming, his hair pointing in all directions, but that made no difference. A house was ablaze, and he was the fire chief. There was no time to waste. Get the fire engine out, start the sirens, put on the blue lights. Drive for all you were worth. Arrive. Assess the situation. Dag had been ready for some time; he had buttoned his shirt up to the neck and was shuffling his feet in the hall.

'Aren't you going to put on any more clothes?' Alma asked.

'There's a fire, Mamma. I don't have the time.'

'But you're only wearing a shirt, Dag.'

That was all she managed to say. He was already out of the door and bounding through the dawn towards the fire station. A few minutes later she heard the sirens merging with the protracted wailing of the alarm. She hurriedly slipped the packed lunches into a bag, which Ingemann grabbed on his way out of the door to the fire engine and Dag, who was waiting behind the wheel.

VIII.

ON 7 JUNE 1978, *Fædrelandsvennen* carries a lengthy interview with Olav and Johanna Vatneli. It is a good two days after the fire. It is the same interview that I remembered when I was standing by the grave, the one in which Olav referred to himself as soft and Johanna as calm.

The two of them are sitting in Knut Karlsen's basement flat. Olav on the edge of the bed, wearing a checked shirt and loose braces, staring into the air apathetically. Johanna on a chair alongside him with her hands limp in her lap and a faint smile around her mouth, as though none of this really concerns her. Behind them a bracket lamp with the plug dangling down.

The previous day they had gone to town to buy clothes. Two summer dresses, a pair of trousers, shirts, underwear. Two pairs of shoes. In addition, they had both been measured for new dentures.

Bereft of everything, Olav and Johanna sit in their neighbour's flat wondering what will become of them.

Johanna talks about the blaze again, the explosion in the kitchen, the sea of flames, the shadow outside the window and the events that followed. Earlier that day, they had received a visit from Alma and Ingemann. This is said in one sentence, never to be mentioned again, yet the sentence seems to lie there, flashing on the page.

Later in the interview they talk about Kåre. I suppose it felt natural to talk about him, after all, they had lost everything else. There, in Knut Karlsen's cellar, it is nineteen years since he died. He was the only child they had. After Kåre there was nothing, and after the house and the rest were gone, Kåre seemed to return.

That is the situation.

The whole business is so unreal. It is unimaginable. Olav struggles to his feet, but as yet he isn't strong enough to venture down and see the scorched ruins. He still wants to wait a few days, then he will go down, and he will go on his own. The outbuilding was saved, you see, he says, and he has a lot of good oak there. He thinks the oak will come in handy now. The only problem is that they don't have a stove in which to burn it, nor a house to heat. In the outbuilding with the wood there is also a bike. I don't know for certain, but it may be Kåre's. He did eventually teach himself to ride.

They are seventy-three and eighty-three years old and have to start a new life. They have a little wood, a few thousand kroner and an old bike. That is all.

It was through the visit to Alfred and Else that I came to Aasta. I wanted to know more about Johanna and Olav, and about Kåre. All of a sudden it felt important. Aasta, Johanna Vatneli's sister-in-law and therefore Kåre's aunt, was forty-eight years old in 1978, and now, fifty years after he died, she was one of the few still to remember him.

On one of the first evenings in November I left home and walked the kilometre or so to the yellow house where Aasta lived. She has known me all my life: she was one of those to visit my mother while she was still at the maternity ward in Kongens gate and I was no more than a few days old.

We sat chatting for several hours. We talked about the fire, and the pyromaniac. I asked about Olav and Johanna. And about Kåre. I took notes.

Kåre's story was as follows. He had an open wound on his leg, from falling on a ski slope, Slottebakken Hill, the one with the meticulously constructed ski jump and the unusually steep landing area. It was a straight plunge. I recalled my father had spoken about Slottebakken, having jumped there himself many times. He was of course one of the very best – at least that was what he said – and he may well have been there on that evening in the 1950s when Kåre called out in the darkness, crouched down and set off.

Kåre had performed an immense take-off and hovered high on his descent. A gasp ran through the watching crowd. No one had ever seen such a long jump. He continued to hover, his overalls filling out like a taut sail across his back, everyone held their breath, then the skis smacked down on the icy landing strip and scattered cheers broke out on that freezing cold evening. He landed safe and sound, but then fell headlong. It wasn't a nasty fall, but was enough for him to call it a day. He sat in a snowdrift holding his leg.

The next day he gave school a miss and stayed at home. It was a Friday. By Monday he was no better. Quite the contrary, he had a high temperature. Some days later he and Johanna went to see the doctor, who had surgery hours from eleven to four on the bend opposite Knut Frigstad's house in Brandsvoll. His name was Dr Rosenvold, he had the gentle but elusive eyes that you never really saw behind his glasses. He was able to confirm that Kåre had a wound which wouldn't heal. A glistening, evil-smelling liquid leaked from it, and for the time being there was nothing they could do. They would have to wait and see. Johanna tore rags into strips and dipped them in a special vinegar mixture and bound them round his leg. It was diagnosed as a *fracture*. Subsequently it transpired that it was a great deal more serious, but they didn't dare to articulate the word. At that time he was fourteen years old and about to change schools and no one articulated the word. Dr Rosenvold visited Olav and Johanna's home, the white house beside the road. It was late summer, the cherry tree in the garden was bulging with dark red fruit and the black car pulled up in the yard between the house and the barn. Dr Rosenvold ascended the stairs in leisurely fashion and went into the room where the boy lay in bed. He closed the door behind him and was inside for a long time. On his return downstairs, his eyes were still gentle but nowhere near as elusive.

A few days later it was decided that the leg would have to be cut off, slightly above the knee. The left one. They had waited too long.

So.

The leg was *cut off*, as they say in common parlance, and some weeks later Kåre was hobbling across the yard, up the stairs and into the kitchen.

He had to teach himself to walk on crutches. Everything had to be re-learned from scratch, and he lost a year. He had to catch up with the rest of his life, and this delay seemed to give him the motivation to teach himself things that were considered scarcely possible. He learned to walk again, he learned to cycle and he even learned to ride a moped. It was as though nothing was impossible any longer. Aasta told me Kåre lived with her and her husband Sigurd for a short period while he went to school in Lauvslandsmoen. After all, he had to attend school like everyone else. That must have been the winter of 1958. It was easier to live there than at home. From Vatneli it was more than seven kilometres and Olav and Johanna didn't have a car, while from Aasta's house the school was only a couple of hundred metres. He slept in the loft, she said, in the room facing west, and they lit the wood-burner there so it was nice and warm. Her face lit up as all these hazy memories returned. She recalled things she hadn't thought about in years: minor details and trifles she assumed would not interest me. Her eyes wandered, as though somewhere in the middle distance she could see life fifty years ago, like a flimsy, shimmering film. She told me she was always so frightened whenever Kåre had to negotiate the steep staircase on his crutches. The steep staircase without a rail, and Kåre wobbling downwards from step to step. But he always managed, and gradually he became a past master at getting around. He hobbled about on his crutches and sang, she could remember that. In the evenings he came down from the loft, singing as he swung, making the walls vibrate with the sound. It was a love song, she believed. Yes, it was; a love song. She didn't remember which, it was in English; the only word that stuck in her mind was *darling*.

'He was so chirpy,' she said, the film in front of her eyes appearing to have stopped.

'How do you mean?' I asked.

'So chirpy, so bright and breezy. How can I put it? There isn't a better word. So chirpy, so chirpy.'

We went on to talk about Johanna. The woman who became the person who never laughed or cried. She was followed by a large, dark shadow. Or she herself had become a shadow. It was as though the birds fell silent when she appeared. Seven years after Kåre's death, Aasta asked her if it felt easier now that so much time had passed.

The answer was no.

She still went around gathering the fragments.

Johanna would have liked so much to have a family photograph. That was after she and Olav found themselves alone, and her greatest wish was that all three of them would be in the picture. She and Olav with Kåre in the middle. She had asked Aasta and Sigurd for help. There had to be a way of doing it, surely? This was in the 1960s. The only way to do it was to cut the old wedding photograph in two and then place Kåre's confirmation photograph between the two halves. Then you could take a new photograph of the two originals. By destroying them you would have a new picture. But they couldn't do that, of course, and as they couldn't Johanna dismissed the whole idea: if Kåre wasn't in, nothing else mattered. It was him in the middle or nothing.

That was Johanna's story. She was serenity itself. Everything she did she did with serene movements. She had an old spinning wheel, and she spun for Husfliden, the crafts shop. The yarn ran forever through her fingers.

Towards the end, after the Vatnelis had also lost their house, Aasta washed Johanna's clothes for her. Johanna no longer had the energy. She had acquired a new spinning wheel, but mostly it stood unused in the corner. In her last months she sat staring blankly at it. It was during this time –

when Aasta was washing her clothes – that Aasta discovered all the blood. Not so many months after the fire. It must have come from her womb.

Aasta accompanied me to the door. It was dark outside; white mist hung over the fields, and above the northern sky you could glimpse traces of light from the floodlit church. I was full of Kåre's story, of his brief but apparently carefree life. I asked her if she knew anyone who could tell me any more. She had to give the matter some thought. In the end, she shook her head. She was the only person. She said:

'You know, they're all dead.'

After Olav and Johanna died she had tended Kåre's grave every summer until it had been levelled. That happened during the 1990s. She had given her blessing. And, of course, one can understand why. Everyone had gone. The entire little family. There was nothing left.

Oh yes, there was. Something was left: Johanna's spinning wheel.

Before I went I gave Aasta a hug. For a few brief seconds we stood in the darkness gently holding each other. Then I walked the short distance home. It was murky now and quite cold. The first frost could not be far away. I thought of all the times I had walked this route as a child. After I had passed Aasta and Sigurd's house it would be pitch black right until I reached the letter boxes. It was a stretch of approximately half a kilometre and my heart was in my mouth every time. The road led first through the spruce forest in Vollan, then opened up. When I was a child I used to sing my way through the trees and all the way to the stream that flowed beneath the road and cascaded down the rocks on the other side. I would be on my way home from a meeting at Von Youth Club, where we had been taught about the damaging effects of alcohol; however, alone in the darkness, I would forget all about the abdominal pains and going green in the face and being abandoned by your entire family. At that very moment I was just filled with a chilling terror, and I hoped that singing would ward off the man I feared might suddenly loom up before me in the night. I sang and sang, an exalted medley of songs from the youth choir, Samantha Fox and Michael Jackson. It was 'What a Mighty God We Have', 'Nothing's Gonna Stop Me Now' and 'Bad', all mixed up. The crucial thing was that I sang. That there wasn't a second's silence. And that I kept it going as far as the waterfall. That was the dividing line. If only I could get past that I was saved.

It was the same on this evening, too, walking alone in the darkness, with the conversation about Kåre and Johanna still buzzing round my head. My childhood system was deeply ingrained: no silence until I had passed the invisible border. Past, past, just get past and I would be saved.

3

I.

ON THE NIGHT OF 19 May 1978, it happened again. A remote storehouse in Hæråsen, to the far north of the region, in the forest. Fire number three. Eight tons of artificial fertiliser, an old carriage, a cart, ten or so wheels, two sledges, a barrel, a stump puller, several roof tiles and poles.

All of it.

The flames could be seen from kilometres away. They billowed across the sky, red and orange, and the sight of it made your blood run cold.

They came too late this time as well.

The hoses were directed at the trees, at the fir tops which were vividly illuminated by the blaze. The creaks and bangs echoed deep into the forest. Now and then there was a tearing sound. Something large cracked and toppled onto its side with a bitter lament.

It was on this night that people realised something was seriously amiss.

Everyone from the fire brigade was there. The cars stood in a line behind the fire engine, just as they had at previous blazes. Dag was holding the hose, the pumps were humming somewhere behind him in the darkness, the water was shooting out at a furious rate. He pointed it towards the centre of the flames where it was orange, almost red and nearly static. The fire hissed like a wounded dragon as it was covered with water. For a moment the flames were beaten back, but then they summoned fresh strength and grew taller than ever. Minutes later the heat became too intense and someone else had to take over. He stood on the margins fanning himself as he watched. He observed the others running about, he heard shouts and speaking and the regular drone of the pumps, and he heard the snapping and crackling of the blaze. He stood waiting for Ingemann. The fire chief had not arrived yet, so Alfred had assumed command. Dag began to get restless. His father had said he would follow in his own car. That was the arrangement. But he hadn't turned up. This was the first emergency call-out without Ingemann. Dag had had to do everything himself: he had switched on the alarm, he had stood in their house at Skinnsnes and called up the stairs, but when Ingemann eventually came down he was clutching his chest and saying he felt unwell. He had gone straight into the living room and slumped on the sofa.

'What's up with you?' Dag had asked.

'I think you'll have to go alone,' his father said.

'Alone?'

There wasn't any time to lose, so he had sprinted up to the garage, driven the fire engine out, switched on the sirens, turned right for Breivoll and sped off with the blue lights tearing gashes in the night sky. And that had been fine, everything had gone perfectly and he had done it all on his own.

Now he was standing on the edge of the scene and scouring the area for his father. His face was lit by the fierce flames, which almost erased his features. Or the opposite: they became clearer. Around him ran neighbours and friends who had seen the conflagration or heard the sirens, but he didn't notice them. He was waiting. But Ingemann didn't come.

In the end, he made a decision and strode resolutely over to Alfred.

'I'm going to have a recce,' he said.

'A what?'

'I'm going to see if this nutter has set any other places alight.'

Alfred was too slow to stop him. Or ask what he meant by *nutter*, because Dag was already running towards the fire engine. In he climbed, as quick as a flash, and started it up. The pumps had been detached and all the equipment unloaded, so strictly speaking they didn't need the vehicle any longer.

He turned around at the end of the road. When he passed the scattering of people the flames had subsided into glowing embers, which coloured the smoke orange.

He sped up. Drove past the church and the road to the firing range a bit further down. The box factory, the long plains of Frigstad, the shop in Breivoll. There was no traffic on the roads. The houses were dark. He gunned the vehicle for all it was worth.

At Skinnsnes, his home, there was a light in the kitchen window. He couldn't see anything of Ingemann and he drove right past and onto the main thoroughfare by the disused shop at the crossroads. After passing the community centre in Brandsvoll he switched on the sirens. He continued all the way to Kilen with sirens and flashing blue lights, and stopped outside Kaddeberg's.

He hammered on the door until the light came on in the shop and a shadow approached on the other side of the glass.

'Fire brigade,' he shouted as the door slid back and Kaddeberg himself stood there, wreathed in sleep. 'Let me in. We need provisions.'

For several minutes he whirled between the shelves in the semi-gloom while Kaddeberg stood behind the till in an astonished state. He stared at the young man, who was so breathless and overwrought that he wasn't even taking anything. In the end, the shopkeeper had to fetch a basket for him, and then there was some progress. Dag snatched items off the shelves. Five packets of biscuits, crisps, sausages, ready-made cakes, a box of soft drinks, a fistful of chocolate bars. He smelt of acrid smoke, his shirt was flapping round his body, and it wasn't long before the whole shop reeked of fire.

'Stick it on the fire service tab,' he said, putting the items in bags.

'Who in the fire service?' Kaddeberg asked.

'The fire chief.'

'Ingemann?'

'Yes,' Dag said. 'That's my father.'

Then he charged out of the door and clambered into the fire engine. The lights had continued flashing the whole time he had been inside. He drove back munching chocolate and crisps and slowly getting into a better mood. When he reached Brandsvoll, he switched off the sirens. There was still a light on in the kitchen window at home, and as he passed he leaned on the horn. He honked three times, then switched the sirens back on and tore the wrapper off another chocolate bar. He drove as fast as the fire engine would allow. The steering wheel vibrated and shook. It was as though he could feel the blood in his very fingertips. He threw the half-eaten chocolate bar out of the window. Outside the shop in Breivoll the fire engine listed dangerously, then a car came towards him and he veered so far into the ditch that sand and gravel were sent flying into the darkness. He hooted a bright, trilled laugh that no one else heard. As he passed the church, he switched off the sirens and changed down. He was getting close. There was no longer a billowing sea of flames across the sky. Instead, day had begun to break. Upon his arrival, he noticed that even more people had gathered. There were cars in the road blocking his path and he had to activate the sirens for drivers to come and move them. Perhaps twenty or thirty people were there now. They stood away from the fire, swathed in jackets and coats. There was a haunted air about them, yet their faces were strangely clear and calm.

Ingemann still had not come. Dag shouted his name as he opened the door and stepped out, but no one answered.

Within an hour it was all over. The fire had been extinguished. Now pungent smoke hung between the trees like early morning mist. The fir tops dripped as if after a heavy shower of rain. Hoses were carefully rolled up. Drinks bottles on the ground collected. Chocolate papers lay strewn over the heather and in the roadside ditches. Two of the neighbours stayed to keep an eye on the smoking pile of debris. They sat under the darkness of a tree with several buckets brim-full with water between them. Slowly the crowd dispersed. Those who had driven there got into their cars, started them up, drove to the end of the road, turned and then came back in one long light-punctuated line. Those who were left lived no more than a couple of hundred metres away. They were the ones who had discovered the fire and dialled Ingemann's number at Skinnsnes. Now they turned and walked back home in a group. They returned to their empty houses and found the front doors unlocked; they sat up for a while until they had managed to compose themselves. Then they crept into bed and switched off the lights. Inhaled a couple of deep breaths. Closed their eyes.

A fire doesn't start by itself, everyone knows that.

A storehouse in the middle of the night. Here. Near us. That's just plain impossible.

When eventually Dag went home in the fire engine it was daylight, and Ingemann was standing in the yard, by the post with the alarm. Dag pretended not to see his father, drove right past, up the tight bend and swung around in front of the fire station. Reversed the vehicle into the garage even though the hoses had been neither taken off nor dried and some of the equipment hadn't been checked. He sat behind the wheel staring into space. That was how he was sitting when at length Ingemann walked over.

'Why didn't you come?' Dag said softly. He was gripping the wheel as though he were still racing through the night with sirens blaring and blue lights flashing.

'It's my heart,' Ingemann said. 'From now on I think you'll have to manage everything on your own.'

'Your heart?' Dag said, perplexed.

'From now on you're the fire chief, Dag,' his father said, laying a hand on the wheel. He ventured a smile, but there was no visible reaction on Dag's face.

Still staring straight ahead, he said:

'Take it easy, Pappa. There won't be any more fires. This was the last.'

The sky lightened, the sun rose above the ridges in the east. Where the two outbuildings had stood was now hot, sticky ash. Ash and the four cornerstones at the bottom of the Leipsland ridge. During the day many came to rubberneck. The news spread.

Another fire? Is that possible?

Cars drove past slowly, almost stopping, with rolled-down windows, and the smell of fresh fire was everywhere, then they moved on. Some youths pedalled past, found an empty pop bottle, smashed it against a rock, took fright and cycled off. Ants crawled all over the broken glass. Mosquitoes and flies danced above the wet ash. Evening came. The sun went down behind the ridge. It was May, summer was not far away. Nevertheless, the night soon drew in. By midnight the region lay dark and still. A translucent white mist hung over the fields. It wasn't easy to say where it had originated from. An animal stood motionless among the trees. Its eyes staring ahead, into the gloom. Windows were still lit. People were settling down for the night, but they left lights on, closed their eyes, folded their hands.

And?

In the distance there was the sound of a car. Was it coming closer? Coming this way? No. It was far, far off. Then it was quiet. Perfectly quiet. Everything is as it should be. What has happened, happened. Let's forget it. Let's not think any more. Just sleep now.

II.

I FOUND THE BAPTISM CERTIFICATE; it was in a brown envelope in a cardboard box in the loft with a host of other childhood papers. In addition, I spotted the dark blue travel bag in which I had slept in the car outside Olga Dynestøl's burned-down farmstead. I didn't bother with the bag; however, I took the box of papers downstairs. I sat for a moment with the envelope on which my name was typed. Inside was the baptism certificate signed by the local priest, Trygve Omland, with my parents' names and the date: Sunday, 4 June 1978.

Among the other papers was a small, green book from the winter when I had music lessons with Teresa. I remembered it well; it had squared paper and *Progress Book* written on the front. After every lesson she jotted something down, closed the book with a bang and gave it to me to take home. I don't remember reading her comments, only that I showed them to my parents. Most lessons received: *Good progress.* Now and then: *Must practise more.* The very last lesson was just before Christmas 1988. Then she wrote: *Plays fluently, yet with some strain.* That seemed a fairly apt description. After that I stopped. It was the same year that Grandad died.

In the loft were also Grandma's diaries. Stored in a transparent plastic box beside the travel bag. The box reminded me of the trays you find at airports, in which you put keys, wallets, belts, watches, jackets and shoes before everything goes through a plastic curtain to be X-rayed. I had flicked through the diaries earlier, in fact, although I hadn't considered they would be of any use, not in *that* way. But it emerged that Grandma had written about the fires as well as about herself and Grandad and the grief that almost tore her asunder when he died.

She often spoke about her diaries. I still remember the last evening I spent with her; I remember the sparkle in her eye, as though there was a diamond in the pupil. The diamond had appeared after a cataract operation, and I don't think she had realised. Perhaps everyone has a diamond there after an eye operation. Or perhaps it had been there all her life and I had only noticed it on the very last evening.

She kept her diary in the kitchen, I recall, on the worktop to the left of the sink, partly covered by a pile of bills. Whenever she went on a trip or holiday she took the diary with her. When she visited me in Oslo, before my father fell ill, she had it in her bag, and after we had gone to bed for the night she wrote about our visit to the National Gallery and the History Museum, the Munch Museum and Akershus Fortress, and she wrote about me and my father: *May the Lord protect them both.* But as a rule she used to write in the morning after clearing the table, washing up, putting something in the oven and sitting down at the table waiting for the hours and the day to pass. More often than not it was just trivial comments about the weather, about who had dropped by, what food she had served, or what trips she had been on, what she had seen and whom she had travelled with. Sometimes in the winter she wrote about a rare guest landing on the bird table. This kind of thing:

WEDNESDAY, 5 FEBRUARY 2003
A little bird I've never seen before. He sat there for a while with the others. Later in the day he was gone.

She loved birds so much.

She was quite proud of these diaries, but at the same time I recall they were highly confidential and somewhat taboo. I'd had no idea what was in them. On several occasions she said she was considering burning the whole lot and that under no circumstances would anyone get to read them until she was dead and gone.

And that is now, of course.

This is what she wrote when her neighbour Ester passed away:

SUNDAY, 9 MAY 1999
Snowing. Ester's unconscious in hospital. God help us all.

THURSDAY, 13 MAY
Ascension Day. Sunny but cold. Ester died at three this afternoon. A bad day.

FRIDAY, 14 MAY
Sunny and cold. Painted ceiling. Yard's deserted and quiet.

Eight months earlier, at half past three in the morning, just after Pappa died:

15 SEPTEMBER 1998
Eventually he was given a morphine injection and that eased things, but he had to have another, and the pain went. He fell asleep and never woke again. The last thing he said was, Mm, that's heaven.

After a visit from the local priest eight years earlier:

11 MAY 1990
Colder. Cloudy. Austad came to visit. Rained in the evening.

Two years before that, when Grandad suddenly fell down dead outside the courthouse:

THURSDAY, 3 NOVEMBER
I wake with a start. Is it true or did I dream that Dad was dead? Well, it's true. I have such pain in my chest it feels physical. Holskog came by later in the day and is going to see to the funeral. It is all going to be as simple as possible. He asks me if I want to see him lying in the coffin. I say no. I want to remember him as the good-looking, youthful man I loved so much. Anna came. I see everything through a fog. The sun was out apparently, but I didn't see it.

Grief.

FRIDAY, 4 NOVEMBER
There were so many people here. I am so tired. It was good when night came. The tablet gave me some blessed hours of sleep. Got away from all the pain for a while.

SUNDAY, 6 NOVEMBER
Day feels so hard to bear. All the things I blame myself for, all the things I failed to do or say will take me to the grave. Night came as a friend with some sleep.

She never wrote as much as she did in the year after his death. It was a natural reaction; it forced its way out and poured over the pages. Everything was possible, all she had to do was write, it came easily, and that was how she kept herself going. In fact, she was writing away her grief.

I flicked back to 13 March 1978:

A boy. He arrived today, a little before six o'clock. Everything went fine. Tomorrow Kristen and I are going to see him.

That boy was me.

She writes briefly about her visit the following day, later almost nothing about the newborn baby. I flicked forwards to April, then May. May 1978, in Norway, the month the entire country was stunned by the Inger Apenes murder in Fredrikstad, the one that was not to be solved until twenty-nine years later, in April 2007, when a man turned himself in and confessed. The month that Charlie Chaplin's coffin turned up after vanishing into thin air from Corsier-sur-Vevey cemetery, Switzerland. The month that the 48th World Cup football championship moved to Argentinian shores. And in Kristiansand Cathedral, Cantor Bjarne Sløgedal was preparing for the annual church festival, which on this occasion was going to have an opening concert with the motet choir and Kristiansand Town Orchestra, as well as the English baritone Christopher Keyte. Later, on 3 June, Ingrid Bjoner was to sing Pergolesi's *Stabat Mater*, and the festival would conclude with a concert by Kjell Bækkelund and Harald Bratlie performing Bach's *Kunst der Fuge.*

It is May and springtime in Norway. It has come late, but the weather is holding nicely, slightly overcast, sunshine. Then the heat comes with a vengeance. Leaves are out. Tractors plough the ground, turning over wings of earth. Hills go green, cows are put out to graze, swallows fly high and summer is on its way.

III.

WHO WAS THIS BOY WHO had just been born?

When I went home in March, only a few days old, the whole district lay under a blanket of snow, and for as long as I can remember I have had this special relationship with snow: a desire for it to start falling, for it to fall while I am asleep, for it to come down thick over the trees, over the house, over the forest, for it to fall deep into my dreams, for the whiteness to cover everything, and when I wake in the morning, for the world to be new.

Snow was part of what I first saw. But then came spring. And, soon after, summer.

Who was I?

According to Teresa, I didn't relax when I played music. But I tried to let my fingers rest over the keys. I did what I was told. There was never any trouble with me. I was dutiful to a fault, and I never contradicted anyone. I did my homework with care, I was always prepared and always punctual. I set off on my bike to Lauvslandsmoen School at just before eight even though it took only four minutes and classes didn't begin until half past eight. I stood in the darkness waiting for Knut, the caretaker, to open up, and as soon as he did I went into the warm corridor, put my rucksack in the classroom and patiently waited for the others to come and the school day to begin at last. Every Monday I had a singing rehearsal at the chapel in Brandsvoll. I stood in the youth choir singing all these songs that I can still remember by heart, without shoving, without pulling the girls' hair and without forgetting the words. Every second Thursday I went to Von Youth Club and sat in the same chapel room learning about the ruinous effects of alcohol. I suppose I was eight or nine years old when I first learned that your face went green from drinking beer, and already then I knew that I must never accept a bottle of beer if a tall, pimply boy offered me one (it was always a tall, pimply boy); already I had learned that there was something called *the darker side of life* and that was where beer belonged. I learned that I had at all costs to avoid the darker side of life, or else beer would have me in its possession and I would be forced to drink it. I knew that I should stay on the sunny side of life, although I had little idea as to how in reality that was to be done. But it sounded like sensible advice to a nine-year-old who had always liked being outdoors in the sun.

I wanted to be like everyone else, I didn't want to stand out in any way, and that was why I was well behaved, that was why I did my homework, that was why I was an able pupil. There was just one snag: I often sat indoors reading. I began to cycle to the library in Lauvslandsmoen. Down around the mountain bends in Vollan, onto the plain, the wind in my hair, past Aasta's house, across Stubekken River, past Stubrokka and across Finsåna River. I freewheeled almost the whole way there, but the ride home with a bag on the handlebars was all the harder for it. I began to read *The Story of* series of books. *The Story of Edvard Grieg. The Story of Madame Curie. The Story of Ludwig van Beethoven. The Story of Thomas Alva Edison.* These were books you could lose yourself in. I read with a passion and voracity no one understood, perhaps not even me. They were books that filled me with dreams. They were books that slowly did things to me, that made me wish myself in other places. Something inside me began to wander. At the beginning no one noticed anything, but something inside me had left a long time ago and I was in a slow outward drift. At the same time there was also something in me that wanted to stay. There was something that would remain forever in the safe and the secure, the familiar and the simple, in the region I, in my heart of hearts, loved so much. I felt so bound to this place, partly because my father was. He often sat leafing through the big, thick tome called *Finsland: Gard og Ætt*, the book with so many names, years of births, marriages and deaths, and he showed me how you can follow father and son, father and son down through the centuries, to his father and himself, and me, the last in the line for the time being. That was how it was. That was how the years passed and I didn't know who the 'me' actually was, except that I was the last in the line. Sometimes what Ruth had said – *You're a writer, that's what you are* – came back to me. The words were still out there, although I had completely stopped telling stories. I didn't dare, for it might be considered that such behaviour might lead me into the 'darker side of life'.

This matter of the 'sunny' and the 'darker' sides of life was gradually becoming quite irksome. For this reason I began to camouflage myself. This worked fine for many years. In a way it was easy. I talked like the other kids, did as the others did. But I wasn't like the others. I read books. In some way I became addicted to them. When I was twelve, Karin gave me permission to borrow books from the adult section of the library. It was like crossing an invisible border. I went straight from reading *The Story of* books to ones by Mikkjel Fønhus, which were about animals, or lonely men who went to wrack and ruin. That appealed to me, a boy who was so well behaved and always stayed on the sunny side. From then on I also read the books we had at home. In the early 1970s my parents had been members of the Book Club, the one where all the books looked identical, except for different colours and patterns on the spine. I began to read all those books that Mamma and Pappa may well have read at one time, I didn't know whether they had or not. The exception to this was Trygve Gulbranssen's Bjørndal trilogy, because Pappa had said I should read it. The idea that Pappa had read precisely these books gave me the motivation to tackle them, and there are no books, neither before nor since, that have gripped me in such a way. I was perhaps thirteen or fourteen, I wanted the books to go on for ever, and I shed solitary tears when the character of Old Dag died at the end of the second volume.

A book had made me cry.

It was unheard of. I was ashamed for a long time afterwards. I couldn't bring myself to tell a living soul, but I wondered if the same had befallen Pappa and that was why he wanted me to read it.

I wanted to live on the sunny side of life; I wanted that more than anything else.

As I grew older it became apparent to other boys that I wasn't like them. They could see it as well, of course. There was something strange, something intangible, something alien. They didn't know where it came from, but they could see it. They knew me. It was me. Yet I was someone else. I wasn't like them and they began to draw away. They began to avoid me, and I was left to my own devices in the breaks between lessons. They left me alone. They didn't bother me, they didn't say anything, they left me on my own. They were interested in other things, in fast cars and hunting and women. They began to smoke, they began to drink at the weekends, despite what had been instilled into us at the chapel some years ago. I went to parties too, I wasn't unwelcome, but I sat there without smoking or drinking. After all, I was well behaved and proper and never did anything wrong. I felt myself that there was an aura of purity around me. Everyone talked about hunting and cars and parties, and even more drinking and booze and beer and moonshine. I sat there and was pure, and I wasn't there. I was somewhere else. I was someone else. All these years, in reality, I had been on the move. All my life I had been someone else.

I remember the very last New Year's Eve I spent at someone's house in the area. A school friend had locked himself in the toilet and then fallen asleep. I was the only person still sober, and I felt a certain responsibility to liberate him. The music was pounding away in the sitting room as I tackled the door with a screwdriver. Somehow or other I managed to release the lock, and when I burst in he was lying on the floor with his trousers round his knees and a pool of sick seeping from his mouth and over him. I locked the door at once so no one else would come in and see him like that. At length I succeeded in reviving him, removing all his clothes and placing him in the bathtub. Where I cleaned him up. We had gone to school together for nine years, we had been in Von Youth Club together, sung in the choir and been confirmed together, and now there I was, washing his lean white body as the thick vomit oozed from his mouth, down his neck, chest and stomach and into his crotch. I don't know if he remembers that night – presumably not – yet I had a feeling that something inside him registered what was happening. Registered that someone had forced their way in, undressed him and put him in the bath, that someone was standing over him and rinsing him down, and that this someone was me. I remember that night and the scene in the bathroom because I knew there and then that it was all over. I knew I had to get away from all of this. Away from the sordid and the base, away from beer, alcohol and moonshine, away from Finsland, away from the simple and the familiar, away from the forests and everything that deep in my heart I loved. I was nineteen years old. In August I moved to Oslo and started at university, and I knew I would never be able to return.

IV.

FOR THE WHOLE OF MAY 1978, Grandma writes generally short mundane comments about the weather, about the dry spring, about what she and Grandad have been doing, who visited them and what she cooked. Nothing about the forest fire on 6 May, nor anything about the Tønnes' storehouse. A brief note on 17 May about the church service, Omland's speech, the procession and the party in the evening at Brandsvoll Community Centre.

After the blaze in Hæråsen on 20 May there was a hiatus. No new fires for thirteen days. No suspicious persons or unfamiliar cars on the roads. It felt as though it was all over. The summer arrived with long, drowsy, sun-soaked days. The lilac trees were in blossom and their sweet fragrance hung heavily from garden to garden for those who walked outdoors in the evening.

Perhaps, after all, it had been a dream?

Neither Grandma nor Teresa made any special comments about the following days. Teresa received her last music pupils before the summer holidays. Grandma and Grandad went swimming for the first time in Lake Homevannet on the evening of 27 May; the water was eighteen degrees. Mamma went for slow walks pushing the pram, generally down to

Lauvslandsmoen, past Aasta's house and back again, and I slept the whole way.

On 1 June the World Cup football championship started in Argentina, with the opening ceremony at the River Plate Stadium in Buenos Aires. Followed by the match between Poland and West Germany.

People still talked about the three fires, but their tone had changed. There is probably some explanation, it was said. A cigarette, for example. Someone could have thrown a lit cigarette out of a car window, couldn't they? Someone could have been inattentive, forgetful, couldn't they? They inadvertently flicked a cigarette end out of the window. Drove on. And with all the dry weather there had been. That was the explanation. Thoughtlessness. Accidents. Of course. After all, the three fires had started by the roadside.

Slowly, the region relaxed.

V.

IN THE END he found himself a job, as a fire officer at Kjevik Airport. It happened a few days after the previous fire. It was almost too good to be true. At last he had somewhere to go; the only drawback was that he had to work nights and sleep during the day. He left home at 6 p.m. and drove for up to an hour to the airport. Before starting work he took a training course over a few evenings. That was all. He knew most things already, though. The only new subject for him was emergency first aid and how to save lives. Then he paid very careful attention.

When he applied for the job he attached a reference Ingemann had written. It said that he had almost grown up in a fire engine, that he had been involved in several emergencies and was already a better driver than his father, the fire chief. He had all the requisite qualifications, and he recommended his son without reservation.

A few days later he was appointed.

Alma was extremely relieved. For over a year he had been at home without a fixed occupation. Now, finally, he had a job outside the house, so it couldn't be helped if he had to sleep all day.

It was a lonely job. Often he was on his own in the duty office with a view of the runway and the flight approach. At around twelve, when the night was at its darkest, although it was still quite clear, he watched planes glide in from nowhere. A flashing dot that at first sight appeared to be stationary, but then the light grew and he saw that the flashing came from two small navigation lights on the wing tips. Then he heard the noise coming nearer, rolling across the sky like thunder. A powerful strobe light was switched on. It was like a boat shining down on the sea beneath it. He counted the seconds. The aircraft fuselage hovered above the black Topdalsfjord. The wings rocked from side to side. He visualised the plane suddenly tilting over, or an engine catching alight, dragging a plume of smoke and fire across the sky before it struck the runway and skidded along.

He stood by the window of the office and felt the glass vibrating. The wheels touched down with two tiny screeches. The plane raced along, the wing tips emitting sparks, then it slowed down, came to a halt, turned at the end of the runway and taxied to the control tower.

This is what he did: he followed every single plane that descended from the skies. He couldn't concentrate on anything else. He had to rub his eyes. In a way he felt tired, yet at the same time he was strangely clear-headed and alert. He rested his forehead against the glass. The planes came. They dropped from the sky. They landed. He thought he could see people sitting behind the small windows, laughing and enjoying themselves, making toasts and singing.

A few hours later he drove home. It was already day by then, but his head was hazy, it was as though he had been to the cinema and seen a film which lasted seven long hours. Every so often he stopped the car at a deserted lay-by, opened the door, walked to the forest edge, lit a cigarette, but tossed it away after a few drags and stood for a moment or two staring into the unmoving mesh of branches.

When he arrived home at Skinnsnes, Alma and Ingemann were sitting in the kitchen having breakfast, and as he took his place at the table he had the sense they had been up all night waiting for him. Alma sliced more bread and poured milk into his glass and steaming hot coffee into the cup next to him. It was almost like the old days when he came home from the *gymnas* and had news to tell them. They asked him how work had been and he said it had been fine. And that was true, of course. There wasn't so much to tell. Nothing did happen. Planes came and went. He sat there keeping watch and nothing happened.

'No fires at Kjevik, then?' Ingemann said in jest.

'No fires here, either?' Dag replied.

Ingemann shook his head. Alma said nothing. Then he went up to his room to sleep.

That was how it was. Ten days passed, and nothing happened.

One night he took a gun with him. It was a saloon rifle. 22LR calibre. He had bought it with his confirmation money and had so far used it only for target practice. In addition, he had bought a telescopic sight, a Hawke. He put the rifle on the rear seat of the car, hidden under some clothes. Then he took it into the office with him. He sat waiting for the last plane of the day. According to the timetable it was due to arrive at 23.34. He was calm, clear-headed, yet tired somehow. He reclined on the much-too-short sofa in the corner, closed his eyes, opened them. He had slept almost all day. Yet still there was this peculiar, stubborn tiredness. He switched on the tiny radio on the window sill and found the right frequency: it was the World Cup in Argentina, Austria versus Sweden. The radio crackled and he had to concentrate to hear what was happening on the pitch. After forty minutes Hans Krankl scored for Austria with a rocket from inside the sixteen-metre box.

Then the plane appeared, a Braathens from Stavanger.

He rushed to the window, but it was nearly impossible to fix the plane in the sights. He had to stand searching the night sky for some time. Then he spotted it again. He followed the plane as it came closer and closer. A large illuminated ship. He could almost see the passengers sitting there behind the small windows. As the plane hung sixty or seventy metres above the fjord he pulled the trigger. There was a cold click. Then he lowered the gun. His mouth was dry. He knew he had hit the target.

VI.

ON THE MORNING OF Friday, 2 June, it began to rain. It was a light, floating drizzle that hung in the air during the early hours, making the grass at the roadside glisten. Then it cleared up. The wind increased from the north-west and blew everything away. Clouds dissipated, the freshly washed sun shone, the road dried. It was just past nine o'clock.

On this morning Dag had returned home a bit later than usual. He had been dog-tired and hadn't uttered a word, just went straight upstairs and to bed. He didn't even have a bite to eat, nor a cup of coffee or a glass of milk, nothing.

Ingemann had gone out to the workshop just after eight as usual, and then Alma was left alone in the kitchen. She had switched on the radio, turning it down as low as possible. It was *Nitimen* with Jan Pande-Rolfsen, the cheery voice of popular entertainment. She wiped the table, then ran the tap in the sink and washed up.

After *Nitimen* was finished she went into the hall and stood at the bottom of the stairs, listening. Nothing. She made some fresh coffee, filled the thermos and went to Ingemann's workshop. Inside, it smelt of oil and diesel and old junk. It was a good smell, it made her feel secure; she liked it even though she was never there for longer than absolutely necessary. She didn't have much idea of what he got up to, and he never enlightened her. This was his world, she had her own, and that was how it should be. They each had their own world, and then of course they had Dag.

As soon as Ingemann heard her coming he rose from the steel chair by the workbench where he usually sat if he didn't have a lot to do or when he was taking a break. He went to the shelf with the screws and nuts and had his back to her as she approached.

'I'll put the coffee here,' she said.

'Yes, do that,' he mumbled.

She waited for a second, until he turned.

'He's still asleep,' she said. It sounded more like a question than a statement.

Ingemann didn't answer. A glass partition seemed to slide between them whenever there was any mention of Dag. He bent over a motor that had been almost completely taken apart, then he found the tiny hole where the screw fitted and tightened it. She stood watching him for a moment.

'I think Dag's ill,' she announced.

'Ill?'

'He talks to himself.'

Ingemann straightened up and looked at her.

'Where did you get that idea?'

'I've heard him.'

'That can't be true,' Ingemann said, returning to the motor.

'It's true. He talks to himself.'

'Dag is not ill,' he said softly, his face close to the black engine.

'I've tried to speak to him,' she said. 'He was on the point of telling me what was wrong.'

'I very much doubt if there's anything wrong with him,'

Ingemann said, found another screw and tightened it hard. 'There's nothing wrong with Dag.'

'How can you know that?' She pulled her knitted jacket tighter around her and crossed her arms.

'Because he's my son. I know him.'

She usually had a quiet cup of coffee on her own in the living room before she prepared a light lunch. She did so on this day too, but she drank the coffee faster than was her wont, even though it was scalding hot. She stared at the black piano, and at the shelf of trophies. Then she put down the cup, found a rag in the kitchen and began to dab at the dust. She wiped the piano, carefully ran the rag over the keys, causing them to tinkle. Went into the hall, stood on the lowest step and listened. She couldn't seem to rest, and it still wasn't much past ten o'clock. Making a swift decision, she put the cloth back in the kitchen, dried her hands, straightened her hair in front of the hall mirror, grabbed her cardigan and walked the short distance to Teresa's.

It was good to be out in the sun and the wind. Her hair lifted off her forehead, the morning was fresh and clean, and the whole world seemed to brighten. Alma and Teresa used to visit each other now and then. Even though they were very different types they appreciated each other's company. They chatted about everyday things, Teresa brewed some coffee and if it was sunny they often sat on the front steps. After which they went about their own business. Today was one of those days when they could sit together in the sun, she thought as she got closer, but when she knocked on the door no one answered.

It was while she was standing on the steps to Teresa's house that the alarm went off. All of a sudden there it was, like a torrent from the heavens.

She couldn't move from the step, she was so chilled and so paralysed and so everything. Dag came charging out of the house, stood in the yard for a few seconds, then sprinted up the hill to the fire station. Minutes later the fire engine lurched onto the road. Sirens. Blue lights. The summer wind in the trees.

He drove west to Breivoll.

She stood holding her hands over her ears, unaware that she was doing so.

Soon afterwards she saw Ingemann walk into the yard alone. He was wearing the dark blue overalls that were black with oil across the chest, and he seemed bewildered. He went to the post where the alarm was, then stood there as it wailed above his head. Alma wanted to shout that he should move away so that he didn't go stone deaf. He stood there for maybe thirty seconds, then turned and went into the house. He was gone for a few moments, then came back out wearing the fire service uniform, headed straight for the post and deactivated the alarm. This he did with an abrupt, almost savage wrench. Afterwards it was as though the sky had fallen in and everything had gone quiet.

VII.

I WAS NINETEEN YEARS OLD, I had moved from home and was finding myself. I was going to study law at the August University in the centre of Oslo, I would be walking across the square where P. A. Munch's and Schweigaard's statues stood surveying the scene, staunch and erudite, I would be starting my real life, I would be a student, and I would become an intellectual. Before leaving I visited my grandmother at Heivollen and was given permission to borrow one of my grandfather's coats; in addition, I had got hold of a pair of glasses, even though strictly speaking I didn't need them. I would never have dared to walk around in a coat and glasses at home, that would have been quite unthinkable, but in Oslo everything was different. There I could walk around in glasses and Grandad's old coat without anyone taking any notice. He had hardly ever worn the coat, but it was more than good enough for me. I used to go out alone in the evening and feel a singular contentment spreading through my body. I strolled along Schwensens gate, where I was renting a little bedsit, and continued up towards St Hanshaugen. I stuffed my hands deep into my pockets, which were smooth on the inside and much larger than one would expect. I could feel how well the coat fitted my shoulders, how comfortable I was inside it, indeed, how good life had become after all, how in the end everything had slotted into place. I crossed Ullevålsveien and proceeded along the narrow paths that wound between the tall, bare trees. I crossed the square in front of the gaping, empty outdoor stage, I passed the statue of the four musicians before tackling the last, steep stairs until I was at the top, beside the old fire tower, surveying the town. It lay beneath me glittering in the night air. I saw the dark fjord; above it on one side rose brightly lit, white Holmenkollenbakken , and on the other side of the hill the pink smoke from the incinerator chimney in Økern. I was so far from home, yet it was as though I could hear a voice inside myself, saying: This is your town. This is where you will be. You will live here for many years, and here you will become the person you really are. And, at that moment, wearing Grandad's coat with my hands thrust deep into the pockets, I could feel very clearly that I was happy.

One evening the telephone rang.

'Just me,' Pappa said. That was how all our telephone conversations started. Either he said that or I did. Just me.

And then it came.

He had been a bit unwell recently, he began. He had been to the doctor in Nodeland, and they did a few tests. From there he was sent to Kristiansand Hospital to have an X-ray. It transpired his lungs were full of fluid. He had been sent post-haste to the acute admissions unit and taken in a wheelchair to a room where he was laid on his side while a drain was inserted in his back. One lung, then the other, were drained of fluid. As he lay there he had seen for himself how the transparent bags had slowly filled with something resembling blood, only it was lighter in colour and mixed with tiny, white particles. In the end, they had drawn four and a half litres.

His voice was as always. Even. It was Pappa. Once it was said, he asked me what the weather was like in Oslo that evening. I felt odd, in a kind of daze, and had to go to the window, open the curtain and look out.

'I think it's snowing,' I said.

'There's a starry sky here,' he answered.

'Mhm,' I said.

'And it's cold,' he added. 'Cold and starry.'

That was all. That was the beginning.

A shadow was found over one kidney, the right-hand one. It was April and the ice had thawed. I had turned twenty. Then he had almost a litre of fluid drained. I couldn't understand how it had been possible to breathe with litres of water in his lungs, he couldn't either, and for that matter neither could the doctors. But he had.

He rang me from his hospital bed. It was evening, but still light. Clear, mild April weather with turbid, almost dirty air.

'Just me,' he said.

Then we chatted for perhaps five minutes. A quiet, gentle conversation about next to nothing.

'I suppose you have exams soon?' he enquired.

'Yes,' I said. 'Soon.'

'And you're studying?' he asked.

I heard the faint sounds of music in the background. It seemed to be seeping through from the recesses of the receiver. Very faint music.

'What's the weather like?' I asked, hearing at once that this was his question, not mine, and even though he was four hundred kilometres or so away, I could feel myself blushing.

'I don't know,' he said, and was as he always was. 'I can't get up. There are loads of tubes and things here. And in Oslo?'

'It's spring here,' I replied.

'Right,' he said. 'I think it's spring here, too.'

At the end of April I went home to see my parents. By then he was back at Kleveland, back at the farm. The first thing that struck me on seeing him was that his eyes had grown. He was lying on the sofa under a blanket looking at me with those new eyes of his, and it took me all evening and large parts of the next day to get used to them. It was as though they could see through everything, yet understood nothing of what they saw.

A few days later I took him for a check-up at Kristiansand Hospital. It was a forty-minute trip, but it felt like longer. We drove through the region, past the school in Lauvslandsmoen which we had both attended, with an interval of thirty years, past the community centre, Kilen, Lake Livannet, which glistened and quivered, though not close to the shore where the water lay still and black. There was an odd, oppressive atmosphere in the car, as if we had both been on long journeys, each in our own way, and had so much to tell one another that we didn't know where to begin, and so refrained. After a while we were nearing the coast, and to the west of the town we could see across the whole of the seaward approach. The sea was grey, lifeless. No boats. It reminded me of something, but I wasn't sure what.

Ashes?

All the smokers were clustered outside the hospital entrance. Dressed in Adidas and Nike tracksuits, they were, one and all, eaten up by cancer. Yet, they had somehow managed to make their way into the fresh air. They cupped their cigarettes in their hands as though someone might come along and steal them at any moment, and they regarded us with large, frightened eyes. As we went in a gust of wind blew, I smelt the smoke coming from them, and it was then that I realised they all had the same large eyes as Pappa.

I sat on a chair in the corridor and waited.

On Pappa's return I saw something had changed. His face was stiff and odd, as though he had been shouting and screaming, or laughing for several minutes. But he said nothing.

'Everything alright?' I asked.

'Yes,' he said. 'Everything's fine.'

Then we walked towards the exit. The smokers had gone, but the smell of smoke still hung in the air. Pappa could do with some new clothes, he said, so we drove through the town on our way home. There was an offer on track suits at Dressman, so we went there. I let him wander around on his own and pick out whatever he wanted. I watched him in front of the stand. There was no one else in the shop. He was flicking through the clothes with a determined mien, seeming to know exactly what it was he was after. Then he pulled out a tracksuit. It was red with a white puma in full leap on the breast. That was the one he wanted. It cost only 200 kroner. He went to the counter, paid, smiled at the young girl, and as he turned, his face still split with a smile, I suddenly knew what had happened. I realised Pappa had been crying. Suddenly it was clear to me: the man I had never seen shed a tear had been sitting in front of a doctor he didn't know, crying.

It was the day he was told there was nothing else they could do for him.

VIII.

HE HAMMERED THE fire engine for all it was worth to Breivoll, to the crossroads where the road divided into three. He jumped on the brakes, did a U-turn and continued down to Lauvslandsmoen. By Jens Slotte's house he almost veered off the road. He skidded round where the road curved down towards Finsåna but managed to stay on the carriageway. When he came to the school the road divided into three again. He stopped and asked an elderly man the way. The flashing blue lights were on and he had to shout from the window. He waited behind the wheel while he was given painstaking directions. Then he repeated them himself. Afterwards he put on the sirens, drove two hundred metres in the direction of Laudal, bore left onto the road to Finsådal, passed Stubrokka and the road ascending to Lauvsland. He raced on, whizzing past Haugeneset and the concrete elk that has been standing at the edge of the forest and peering out for as long as I can remember. Then he sped onto the flatlands of Moen where Teacher Jon's house lay all by itself. Two women were walking on the road ahead of him. It was Aasta and her mother, Emma. Emma was hard of hearing, nearly deaf, and she couldn't hear the sirens. Aasta turned to see a cloud of dust and smoke approaching at a menacing speed. She just managed to shove her mother into the ditch in time, and seconds later the fire engine screamed past. They had been a hair's breadth from being mown down, both of them, and stood gawping in the haze of dust and exhaust fumes.

*

The barn in Skogen, which was situated over the municipal border, in Marnardal, started to smoulder after sunrise, it was said, and that didn't fit the pattern of the previous blazes. The fire engine appeared at a little after eleven o'clock, and by then the building was well and truly alight. Several hundred metres of hose had to be rolled out to a small lake nearby, and while this was being done they had to use the water from the fire engine. The 1,000 litres were pumped out until the tank was empty, after which they had the muddy water from the lake in the pipes, but by then it was already too late. The barn burned to the ground, while the farmhouse was severely damaged. The heat was so intense that the wall caught fire even though it was quite a distance from the burning barn. The external cladding had to be hacked at and cut away with fire axes, the tiles had to be torn off, and then the house was sprayed with water so that everything inside – the porch, the hall and some of the kitchen – was left soaking wet.

The question afterwards was why the blaze had started in daylight. That was quite new.

Later, after the fire had been put out, Lensmann Koland made a statement to the newspaper. Only now, after the fourth blaze, had this become a matter for the police. There was no longer any doubt. Koland said the police were sure that the Tønnes' barn near Leipsland had been deliberately set alight. The same could be asserted with reasonable certainty about the summer storehouse in Hæråsen. And now there was the barn in Skogen. Three fires since 17 May. Four in total. There was good reason to believe they were dealing with an arsonist. It had been confirmed that all four fires had occurred within a radius of ten kilometres from Lauvslandsmoen School. From this, one might conclude that the arsonist lived in the vicinity and was familiar with the area. The police were interested to hear from anyone who had seen anything suspicious by the roadside. A search had been mounted to identify cars which had been on the six-kilometre stretch from Finsådal to Lauvslandsmoen between two o'clock and ten o'clock on Friday morning. Everything was of interest, even those things which at first sight might appear to be of no consequence. Furthermore, people were being warned to keep their eyes peeled and report any suspicious persons. That was all for now. No panic as yet.

IX.

TERESA MADE AN ENTRY IN HER DIARY. Five lines. It was Friday afternoon, a few hours after the fire in Skogen had been extinguished, but before all hell broke loose. In the morning she had been to the church to rehearse for a funeral – Anton Eikeli was due to be interred – and it was while she was sitting alone at the organ that the alarm had gone off. But she hadn't heard it; she was in the middle of 'Lead, Kindly Light'.

The five lines are about Dag and Ingemann. From her window she saw them lying side by side in the yard on the Friday afternoon shooting at a target. She describes the scene in precise detail. The bodies recoiling with every shot, the ear-piercing crack of the bullet, the echo that rolls around between the mountain ridges. The way they got up afterwards and march across the field to study the two targets. It is a distance of 100 metres. Dag first, his rifle slung over his shoulder; then Ingemann, his hands thrust into his pockets. She thinks Ingemann suddenly seems old. This procedure is repeated a few times. Then Ingemann walks alone across the field to check the targets. He walks with his hands in his pockets as the swallows swoop and the grass sways in the wind. And she sees Dag lying with the rifle sights to his eye. He is motionless as Ingemann crosses the field. Dag takes aim while Teresa watches from the window and Ingemann ambles onwards. This lasts for perhaps fifteen seconds. Nothing happens. But she is sure. He aims at his father.

Reading Teresa's description I was reminded of the time Pappa shot an elk right through the heart. I would have been around ten years old. Some days previously he had been lying in the yard and breaking in his rifle. I stood a few metres behind him and felt the gunshots like a clenched fist in the solar plexus. I stared at his cheek resting against the rifle stock. I had never seen him rest his cheek against anything or anyone in the same way as he did against the smooth rifle butt. So sensitive and gentle and careful against the untidy wood grain. It was as if he were settling down to sleep before the first shot shattered everything. I looked at the smoking spent cartridges that were ejected, empty, red-hot, all of them accompanied by a strange, hollow song, like a kind of cheer. Five shots in all. Then he got up from the old beach mat he had been lying on, put the gun down with care, walked across the field to the target and studied it closely while I picked up the cartridges, which were still too hot to hold to your lips and blow on.

A few days later he took his shooting test. I was with him at the range, the one that lay secluded about half way between the church and the shop in Breivoll. He lay down on his front and fired a series of ten shots at the silhouette of an elk that appeared from a pit. It transpired that all the shots were within the magic circle drawn around the heart and lungs.

He had passed.

The man who had never shot an animal. The man who had never been interested in hunting. Yet he turned out to be an accurate marksman. The question is: what prompted him to take a shooting test and go elk hunting? This was a conundrum for me. It still is, even now, more than twenty years later. I knew he wasn't interested in hunting. He wasn't like that. He was too gentle, too much of a dreamer. He might perhaps have dreamed of doing it, thought about it, talked about it. But not of actually going through with it. Yet he did. He did go through with it. Pappa became a hunter. And when, a few weeks later, he was in situ with a rifle resting on his lap, I was sitting right behind him. I remember staring at his back and thinking it wasn't Pappa there, it was a stranger, someone I had never met; however, if he turned I would immediately see that it was him.

X.

TWO DAYS AFTER Pappa had bought the new tracksuit I returned to Oslo. It was May 1998, exams were approaching, but I couldn't concentrate on my studies. I couldn't concentrate on anything. After the first weeks it was as if all my willpower had crumbled inside me. I had a lie-in every morning, and didn't get up until the sun peered in through the window. I got dressed, ate whatever food I had lying around and didn't go to the reading room before twelve. I found a free seat, piled my books in front of me and sat staring at the steady flow of traffic down St Olavs gate. I couldn't read. I could barely open a book. My brain was absolutely blank. It was frightening. I had never experienced anything like it. I was on the point of losing control, but I was still absolutely unperturbed. Why was I reacting in this way? There were many other people in similar situations. There were many people who had a dying father at home, weren't there? There were many people in the same situation as I was who had to take exams and still managed to work in the reading room, and who lived apparently normal lives.

Weren't there?

I forgot both my grandfather's coat and my new glasses. I completely forgot to be intellectual. I forgot about everything and everyone. Now there was only me. I didn't know what was going to happen; however, I was quite unconcerned. I sat in the canteen and ate meals with the others, as usual. Queued up like a good boy, took a plate with three potatoes, a pile of grated carrots and pollock fish cakes in sauce, and moved on to the till where I paid. I placed my tray with the food on the table where the others were already sitting, poured myself a glass of water and fetched salt, pepper and serviettes. I was as before. I ate as before, talked with the others as before. The only difference was that I was prone to sudden fits of laughter. If someone told a joke, or a funny story, I could laugh so much I almost fell off my chair. The others looked at me and smiled. Food went down the wrong way and I had to go to the toilet to recover. But, aside from the fits of laughter, everything was fine. The exams were getting closer, and I hadn't read a line for many weeks. The books stayed in my bedsit. I didn't open them any more. I was unemotional all the time, and discovered how easy it was. It was easy, I was unemotional and in a way I was in control. I walked through the corridors outside the reading room in the Domus Nova building in the centre of Oslo, in the centre of the town that was supposed to be mine, and let absolutely everything slide.

A frenetic, nervous atmosphere began to spread through the corridors, the reading room and the canteen. I caught fragments of conversation. Now and then someone asked me something. *What's mea culpa in tort again? What does Falkinger say about it? Is there anything about it in Lødrup?* Yes, I answered without any qualms. I was positive that there was something in Lødrup, and perhaps also in Falkinger. I said I would go home and check. When I was home, however, I did nothing. I had let everything slip. All my dreams. My ambitions. Everything I had imagined. Everything I was going to work towards. An education. A career. A future.

And all because of Pappa.

My books gathered dust at home while I went out walking in town. I crossed St Olavs gate and continued down Universitetsgata, past the National Gallery and the large grey edifice housing the Norwegian publisher Gyldendal, and I squinted up at those sitting behind the windows deep in concentration. Perhaps they were reading a manuscript?

Something that would one day be a book, a collection of poems, a novel? I remembered Ruth's words from years ago, the ones that had never quite lost their hold on me. But I had never dared to believe them. I had even promised myself then that I would never tell another lie, and I had no dreams of becoming a writer. Quite the contrary. I was going to become a lawyer. I was going to have order and lucidity. I was going to know my law backwards and make a distinction between right and wrong. I was going to be someone quite different. I had no time for so-called artists, whom I considered drop-outs, people who hadn't been capable of completing an education, who had started painting, or writing, or some other endeavour that was supposed to give their lives a semblance of meaning and dignity.

All of those people who had ended up on the darker side of life. This concept was still ingrained in me.

And now, there I stood, staring up at the grey Gyldendal building that had acquired some allure in the hot May sun, and as I turned to go I realised it reminded me of the balcony on the old shop in Brandsvoll, the one with the flagpole mounted over the road. I had dreamed so often of standing there and looking out.

I walked on past the Norwegian Theatre, and eventually arrived in Akersgata. I mounted the broad steps by the government building and finally reached the Deichman Library. That was my destination. When I entered, everything was very quiet, not just around me but also inside me. Everything went quiet. I became placid and calm, and sat for several hours reading novels and poetry until my head was spinning. I did exactly the same thing the day after, and the next, and the day after that. I can still recall the dank atmosphere in the stairwell, the carpet in the middle of the staircase that was wet and squelched at the very bottom but was dry at the top, the banister that was worn and shiny from all the hands. And I remember all the shelves of books, probably several hundred times as many as in the library back in Lauvslandsmoen, and the unruffled woman's voice over the loudspeaker just before eight o'clock every evening, the one that announced it was time to make your way homewards because the doors were closing.

The day before the exam he rang. It was in the evening and I had just returned home from Deichman with a bag of books. The mobile phone emitted its cheery ringtone in my pocket, and I put down my bag and went to the window.

His voice was more relaxed, as though he had been drinking. But of course he hadn't; Pappa never drank. I stood by the window looking out at the lamp swinging on a wire stretched taut across the street.

'Tomorrow's the big day,' he said.

'What do you mean?' I asked.

'You've got an exam, haven't you?'

'Of course,' I said.

'And everything's under control?'

'Near as dammit,' I said.

'Good luck,' he said.

'Thank you.'

We chatted about other things, I have no memory of what, and then rang off. Him first. I stood for a long time with the phone in my hand. Then I grabbed my jacket and went to the

Underwater Pub, which was close to where I was living, and ordered a half-litre of beer. It was the first time I had done this, and I am sure it was obvious. I didn't know whether to say *Beer, please.* Or: *A pils.* Or: *Half a litre.* In the end I gave a brief nod of the head in the direction of the beer tap behind the bar, and the young girl working there probably thought I was a foreigner who couldn't speak Norwegian or English. I waited at the bar, not quite at my ease, for the glass to be filled, then occupied a seat at the back of the room and took long swigs. Afterwards I got up, paid and went out into the mild evening air. I was scared someone I knew would see me, or I would meet someone from home, even though that was completely inconceivable. As it happened, I didn't bump into anyone on the way and reached home without mishap. Where I stood in the middle of the room for a long time.

The following day I appeared for the exam at eight thirty on the dot. It was held in a large West Oslo gymnasium and I took a seat next to the wall. I printed my name and candidate number very clearly. Then I handed everything in and walked out into the sun. I had recently turned twenty, life was about to begin, real life. I had left my old life behind me to become the person I was. But, coldly, unemotionally, with my mind as clear as a bell, I wrote my name and handed in all the sheets of paper utterly blank. I walked in the hot sunshine listening to the birds twittering in the rose-hip bushes, went to the tram stop, the regular rumble of the town in my ears, and stood alone waiting for the tram to take me to the centre. My mind drifted. Wasn't I the one who was going to become a lawyer? Wasn't I the one who had travelled to Oslo to find himself? Yes, I was. However, it hadn't happened. I was now sitting on a tram to the city centre, but in reality I was on my way into an unknown world. As the tram disappeared beneath the town I stared into my own hazy reflection, and when I surfaced in daylight in front of the fountain by the National Theatre, I knew: now you're on the darker side of life. It will carry you away. No one can help you. You are where you vowed to yourself you would never end up. It is too late.

That afternoon I sat in the Underwater Pub until I felt I was a little more myself. Then I went home and rang Pappa.

'It's over now,' I said in a bright tone which wasn't my usual one. But the 400 kilometres between us saved me, and Pappa was unaware that anything was wrong.

'Congratulations,' he said.

'Thank you,' I answered.

'How does it feel?'

'I'm not quite sure,' I replied.

'I'm proud of you,' he said, and he could never have said that if we had been in the same room, that I do know. I didn't answer.

'Now you've done what I've always dreamed of doing,' he said.

'Have I?' I asked, staring out at the swaying street lamp, just as I had on the previous night.

'I always dreamed of studying in Oslo when I was young,' he said.

'Did you?'

'I dreamed of becoming someone, you know.'

'But you did become someone,' I said, immediately hearing my mistake. 'I mean, you *are* someone.'

This time it was Pappa who didn't answer. There was a

silence, and I was unsure whether he was there, and again I thought I could hear faint music coming from somewhere as far from my father as it was from me.

XI.

I WASN'T QUITE finished with Kåre Vatneli. It emerged that he attended a confirmation service with Pappa in the autumn of 1957, barely two years before he died.

He got as far as being confirmed, he passed the start line, so to speak, and for confirmation he was given a long, black coat and hat, and this was for him, as for the other confirmands, a definitive indication that the world of childhood had now been left behind.

That was September 1957, the first year that white confirmation caps were worn. Pappa had just entered his fifteenth year, Kåre his sixteenth. After the ceremony they would finally be regarded as adults. As they entered the church they were ranked according to height, the tallest first. Medium height, in the middle. The smallest, last. First of all came the priest. Absalon Elias Holme, a name worthy of a priest. Then came Kåre. Pappa was quite close to the front. Grandma and Grandad were in the pews and had risen to their feet along with everyone else. Teresa was in the gallery playing the organ. The confirmands proceeded up the aisle, took their seats in the front rows beneath the pulpit. The music faded. Holme turned, made the sign of the cross and the service could begin.

*

Many more people than Aasta remembered Kåre Vatneli. At a later point I visited three of his childhood friends. It was November, I was at Otto Øvland's house. I wasn't aware that he and Pappa had been christened on the same day, with the same water. That was one of the first things Otto told me, as though it was important for him to say it at last.

Tom and Willy Utsogn were there that evening, with Otto, in his warm house. Both Otto and Willy had been to Kristiansand Hospital to visit Kåre that time in 1959. Tom, who was a bit younger, remembered the vehicle that came home with the coffin. He had no memory of the coffin itself, only the car. The car made a stronger impression on him. And that Kåre was lying in it.

They were able, incidentally, to confirm what I had already been told about Kåre: the carefree attitude, the unbelievable cheerfulness. When everyone around him was so marked by his illness, by the amputation, by what lay in the offing, why wasn't he? How did he manage to retain his cheery spirits when both Johanna and Olav were barely able to keep themselves upright? There was no explanation. Kåre's life, for me, was an enigma, baffling. It was inexpressible, almost erased, but also somehow beautiful. Like laughing in the shadow of death. Or it was a love song. His life had been a love song of which all that remained now, fifty years later, was the word *darling*.

In addition, I was told the moped story:

They were going to see the priest for confirmation lessons, and everyone cycled together to the church. They always took their time, and when they arrived the church door was generally open. I remember Pappa telling me a story, I didn't know whether it was true or not, about one occasion before the lesson when they lifted their bikes up the church steps and cycled around inside the church. Otto laughed and corroborated its authenticity. But that wasn't all, he said. Someone rode a moped in the church, he recalled. *A moped?* Yes, indeed. *In the church?* Yes. Yes. *And who did that?* It was Kåre. The happy, easy-going Kåre had ridden his moped around the church. The one he had been given because he couldn't cycle all the way with only one leg. So he had taught himself to walk again, then to ride a bike, then to ride a moped. He was still officially too young, but the local police authority had given him a dispensation because of his leg. He taught himself to ride a moped, and in the end, as one of very few, to ride a moped in church. The central aisle was very narrow, so it wasn't easy to keep your balance. The others had looked on, stunned. He had crossed an invisible line, and the others stood holding their breath. First of all, he drove up the nave, then he turned by the altar, drove into both arms of the transept and back up to the altar. The church interior slowly filled with exhaust fumes which mixed with the bright peals of laughter. All of a sudden Holme was there. He advanced from behind the altar, white-faced, but still controlled. You can't lose your temper with a one-legged fifteen-year-old. Even if he has crossed the line.

This had been merely one of many pranks, but people never talked about Kåre's illness. And no one ever said the name of his illness aloud. It was taboo, it was the worst, it was as if it might infect others if it were mentioned. Kåre himself didn't seem particularly bothered. The leg was amputated but he carried on. Evidently it would take more than that to worry him. To worry the boy who had been given a special dispensation to ride a moped by the lensmann himself.

Right up until some days before he was admitted to the hospital for the final time he was talking about how he would probably get a car when he was discharged. The car would be in the yard waiting for him as soon as he returned from hospital. Most probably a Triumph Herald, or a Chevrolet Impala, or perhaps a black Buick. One of the three. Most probably. It was Olav, his father, who had sat at his bedside and told him that. Father and son had imagined them, all polished and shiny, standing in the yard between the house and the barn. Then Kåre had got in behind the wheel and started the engine, Olav slipped into the passenger seat, and they had raced off.

Willy had been the last person to visit him. On the day before he died. Willy had been no more than fifteen years old and he travelled to Kristiansand with the sole purpose of seeing him. The visit lasted maybe half an hour. They didn't exchange one word. Kåre lay under a white rug, skeletal. There was almost nothing left of him, only his chest rose above the level, white bed and resembled a rock beneath snow. And the head. And the eyes. He seemed to be floating. They didn't say anything. Not even about cars. They just looked at each other. That was all. Johanna had been there with them. Willy remembered that he and Johanna had spoken, but not what they had spoken about. Most likely about quite ordinary things. The weather. The bus trip to town. Nothing one might remember fifty years later.

Johanna had been calm. Quite calm.

Then Kåre died, and the incomprehensibly happy and cheerful boy was gone.

As I was about to go Tom and Willy started to talk about Pappa. They had both known him, it transpired, and something happened to them when we touched on the subject. I don't know if it was out of consideration for me, but they talked about him in an affectionate yet measured way. They talked about his ski jumping, for which he had evidently become well known.

'No one could jump like your father,' Tom said, and I understood that I should take that as a very special compliment. They went on to say he could do things others never achieved. Or dared. As soon as he took off from the ski jump he leaned perilously far forwards. It had been scary standing on the flat and watching, the tips of his skis were tilted so far upwards they were almost in his woolly hat, and that was how he lay, waiting for the lift that came once he had left the ramp. He leaned forwards and the lift came, and he floated for longer than anyone else. He had done the Slottebakken jump, and he had jumped off Stubrokka, they told me, and he had done many more ski jumps, and they reeled them off, but I have forgotten what they are all called. It was as though they wanted to tell me this, it was important for them to say that Pappa had been such an exceptional ski-jumper. That no one jumped further than he did, and that his secret was that rare combination of daring, courage and recklessness, and all of this carried him further than anyone else.

Or was there perhaps more to it? Something they didn't say, something they thought, but omitted to say. That Pappa had actually crossed a line with these ski jumps. That something could easily have gone wrong. Terribly wrong. That it was his sheer good fortune that he had got down unscathed every time. That in fact they had never really understood it at the time: why he did it, what was so important to him about these ski jumps. That everyone was standing at the bottom while he climbed up the tower alone, with his skis on his shoulders, higher and higher in the darkness until he stood at the top, fastening on his skis. That no one really understood him when he launched himself, crouched down as his speed increased and the ramp approached, when he took off and immediately leaned into the wind and the noise and the cold, which drove into his face.

After the visit I got into my car and drove west to Hønemyr. I felt as if I was somehow outside myself, and that the conversation about my father had led me there. It was as though I was contemplating everything from the outside. It wasn't me driving in the dark, it was the person who used to live here, who was left behind when I moved, perhaps the person I really want to be but can never be.

I came to the crossroads where the road divides into three, turned down towards Brandsvoll, passed the army camp and the disused firing range and continued towards Skinnsnes. As I drove I remembered the weeks in the summer of 1998 when I had driven around in my father's car, stopped and tried to write. That all seemed such a long time ago now, but it came closer as I drove through this countryside where everything had happened.

After passing Sløgedal's house, acting on a spur-of-the-moment feeling, I braked and turned into the area in front of the fire station. Then I switched off the engine and got out. It was cold and I wasn't suitably dressed. I lingered for a while, examining the dark building. Some grass had grown between the gravel in front of the garage door, and it must have been a long time since the fire engine had been given an outing. There were almost never fires. I tried to peer through the frosted glass in the door, but I couldn't see anything; it was completely black inside where the fire engine was. Instead of getting back into the car and driving home I began to walk up to Sløgedal's house. I had never taken this path before, and it turned out to be further than I had imagined. I was walking in the dark. I could hear only the sound of my own footsteps. So I started humming. It was a tune without beginning or end, I just made it up on the spot, and then, after a while, it was gone. Soon I had walked far enough to be able to discern Sløgedal's house, a large, grey building somewhere in front of me in the darkness. Gradually I began to distinguish the window frames, which had been painted white, and I glimpsed the outline of the barn, which had been erected on the ruins of the old one. I decided to go right up to it. Just as I had made my decision I saw the lights of a car approaching from the north. I don't quite know what happened, but I was immediately gripped by a kind of panic. It was, as I said, too late to turn and go back, and it was still too far to the house – the car would be round the bend before I could take refuge behind the corner of the house. In the end I broke into a run. I sprinted as fast as I could to Sløgedal's house while the light from the car grew and spread across the sky, and I was reminded of the sea of fire from the summer thirty years ago, about which so many first-hand witnesses had spoken. As I was about to leave the road the car lights appeared before me, and with that I came to a halt. I was caught, and some way from the house. The headlamps shone into my face, I stood there staring helplessly into them, for several seconds I was blinded, the car slowed down, loomed nearer, for a moment I thought it would stop, and I strove to find something to say. However, it didn't stop, it drove slowly past, and I was left in the darkness as the car snaked down to the fire station and was gone.

XII.

AT SHORTLY AFTER SEVEN O'CLOCK he set off down to Kilen, filled up with petrol at the Shell station, bought cigarettes, a few sweets and the latest Donald Duck comic, then continued past the community house, towards Øvland. It was a warm evening, Friday evening what was more, he was free, he had no plans and he didn't have to return to work in Kjevik until Monday at 6 p.m.

He accelerated, caught up with some young girls on their bikes, waved to them, noticed that they giggled back. That was all. Reaching the brow of the hill, he switched on the radio. There was a live transmission from Argentina tonight as well. That was why it was so deserted and still: everyone was indoors watching TV. The match had kicked off at seven, Italy against France in the Mar del Plata stadium, which had been transformed into a seething cauldron. He pulled into a lay-by and listened as he ate the sweets and flicked through the comic. After twenty minutes or so the match began to bore him – no goals, no chances, nothing. Just the endless roar of the stadium. It made your mind go fuzzy. At length he got out of the car, lit a cigarette, leaned against the bonnet and stared into the forest, at the straight tree trunks glowing with the heat of the sun, the unmoving branches.

When he drove on it was slightly after eight, and half-time in Argentina, where the score was 0–0. He crossed through Hønemyr, came to the crossroads where the road split into three, and turned down towards Brandsvoll, skidding the car and, in the mirror, saw the gravel flying. He turned up the volume on the radio. Turned it down. Switched it off. He stopped at the old shooting range, lit another cigarette, but dropped it after a few drags, trod it hard into the gravel until it stopped smoking. He stood listening for a long time. Dogged tiredness was spreading into his arms like a kind of poison. Then he spotted the rifle on the back seat. He adopted a stance leaning on the car roof, took careful aim, then fired. It must have been a good hundred metres to the road sign with the black elk. Then he got into the car and drove over to check the result. There was a dark hollow in the middle of the triangle, in the middle of the black animal. A perfect bullseye.

He drove slowly down the long hills past Djupesland; no one to be seen there, either. It was as if the whole region had been abandoned, everyone had gone, there wasn't a single person left, only him. He passed Sløgedal's house, which lay empty and still, and turned finally into the fire station. He waited for a few minutes with the engine idling. Night had begun to fall. The sky was still light in the west, but the forest was dark and uniform, the trees merged into one another like shadows, forming a black, impenetrable mass. Then he killed the engine, groped in the glove compartment, found the fire station key and let himself in. There was a smell in the gloom of lubricating oil, diesel and stale smoke. It had smelt like that inside for as long as he could remember. Whenever he wanted he could close his eyes and recall this precise smell. The fire engine seemed to be gleaming in the light from the outside lamp, shiny and red, almost black. He ran his hand down the side. The metal was cold and smooth, providing hardly any resistance to his fingertips. Then he opened the sliding door at the back of the vehicle. He had to use force. In all there were three jerrycans in the boot; he lifted them one by one. The can on the left was half full, not too heavy: excellent. He picked it up without a sound and carried it to the car. Put it on the floor at the back and threw some clothes over it. Then he locked the garage door, got into the car and drove the few metres home.

He went up to his room, turned on the radio and remained upstairs for several hours. The next match from Argentina started at a quarter to eleven. Alma and Ingemann were in the living room watching TV. It was Holland versus West Germany, and there was a constant cacophony coming from more than 40,000 spectators.

Alma sat with her knitting in her lap, only looking up every time the commentator – it was Knut Th. Gleditsch – raised his voice. It was a draw, 1–1. It had just gone half past eleven. Frenetic knitting needles were clicking. Alma thought she could hear Dag's voice upstairs. Her fingers stiffened and she looked over at Ingemann, but he was slumped in his chair and his eyelids were fluttering. She put down her knitting, got up in a flash, went into the hall and stood listening with one hand on the banister. She could hear him talking upstairs. It was unmistakeable. It wasn't the radio. It wasn't the television. It was him. She went to the kitchen, glanced at the clock, ran hot water in the sink, then just stared down at the water before pulling the plug, drying her hands on the kitchen towel and returning to the hall. It had gone quiet upstairs. No voices, nothing.

Then the door opened and he slowly descended the staircase.

'Are you down there, Mamma?' he asked.

'Yes,' she said, trying to catch his eye.

'Aren't you watching the match?'

'No,' she replied.

'It was a damned draw,' Ingemann shouted from the living room, suddenly awake and stretching in his chair.

'They got what they deserved,' Dag said.

'Who did?' asked Alma.

'The ones who were unable to win.'

Alma fixed her gaze on him. He seemed tired. His eyes were red and swollen. One eye was slightly smaller than the other. It went like that when he hadn't slept. It shrank. He had been like that ever since he was a child.

'You look tired, Dag,' she said.

'Do I?' he answered. There was a hint of merriment in his expression, she recognised it from the time he had tiptoed up behind her and placed his hands over her eyes.

'Aren't you going to bed? You need the sleep.'

'To bed?'

'It's close on midnight,' Ingemann said, struggling up from his chair. 'We'll have to hope it's a quiet night.'

'I'm going to scout around for anything suspicious,' Dag said, going into the kitchen. She heard the fridge door open.

'Surely you don't want anything now, do you?' she said, following him. He was leaning against the fridge door and staring into the dim light.

'Someone has to keep watch,' he said, closing the door and turning to her. He peeled a banana and devoured it in a trice. 'If no one keeps watch there'll be another fire. There's no knowing what the nutter might get up to.'

'But not tonight,' she said. 'You . . . you've got to sleep as well, you know.'

He scrutinised her, and at that moment she thought she detected a change in his face. She recognised it straightaway. Just for one brief, chilling instant, it had gone hard. Then it softened. He went over to her, so close that she could smell it on him. Exhaust fumes, diesel and a faint whiff of banana. He was almost a head taller than her; she could feel his breath in her hair.

'Mamma,' he said, so softly that only she could hear. She had a sudden sense of feeling unwell, as though she couldn't get enough air.

'But, Dag,' she whispered. 'Dag, my love, you need your sleep.'

He laid his hand on her shoulder, and it was so heavy it might have forced her through the floor, and yet so light it could have made her float. His hand filled her with warmth, a warmth she had never experienced before, a warmth that could only come from Dag and in the whole wide world only she could receive it. And she was the only person in the world who heard his voice. It whispered close to her ear:

'Mamma, Mamma, good little Mamma.'

XIII.

THE NIGHT AFTER the examination I joined the others at the post-exam party in the cellar under the old university buildings. First, though, we got into the mood in a cramped bedsit by the square known as Tullinløkka, and after a few hours and several beers we continued in the city centre. I sat with the others and yelled one *skål* after another, draining my glass, getting a refill and *skål*-ing again. I noticed the others sending me looks, their eyes a touch apprehensive but kind. They had never seen me like this before, after all. Everyone was happy and excited and exhausted after weeks of studying. No one talked about the exams or the questions we had been set. Most of them were just relieved to have them over and done with, and were looking forward to the summer and the long holidays, and thereafter the autumn semester with its new challenges, like another step on the ladder that would lead to the final goal. I sat there smiling and *skål*-ing and singing along to the music that pounded through the vaulted cellar, but in reality I was drifting quietly away. All the time I was strangely clear-headed and focused, despite the mounting inebriation. It was indeed this clarity of mind that characterised the state I had found myself in since my father had fallen ill. I was clear-headed and distant and strangely outside myself, and in a break between songs I remember I stood up with a large beer in my hand. *I didn't write a line!* I shouted. *I handed in blank papers. That's me for you.* Skål *to that!* There might have been a couple of seconds' silence as people looked at each other, a couple of seconds of bewilderment, no more, before they burst into laughter. Everyone laughed, they raised their glasses and *skål*-ed, and I laughed and *skål*-ed with them. The party continued at an ever faster pace, and with ever vaguer images, faster music, warm bodies, roars of laughter, long embraces, lips to ears, all as I drifted quietly away. At some point we left the university cellar and carried on partying in the city as my head grew more and more fuzzy. I didn't know what the time was, but it was a cool evening at the beginning of June and I remember smiling faces and laughter in the streets. I remember a large crowd of people, a swaying dance floor, sharp flashes of light, sweaty bodies, hair over my face, arms round my shoulders, the scent of perfume and the bass vibrating deep in my stomach. I was surrounded on all sides by a hot, pulsating darkness and people shouting and laughing, yet I was quite, quite alone. I was drifting away. And no one noticed. And no one imagined. It was a party. We were on the town to party. I drank four cocktails in quick succession, all with a little umbrella which I tossed over my shoulder. I had no idea where the cocktails came from, whether I had been given them or bought them myself, but I remember the tiny parasols and I remember the floor beginning to whirl. I screamed into the face of a girl with long, dark hair and blurred eyes. She was standing right up against me as I shouted something or other, yet she didn't seem to hear a word, or perhaps I was mistaken, perhaps I wasn't shouting at all, perhaps it was me standing there with my eyes blurred, not saying a word while she shouted. I'm not sure. Shortly afterwards, however, everything went black.

There are a few minutes or hours missing from my memory before I found myself again, walking along the deserted street from St Olavs plass in the city centre. I walked, trying to support myself on tenement walls, as the world around me rocked and swayed. I was surrounded by a sudden silence; all I could hear was my own unsteady, shuffling steps. *Silence*, I remember thinking. *Silence. Silence. Silence.* I met scattered huddles of people, I saw them approaching like shadows and from far away, and then there they were, in front of me, I shouted something, brandished my arms and barred their way, I don't remember what I was thinking or what I wanted to accomplish, but straight after I felt a stinging pain on my cheek, by my ear, and realised someone had punched me in the face. Again I was alone, the people had gone and the world was moving sideways. I tried to establish what had happened. Someone had punched me. I had no idea why. All I knew was that my cheek was throbbing. Eventually I reached Ullevålsveien and took a left. I didn't have a clear thought in my head, yet there was something in me observing all of this. Something that was always lucid and rational. It was this lucidity I had had when I walked out of the exam, and it was the same lucidity steering me across the street and through the gates of Vår Frelser cemetery. *You failed the exam on purpose*, a sober voice said inside me. *You failed the exam and you've drunk yourself senseless. You've lied to your father, and you've just been knocked to the ground and now you're going into a cemetery.* Inside it was as black as pitch. There had been a number of attacks here recently, but that didn't deter me. I rather wished that someone *would* attack me, that someone would sneak up on me from behind, hit me over the head with a hard object, causing me to lose consciousness and keel over. I hadn't felt much of the punch to my cheek and now I wanted a bit more, with some oomph, a real belter from behind to make glass shatter and stars spin. So that someone would find me the day after and by then it wouldn't really matter if I was dead or alive. Such were my thoughts as I staggered along the gravel path leading to the Grove of Honour, where all the great authors and composers were buried. My thoughts were unclear, fuzzy, yet in fact strangely clear. I lurched around in the darkness among the gravestones, not knowing where I was going. Occasionally I registered a car passing in Ullevålsveien, but it was only as a distant puff of air from another world. Then I straightened up and had a pee. I didn't know what was in front of me. That is to say, I knew it was some grave, but I had no idea whose. I was just having a pee. It felt wonderfully liberating. Afterwards I sat down on a headstone with both shoes planted in the flower bed. Part of me was aware of the recent additions there, the pansies arranged neatly in groups in soft, wet earth. Then a chilling sensation took root in me: this was my father's grave. He was dead and had been buried without my knowledge; attempts had been made to contact me but I had been unreachable, and so they had buried him, and now I was sitting there convinced that it was my father lying beneath the soft earth. I hardly dared look to see what was inscribed on the stone.

I just knew. It's him, I told myself. It's him. It's him. In the end I bent forwards anyway, until my head was between my knees. I managed to read the name on the stone. It was a very simple name, so it couldn't be him. Then I vomited. It gushed over my shoes and the flowers and splashed onto the soil. I stood up and stumbled a few metres, then vomited a second time and stooped over another gravestone. I immediately felt a bit better, but my mind was still at sea. I walked between two dark trees weighed down with foliage and with large branches that spread low over the ground. I knew that the writer Bjørnstjerne Bjørnson was buried beneath these trees. I walked under the branches and sat down on a big block of stone, which was his grave, with a stone flag spread across it. I was sitting on Bjørnson's grave and felt that I was still drifting away. I leaned back. That was good. Immensely good. It was as though I had been waiting all my life for just this moment. I lay back, stretched out my arms and felt myself getting heavy, and in the end I must have fallen asleep, stretched out like an angel, for I remember nothing else.

XIV.

AS HE PASSED LAUVSLANDSMOEN SCHOOL he switched off the headlamps. At first he couldn't see anything, then his vision improved, and soon he could see without a problem. He just had to get used to it. He switched the lights on again. By the playground he turned left onto the Dynestøl road. The fence by the football pitch was damaged in places. The school buildings lay shrouded in darkness. Whenever he drove past the school it felt as if he had hardly left it. Everything seemed to come back to him, even though it was nine years ago now. He remembered what it had been like. Being the best in all the subjects, being at the top, on his own. Sometimes he could still hear Reinert's voice: *Could you read for us, Dag? Could you play the first bars for us, Dag? Could you write this sentence on the board, Dag, as your writing is so neat?* It had been Reinert who had given him the belief that he could be whatever he wanted to be. It had been Reinert who had seen him. Who had understood who he was, what he was good at, that he was quite unique. He wasn't like the other children, and Reinert had realised that. The others would be farmers, electricians, carpenters and plumbers, and perhaps police officers.

But him, Dag? What would Dag be?

Now and then they would sit round the kitchen table at Skinnsnes discussing his future, and it was as though they were inside a magic circle. It didn't happen so often any more, but he remembered the feeling that they were all filled with something great and rather solemn. And he knew that this greatness and solemnity lay in his hands. What he would achieve in his life, what he would become, everything lay in his hands.

Ingemann had wanted him to be a doctor. Or a lawyer. *You can be whatever you want, you're so clever*, his father had said. *You can be whatever you want, except a fireman, because that's what you are already*, he had said. And then they had all laughed. But he knew his father was right. At that moment he had felt anything was possible, he had unlimited gifts, the world lay at his feet, all he had to do was start walking.

He drove into the playground. Stopped the car, got out. It was dark everywhere, and quite, quite still, apart from the ticking of the hot car engine. He strolled past the building, peered in through the dark windows and glimpsed the rows of tables, the teacher's desk, the board, a line of letters, some children's drawings on the wall.

What would he actually be?

It would have to be something impressive, something that would make people open their eyes wide. He could hear what they would say: *Has Dag become a doctor? Has Dag become a lawyer? Well, we knew he had it in him.*

There were no limits. He could move to Oslo and start studying medicine this autumn; he could finish the course in two, three years. No problem. He could take piano lessons on the side. Or he could start a law degree. Or, vice versa, he could concentrate on music and do a law course in the evenings. That was another option. Perhaps it might be best to focus his efforts on law. After all, it was so useful. He could find himself a job as a top lawyer. In the Ministry of Justice, perhaps. Or in the Ministry of Foreign Affairs. He could apply to do a course with the ministry. Learn French properly, or perhaps Spanish. Get a posting to Paris, or Madrid. He could be a diplomat. He visualised Alma and Ingemann going to the Norwegian Embassy in Paris to visit him. He drove the black embassy car and picked them up at Charles de Gaulle Airport; his mother would clap her hands, hug him and whisper: *Is this really you, my boy?* Then they would drive to Paris while he showed them where everything was, all the places they had heard of: the Tour Eiffel, the Champs Élysées, the Arc de Triomphe. The daydream always stopped there, at the Arc de Triomphe; he had never been to Paris, of course.

He could be a diplomat. Or why not a defence counsel? After all, he had seen the famous lawyer Alf Nordhus on TV, and had instantly been fascinated. The caustic wit, the beard and the smoking cigarette. He imagined himself wearing a black cap and conducting some court case. That role would have been right up his street. He had the ability to defend anyone. Even if it was a murderer. He could persuade everyone that he was right and the others wrong. Prove that the murderer had behaved in a rational way. Contend that the others should understand what lay behind his actions. If they did, there was no longer a crime. And the murderer was no longer a murderer. He would be acquitted, and Dag would bask in the glory and the amazement.

He could imagine it, hearing his own voice. All that was required was some understanding. The murderer wasn't a murderer; the murderer was a human being. Was that so difficult to grasp?

He got back into the car and drove on towards Dynestøl. He took the long road past Lake Homevannet. A white veil of mist hung a few metres above the surface, as though it had detached itself from all the darkness and was now rising to the sky with infinite languor. He couldn't see land on the other side, just a black wall of forest. Then he extinguished the lights. He passed the cabin belonging to Kristiansand Automobilklubb, or the KAK cabin as it was called, and immediately below was the bathing area with the underwater rock jutting thirty metres out from the shore. The cabin was inhabited, he could see – there were several cars parked higgledy-piggledy outside – but everyone was asleep. It was just past one o'clock. He had switched off the radio, and proceeded towards Dynestøl. The road was narrow and winding, and a line of grass grew between the ruts made by wheels. Birch branches brushed the side of the car, making him jump; they sounded like limp human hands. There was no light anywhere. No houses, no outside lamps, nothing. He decided to drive back, and started to look out for a suitable place to turn.

That was when he caught sight of what he supposed was a house. It was on the side of the road a bit further ahead in the darkness, atop a small mound. There was a barn as well, which he didn't see until he was nearer. Slowly, he drove right up to it. Then he stopped and got out. The night was chilly, and he was wearing only a thin shirt. He buttoned it to the throat and rolled down the sleeves. That helped a little. In addition, he found the jacket he had thrown onto the rear seat, put it on, and then he was nice and warm. All around him there was silence, again just the hot engine clicking as it cooled, otherwise nothing. He drew closer. It was an old house, you could see that even in the darkness. And it was big. The foundation plinth was massive, with small windows looking into the cellar. Steps with a handrail led up from the long grass. Between the house and barn there was a tractor, while the barn itself was tall, narrow and very black. That was all. He walked down a slight slope to the back of the barn. Beneath the building was an open space with hundreds of poles and other old junk piled in the murk.

He hurried back to the car, and uncovered the shining white jerrycan on the rear seat. It was easy to carry when it was only half full. Returning to the slope behind the barn, he lowered the can to the grass for a moment. He spotted a door and groped towards it, carrying the jerrycan. It was unlocked. He slipped into a dark room with a wooden floor. It was impossible to see a thing even though he waited patiently for his eyes to adjust to the darkness. Then he struck a match. It flared up. The room was empty. A low ceiling. Some straw on the floor. Two of the walls were the foundation wall. There was a smell of mould, decay, animals. Then the match went out. The cap on the jerrycan was stuck, but after a bit of fiddling it finally came off. He couldn't see where he was pouring, but he heard the petrol splashing on the planks. When he had finished he went outside, put the can down on the ground and wiped his hands thoroughly before returning to the barn. The night was at its darkest now; in a while the light in the sky would slowly awaken, and then the birds would start singing, even though it was still night. He heard his own whispering footsteps in the long grass. His legs were wet up to his calves, and as he stood at the door, taking out the box of matches, he could barely see his own hands. Unhurriedly, he counted in his head. Then he struck the match. The flame was blown out straightaway. The same happened to match number two. He must have blown them out himself, for there wasn't a breath of wind. He cursed through clenched teeth. Struck three at once. Got one decent flame, which seemed to soar straight up from his hand. He stepped back, opened the door a fraction, then threw the matches inside, shut the door and retreated until he was some way into the field. He had never dreamed that it could be so quick. The little room exploded. Then all was quiet, until a distant noise grew somewhere inside the barn. After two or three minutes the smoke began to seep out between the cracked outer cladding, and a few minutes later the first yellow tongues of fire broke through the roof. Gradually, the light became stronger. He saw the car parked on the road, the dense forest around him, the nearest trees, which seemed to become more distinct with their extended branches in the unreal glare. His face was white and shiny. His age was somehow erased. His eyes shone. The pupils were black. An unseen wind issued forth from the old barn. He recognised it. The hair over his forehead lifted. He had first felt the wind when he was sitting alone in the tree. That was while the dog in the kitchen was still alive, and the heat was billowing towards him. The wind was both ice cold and burning hot. The wailing and the singing tone would come much later. When everything was on the point of collapse. By then he would have made it home.

He tore himself away, ran to the car, replaced the petrol can and drove off without a second glance in the mirror. He didn't switch on the headlamps until he reached the Løbakke hills. Once there, he stopped, got out of the car and looked back. The sky above Lake Homevannet was still dark. Not a sound. Not a puff of wind. There was an old storehouse just a few metres away, at the edge of a field. It was almost completely black, in the darkness, and couldn't have been painted since the war. He opened the rear door and took the can. There was a fair bit left. Not a lot was needed; what was important was where the fire started. He broke down a door at the back and entered an ink-black room. It stank of old hay. And lime, and marsh and damp soil. That was how the grave must smell, he thought, and had to smile. He took a few soundless steps in, but then came to a sudden halt. It felt as if there was someone inside. Someone was watching him. Intense staring from the darkness, and in a flash he thought of the gun he had left in the car.

'Hello?' he whispered.

No answer.

'Who are you?'

Still nothing.

'I know you're there. Come out, wherever you are.'

He glared into the darkness. He thought he saw something move. Someone was standing there, reluctant to come out.

'Are you afraid?' he asked.

The figure didn't answer. He suddenly realised who it was.

'Pappa?' he said.

The figure came a little closer. Reached out his hands while he himself was rooted to the spot.

'Don't come any nearer,' he growled. 'Do not come any nearer.'

The figure glided slowly towards him.

Then he lit a match. The room flared up around him. No one there. Neither Ingemann nor anyone else. Just old tools and other scrap leaning against the wall. But when the match went out he could see his father again. He seemed to be kneeling.

'Pappa? There won't be any more fires, Pappa. Do you hear me?'

No answer.

'I'm telling you there won't be any more fires.'

He lit another match, his father disappeared, and in the

few seconds the flame lasted he managed to locate a suitable place.

Then the match died and his father reappeared, kneeling in the darkness.

'I don't want you here, I said.'

He saw his father get to his feet, stand in front of him and reach out his hands.

'Get out. Otherwise you'll be burned alive!'

His father stood with hands outstretched, motionless.

Then Dag lit another match and the bare room returned. There was an old horse cart in the corner with several empty crates and planks piled on top. He slopped some petrol over a wheel, a shaft and the planks. He managed to close the cap and get out before the match burned down.

'If that's the way you want it,' he said to his father in the darkness. 'Don't blame me.'

Then the room flared up again, but this time it was utterly and irrevocably lit. Once more he had chosen the perfect spot. The flames rose at once. It was as though they had been hiding somewhere, waiting for this moment. The wheel was alight, and the planks and the empty crates, and the room was hot and intensely alive. So far, only the cart was well ablaze: the spokes in the wheel glowed red and began to spit onto the floor, but then the flames seemed to regroup, gather their strength. The old hay immediately caught and the fire raced towards the wall. In a few seconds the flames whooshed up the wall, so high that the topmost tongues were licking at the roof. And now it had begun, the rest would take care of itself. He backed towards the door.

'Do you hear me, Pappa? Praying won't help!'

He hesitated for a few seconds as he stared into the inferno. The room was aglow in the unreal, flickering light. He saw the rafters and girders in the roof, and along the cross-beams small, black holes. They were swallow nests. He stiffened for an instant when he saw the tiny birds' heads peering over the edge of a nest, he saw the beaks opening and closing, he heard the reedy cheeping, and then he spotted the swallows desperately circling in the dense smoke beneath the roof.

He got out and slammed the door behind him. Staggered backwards, rubbing his eyes. He had petrol on his fingers and it stung; it felt as if his entire face was on fire. At length, he sank to his knees, snatched at tufts of wet grass and wiped his eyes, and soon the worst was over. That was when he discovered the eyes. They shone.

'So that's where you are,' he said to the quiet, black beast and then saw that there were several cows in the field. They were scattered around, standing or lying in the gloom, but only the nearest of them had seen everything. The cow lifted its black head and stared at him until it lost interest and resumed munching at the grass by the fence.

He didn't have time to wait. The noise inside was increasing. He ran to the car and drove slowly towards the school. After a few hundred metres he stopped the car and looked back. The sky above Lake Homevannet was still dark. No smoke, no sea of fire. Nothing.

Reaching the school, he pulled up in front of the little outhouse, opposite the old school building where they used to have woodwork in the cellar and PE on the ground floor and at the top there was a loft you could sneak up to and sit in peace. He got out of the car and stood for a few seconds gazing at the school building, then turned on his heel and walked towards the outhouse.

He made short work of it. There wasn't a moment for anything else. Cars might pass by on the road at any moment. He doused a number of poles with the remains of the petrol. A single match and the flames raced high up the wall. The wood cladding was cracked and tinder-dry and burned as easily as cardboard. It couldn't have been simpler. A couple of seconds and it was done. He had an effervescent feeling inside as he hastened back to the car, stowed the can on the rear seat and drove slowly and with composure across the plain, past Lake Bordvannet and past the house belonging to Anders and Agnes Fjeldsgård in Solås. At the junction in Brandsvoll he switched on the headlamps. His eyes had grown accustomed to driving in the darkness, so the sudden light was overwhelming. Now he could see everything. Whirring insects, the sharply defined grass at the roadside, the trees and the network of branches woven into the night. As he turned left at the Brandsvoll crossroads the headlamps swept through the fragile windows of the disused shop, and he saw the old shelves and drawers that had once been stacked with flour and peas and oats and coffee, but which now lay gathering dust. Soon afterwards he passed the house belonging to Alfred and Else, and he saw the light from a solitary bulb in Teresa's house. Then he turned right, crossed the bridge and the tranquil river, and he was home. He tiptoed in, went to the bathroom and washed, stood for a moment studying some cuts and grazes to his forehead; his fingers still smelled faintly of petrol. His eyes were radiant and the tiredness was gone. There was grass in his hair. He shut his eyes and saw the swallows circling in the smoke under the roof. Then he switched off the light, mounted the staircase in four strides, had enough time to fling off his clothes, creep under the cool duvet and lie with closed eyes before the telephone started to ring in the hall.

4

I.

ON THE MORNING OF 3 JUNE, Grandma writes in her diary:

Olga's old house has burned down. The outbuilding as well. It's not possible. But it has actually happened. Kasper Kristiansen owns it now, but I can remember Olga living there so clearly. I remember when Kristen and Steinar and I accompanied Olga to Oslo with a patient. It was a girl who had been too difficult to have at home. She had to go to Gaustad Asylum. So we drove all the way to Oslo. It was just after the war. And now Olga's house has burned down. Lord help us all.

Fædrelandsvennen, Saturday, 3 June. Front page:

At eight o'clock this morning, Lensmann Knut Koland and his officers gathered for a crisis meeting at his Søgne office to discuss last night's blazes, in addition to other recent incidents in Finsland. An arsonist is on the loose in the district. So far he has limited his activities to unoccupied houses and agricultural buildings. Last night a farm, an outhouse and a storehouse were set alight at Lauvsland and Dynestøl, in Finsland.

The Oslo newspapers are beginning to mention the case. One short item in *Aftenposten*. An article in *Verdens Gang*, both relatively unemotional accounts without photographs. NRK radio broadcasts a longer report, but no TV reports as yet, not until Monday evening.

II.

I HAD HEARD THE STORY of the female patient who had to be taken to Gaustad, but I wasn't aware that Pappa had been involved. Nor was I aware that they had transported her from the house at Dynestøl; nor that the patient had lived there with Olga and that it was from this house that she took the ash from the wood-burning stove.

Having mental patients living in your house wasn't so unusual. Most of them came from Eg Hospital in Kristiansand, and they were taken on by farms in the hope that this would have a beneficial effect. It was the old idea that work was a blessing. They should be taken out of their grey, passive institutional lives. Into the fresh air. Into the sunshine, into the rain, into the wind and cold. So that they could use their bodies and give a helping hand. And perhaps, slowly but surely, they would get better. Perhaps even recover and return to their normal lives. Furthermore, you got a few kroner for keeping them. It was a kindly thought, but often things didn't go as hoped. There are many stories about patients, but the details are vague. I know that Olga had several patients over the years, but I know almost nothing about them. What their names were, who they were, what they did at her place. How long they stayed. Where they went afterwards. If they are dead or alive. I know nothing, and no one I have asked can provide any more information.

Except for the ash anecdote.

This one is true.

Things had got to such a pass with the patient that Olga was unable to have her living on the farm any longer. The patient had started having loud discussions with Our Lord; apparently this had been going on for a long time, but when she repeatedly tried to knock Our Saviour off the heavenly throne with a pole, things boiled over for Olga. The patient couldn't stay there any more; however, there was no room for her at Eg, either. This went on until she had to be transferred to Gaustad in Oslo. It was a trip of more than four hundred kilometres, and Olga didn't have a car, of course. So she asked Grandad – who had a Nash Ambassador from 1937 with the split windscreen – whether he would consider undertaking the long journey to the country's capital with her and the patient. Grandad said he would, and Grandma went along as well, and my father too, because there was no one to look after him. So, early in the morning one June day in 1947, the black car started up in the yard, and the small family set off. After some kilometres they parked in front of the house at Dynestøl. Grandad got out and knocked on the door. It was quite a while before Olga answered the door. It transpired that she and the patient had cleaned the whole house, from cellar to loft; all that was now left was to remove the ash from the wood-burning stoves, and that was what they had been doing when Grandad knocked. They had to wait a few more minutes until everyone was ready to leave, and moments before the female patient got in she took the ash from the sitting room stove, filled a tin can with it and deposited it in her handbag. Then she, too, was ready. It was the only thing she wanted to take with her: a tin of ash, which she put in her bag. Whereupon she sat, squeezed up against the others, for a good four hundred kilometres with the bag on her lap.

After Grandma died, in the winter of 2004, a photograph appeared from nowhere. I had never seen it before. It was of Pappa. He must have been about four years old that summer because he was wearing knee breeches and a short-sleeved shirt. He was sitting on one of two bronze lions outside Kunstnernes Hus, a contemporary art house in Oslo, laughing. As I held the photograph in my hands I knew nothing about the two lions, I didn't know they were still there, in exactly the same place, clutching the flagpoles on either side of the entrance. Pappa had the same wavy hair as in his baby photograph, which had been taken by Harme of Kristiansand and was hand-coloured and not quite true to life, making him look like a little bronze angel. As a child I flatly refused to believe that it was my father in the baby picture. I insisted it was an angel.

The new photograph must have been taken during the stay in Oslo, presumably after the patient and the ash had been delivered to Gaustad Mental Hospital. The long journey was over, finally they had arrived in Norway's capital city, and I suppose they wanted to see the Royal Palace. Which must have seemed like life's greatest experience, both for Pappa and for my grandparents, and I presume also for Olga Dynestøl, who had never travelled anywhere. After all, it was only two years since the war had finished, and they wanted to see the Royal Palace and the guards in their black uniforms, standing as silent as the grave in the broiling hot sun. Afterwards they wandered around the Palace Gardens, strolled past the residence where the great Arnulf Øverland lived, and then saw the lions. And what could be better than to take a photograph of a little boy on the back of a snarling lion?

That was how it was. The story of the long journey, the photograph of Pappa and the story of the ash from the stove at Dynestøl. The stories intertwine and are all connected with the stories of the fires. It was ash from the same chimney that on the morning of 3 June 1978 was left blackened and solitary like a tree denuded of its branches.

You gather all the fragments, even ash.

III.

I PHONED KASPER KRISTIANSEN, but it was Helga, his wife, who answered. She knew who I was, of course, as did Kasper; they have both known me since I was born. Kasper might also have remembered me from the elk hunt when I was with my father, when Kasper held the bloody heart in his hand.

I went into great detail explaining what I was after. Said that I was in the process of writing about their house, which they lost early in the morning of 3 June more than thirty years ago, and asked if they would mind telling me what happened. I had no idea how they would feel about this, whether it was something they could discuss or whether it was still too painful.

The answer, however, was: *Not at all.*

They received me the very next evening.

We chatted for ages. Not only about the fires; other stories also came up, interwoven into previous ones, and in this way the conversation extended into a picture that grew bigger and bigger, and in the end it was unstoppable. It was as though I had touched upon something that had gone missing long ago. Something I was closely related to, yet of which I still knew very little. We talked about Grandma and Grandad, whom they had both known, and about Great-Grandfather Sigvald, who tanned leather in the loft at his Heivollen home, and about Great-Great-Grandfather Jens, who was so gentle.

However, it was the Dynestøl blaze I had come to hear about.

At just after one o'clock on the morning of 3 June 1978, the telephone rang in Helga and Kasper's house. They were then living in Nodeland; they had bought the Dynestøl house from Olga a few months earlier, but had barely begun the renovation work on it. Kasper had bought, among other things, new double-glazed windows for the entire house, but they hadn't yet been installed and were standing outside Dynestøl, leaning against the house wall. In addition, Kasper's tractor, a Fiat, was parked in the yard between the house and the barn.

Helga picked up the phone. At the other end was a voice she recognised. It was Olga Dynestøl. She sounded distant and subdued, as if she were ringing from another world.

At first Olga could only utter four words:

Dynestøl is on fire.

Then she collected herself and said she had seen and heard the fire engine. She had dashed into the yard outside her house in the Løbakke hills. She had seen Per Lauvsland's burning storehouse, which was across the field, and next the billowing sea of flames over Lake Homevannet, and she knew. Soon after there were four terrible explosions, with an interval of a few minutes between each one, and each explosion caused the flames to boil over. Alone in the yard, she realised it was her old house in Dynestøl that was on fire. The house where she had been born seventy-three years before, her brother Kristen the year after, and from where both parents had been carried out feet first. She stood watching the flames across the sky while reciting something akin to a prayer. Her lips scarcely moved. Then she turned and went indoors. She had not spoken to anyone before ringing Helga and Kasper. No one had come to tell her what was happening. She simply knew.

Kasper and Helga jumped into their car and drove off to see for themselves what had happened. They passed through Nodeland, Hortemo, Stokkeland. Kasper stayed calm. He didn't believe it could be true. The buildings at Dynestøl? They were set apart and were so quiet and peaceful. Olga must have been dreaming. That was the explanation. Or it was something she had imagined while she lay in bed unable to sleep. She was getting on in years.

As they motored down the slope towards Kilen it was light enough for them to see the clear sky and the undulating hills to the west. They couldn't see any smoke or any sea of flames. Nothing. Kasper was becoming fairly confident that his surmises were correct, but when, a few minutes later, they passed the school in Lauvslandsmoen, they spotted Hans Aasland's burned-down outhouse, the one opposite the school. There was nothing left of it, just a black stain on the ground, from which rose thin, grey smoke. They turned towards Dynestøl, and after a couple of hundred metres they were met by the sight of Per Lauvsland's razed barn. There was no one around. Everything was destroyed, and here too smoke rose from the collapsed structure. There was a strange abandoned atmosphere. The cows were grazing in the field, apparently unconcerned. Behind, they could see the house where Olga now lived, but there were no lights in any of the windows. That was when it slowly dawned on them what was awaiting them. They drove the last few kilometres. Lake Homevannet lay black and still, with the mist hovering above it, and around it pine trees stood in distorted poses, seemingly stretching out their branches to try to hold on tight. Neither of them said a word. They couldn't see any flames. Nor any light. Nor people. Nor cars. They couldn't see anything. It was as if they were in a dream. Olga had rung them in the dream to say that her old house was on fire. Now they were driving slowly along the road in the dream, and when in a while they arrived they would wake up at home in bed. They would be lying there blinking up at the ceiling as the dream gently sank back to whence it had come. Then they could get up and start the day.

But, of course, this was no dream.

As they approached the last hill they saw that the gravel had been gouged up. A large vehicle must have been there before them. Then they reached their destination. Kasper stopped the car. They got out, leaving the doors open. Helga said nothing. Kasper said nothing. It was chilly, almost cold, they should have brought warmer clothing, they realised that at once. Helga had only her thin woollen jacket, Kasper a faded shirt. They walked the few metres to the firemen standing around in a ragged group. The men had finished hosing down the house, or they had given up long ago. They seemed exhausted, their faces were drawn, and blackened with soot and smoke, their clothes filthy, their shirts unbuttoned. They gave the impression of just having awoken, and that what they had awoken to was way beyond their comprehension. They were barely recognisable, even though Kasper and Helga knew everyone. That was Knut. There was Arnold. And there were Jens and Peder and Salve, and several others. Helga suddenly felt dizzy. No one could utter a word. There was as good as nothing left of the house or the barn. There were just the foundation walls, and the chimney, immovable and blackened with soot. The whole site was transformed. Now it was impossible to see how everything had actually been. The house with its shiny windows, the barn with its moss-covered bridge, the few tiny doorsteps from the grass leading inside. The door with the faintly squeaking hinges, the cold porch, the hall with the rag rug, the kitchen with the white utility sink, the steep stairs to the loft. But it wasn't just the buildings; the whole landscape appeared to have changed – the sloping fields, the road, the green hills, the surrounding forest, everything was different now that the house and barn had gone.

They caught sight of Alfred. His shirt was open, showing all of his pale chest. He came over and shook hands with both of them.

'There was nothing we could do.'

'I didn't believe it was true,' Kasper said.

'No, none of us did,' Alfred replied.

'What do we do now?' Helga asked, but no one answered.

What could you say? What do you say to two people who have just lost their house?

'We were too late,' Alfred said in a low voice. 'We were too late.'

They stared at the chimney towering up in the half-light. The tractor was there too, black and burned out, resembling a beetle that had slowly rotted in the sun. It was a Fiat, 1965 model, but as good as new. It was the tractor that had produced the four explosions. The tyres had caught fire, they must have been alight for some time, all four of them, before they burst with enormous force. That was what Olga had heard. That was what had made the flames boil over.

It was then that the fire engine returned. They heard the sirens approaching. Next they saw the flicker of the blue lights and heard the roaring of the motor up the last inclines. Not until the vehicle was stationary were the sirens and blue lights switched off. Out jumped a young man, though more a boy. They recognised him at once: it was the son of the fire chief, Ingemann at Skinnsnes. Inside the cabin he had a carrier bag full of food.

'Have you been shopping?' someone asked, but the boy didn't respond. He put the bag down on the ground. It toppled over as soon as he turned his back. Kasper and Helga watched him roam around the site for a while. Then he came back and searched for something in the bag. They hadn't noticed, but there was smoke still rising from the house and the barn. It was thin, grey smoke, almost like steam, and it dispersed at once.

'Who wants a hot dog?!' the boy yelled.

He had to step into the trees to find a suitable stick. Then he poked it through a sausage from the bag and lurched into the ruins, more or less where the living room had been. In his white shirt he wasn't warmly dressed, and he held out his arms as if he were walking on glass. He walked along the foundation wall for some of the way, but then turned and came back. There were no flames left, just ash and the thin, grey smoke. He cursed aloud. He had driven all the way to Kaddeberg's to buy sausages and now there weren't any flames or embers to cook them over! What the hell was going on? No one spoke. He started laughing. The firemen watched him, turned away and pretended there was work to be done. Helga wrapped her jacket tighter around her.

'Then we'll have to eat them cold,' the boy continued, clearly miffed. 'What do you say? Cold sausages!' He jumped down from the wall, went from one fireman to the next offering cold, slippery sausages straight from the packet.

IV.

IT WAS LATE SUMMER, 1998. I had been at home since June and seen how he was slowly getting worse. His eyes were growing, and when I was sure that had to be it, they couldn't possibly get any bigger in that emaciated face, they grew a tiny bit more. I had told neither him nor my mother about my exams. A few days after the night in Vår Frelser cemetery I caught the train home from Oslo, and during the first evenings I lay in my old room listening for sounds from my parents' bedroom. My father was alone there now, while my mother had rigged up a bed on the sitting room sofa. He slept so badly and was always in pain. I heard him mumbling to himself, but couldn't catch what he was saying. I lay awake during the light summer evenings, unable to do anything at all. I had no contact with my old classmates from school. I had grown apart from them, and they had no doubt grown apart from me. I had nothing, other than my books, which I had left here when I departed for Oslo. I lay for hours in the darkness flicking through the books I had once read with such incomprehensible voracity.

I read a bit of *The Troll Elk* by Mikkjel Fønhus, and re-started Trygve Gulbranssen's Bjørndal trilogy, skimming the pages for the place where tears had begun to flow when I was thirteen, but I couldn't find it, and in any case the story now seemed empty and devoid of meaning. I lay reading, but only managed to concentrate for a few minutes at a time before my mind filled with thoughts that went their own ways.

Then, one evening, I took out my lecture pad, tore out all

the pages of notes, settled down and started writing. I remembered the words Ruth had sown in me long ago when she held me back after class. I hadn't forgotten them, and now I was trying. I wrote one page, two. Tore out the pages, and lay down to sleep. The following day I read through everything I'd written and was ashamed. It was deeply, deeply shaming. But, come the evening, there I was again with the pad on my knee, writing. I don't remember what about, or even if it was about anything. I just wrote. It felt good in a strange, remote way, as though actually it had nothing to do with me. And that was how the summer continued. My father's health deteriorated and it became a strain living in the house with him. In the evenings I would take his car, the old pickup, and go on a long drive. I took my pad with me, and stopped here and there to do some writing. I drove to Brandsvoll, turned left by the old shop, passed Else and Alfred's house, turned right in front of Teresa's house, and drove past the quiet, white house where I never saw anyone, what people called *the pyromaniac's house.* Next I passed the fire station, Sløgedal's house, and drove uphill towards Hønemyr. Then I turned into the square outside the military camp and sat there with my pad on the steering wheel, writing.

In August, Pappa became so unwell that Mamma could no longer cope with him at home. He had been on a sickbed in the middle of the sitting room for some weeks, and when the ambulance came to collect him, she wasn't at home. I think she may have been out shopping; at any rate, there were just the two of us in the house when the bell rang and I went to answer the door. On the steps were two men of my age who said they had come to collect my father. Then it all became too much for me. I don't remember exactly what happened, just that I let them in, showed them the way, then left them in the sitting room with him while I went to the cellar. I heard them talking in hushed tones, as if they were planning a burglary. I heard my father's calm voice and the cold snap of the metal legs as they folded them and lifted the stretcher off the floor. I could hear them trying to carry him through the front door, but it was too narrow, so they had to trudge back and put the bed on the floor while they discussed another solution. I stayed in my room in the cellar staring into space. I couldn't face going upstairs, for I knew it would be the last time, and I knew in my heart that I wouldn't be able to watch him being carried out of the house, and I imagined that he wouldn't want me to see that, either. Eventually, after a fair bit of to-ing and fro-ing, they got him and the bed through the veranda door, and once they were outside I coolly ascended the stairs and just caught a glimpse of his legs disappearing into the ambulance. Then they closed the doors, got in on opposite sides, and drove off, and Pappa had nothing at all from the house he had lived in since the summer of 1976, not even a small handful of ash.

My very last visit to see him was in the middle of September 1998. At that time he had a room of his own at the rest home in Nodeland, where ten years earlier I had sung with the youth choir in front of an audience of elderly people. I had been back in Oslo since the middle of August, although I hadn't resumed my studies. I had also given up writing. The days were spent in the Deichman Library, I sat there reading and was transported, and every evening I was roused by the voice saying that they were closing the doors.

One Friday I caught the train home to Kristiansand. Deep down I knew this would be the last time I would see him. Mamma came to pick me up at the station, and on the next day I drove down to the rest home in his red pickup. I passed through Finsland feeling people's eyes on me. After all, they knew the vehicle, no one else in these parts had a red pickup, and they must have thought my father was at the wheel, but just as they raised their hands to wave they saw that of course it wasn't him. They saw that it wasn't him, but they waved anyway. And I waved back. I passed the disused chapel in Brandsvoll, the one that had now become a sort of agricultural building, and I wondered what had happened to the bottle-green lectern, and the picture of the man with a hoe, the man with an angel of the Lord hovering above him, the one that hovered above us when we sang there; I passed the community centre, which was hardly used any more, just for the odd bridge evening, a meeting of the Farmers' Association, the Nynorsk Language Society, that was all. I drove across Fjeldsgård Plain, arrived at the new chapel, which had been erected as a community project in the mid-1990s. I passed the bank, where ten years later I would be writing this. I came to Kaddeberg's old shop, which had been abandoned years ago, and had a sudden vision of Kaddeberg in his old blue smock and horn-rimmed glasses with a stump of a pencil tucked behind one ear, mumbling pleasantries behind the counter. I remembered all the times I had stood on the worn floor in front of the till with Pappa, when a bar of chocolate was thrust into my hand, a Hobby or a Stratos, or one of the small chewing-gum balls with the sweet-smelling wrappers, and my whole being must have brightened because I remembered that old Kaddeberg always used to remove his glasses and keep rubbing them on his shirt front. Everything seemed to come back to me. My entire childhood, the entire landscape, the forests, the lakes, the sky, everything was too long ago, and everything was still there, bathed in the gentle September sun. My new life in Oslo was so far away all of a sudden. I had left Grandad's coat in my bedsit, together with my new glasses. I didn't need either now; they felt completely out of place. I changed down, drove slowly uphill and saw Lake Livannet beneath me, saw it glittering in a gust of wind that swept from east to west.

I was early, turned left and parked just a few steps from the fountain. I walked through the corridor of the rest home, where the smell of coffee, musty old clothes and pee met me head-on; the sounds of TV from rooms, laughter and community singing seemed to come from somewhere deep below ground.

Pappa looked better than he had for a long time; when I opened the door he was sitting on the edge of the bed in his red tracksuit and dangling his legs.

'There you are,' he said jauntily.

'I hope I'm not too early,' I said.

'Early, not at all,' he replied. 'I've done nothing all day except wait for you.'

He said it in such a robust, casual way that we could both hear it was not his normal tone, yet we behaved as if nothing was different. I had a bag of Freia chocolates, which I knew he liked, or at least he had done. As I went to empty the bag into the bowl I had filled the previous time, I saw it was still half-full.

'And are you alright?' I asked.

'I'm alright,' he said.

'Shall I take off my shoes?' I asked.

'No, no,' he answered in the same robust manner. 'It's not me who has to do the cleaning here.'

We laughed, and I felt a need to follow up in the same tone that he had set.

'Stay here much longer,' I exclaimed, 'and you'll be sporting a perm.'

He gave a faint smile but didn't laugh as I had hoped he would; he slid to the floor and poked his feet into the same slippers he had shuffled around in at home. When he was upright I could see how thin he had become; the cord in his tracksuit had been pulled tight around the waist, and his watch hung loosely from a wrist. It was as though neither the tracksuit nor the watch belonged to him but were stolen goods, things he had snatched in a hurry and which didn't fit. He walked unsteadily to the open window, where he stood holding the sill and looking out. From the window it was only fifty metres to the railway line; a long goods train thundered past, and in the enormous din it seemed as if he might snap in two or crumble to dust at any moment. When it was quiet again he turned, shuffled back to the bed and picked up a chocolate with fingers resembling delicate claws, which shook so much that several of the chocolate balls spilled out of the bowl onto the floor and rolled off in all directions. I scrabbled around on my knees picking them up, some under the table, others in the middle of the floor, the last under the bed, right next to a glass bedpan, a kind of carafe with a kink in the neck, partly full with dark urine, and beside it lay the sweet, looking like the head of a tiny seal popping up from the sea.

'I thought we could go for a little drive,' I said when all the balls were back in the bowl.

'A drive, yes,' he said.

'In your pickup,' I said.

He nodded, and I said no more, for I knew my voice would crack, and neither of us wanted that.

I pushed Pappa in the wheelchair he usually kept in a corner of the room, one that could easily be folded and unfolded. I pushed him gently and noiselessly along the shiny floor of the rest home corridor, and at that point, on the short trip from his room to the front door, we were all alone. He was no weight, he seemed to float along, although, slumped there, he might have appeared heavy. He floated in front of me, and I floated behind him, and at a point some way from the door I gave the chair a firm push and let go of the handles and Pappa sailed away, a couple of metres perhaps, without noticing that I wasn't holding on. He was wearing his jacket with the Lillehammer Winter Olympics logo on the sleeve and chest. The jacket hung like a sack over his bony shoulders and rustled like newspaper whenever he moved. He had bought it because in fact he had considered going to Lillehammer. He had wanted to see ski jumping from the large hill. That was all. The man who in his youth had set off down old Slottebakken, the slope that was later adjudged to be too dangerous, where you could jump to the very bottom, almost down to the plain if the wind got hold of you, and for that reason it was closed down, people were simply jumping too far; that was in 1960, six years after Kåre Vatneli fell and fractured his leg, and the year after he died. But three years before the new ski jumping slope in Stubrokka was built and Pappa climbed up the tower and set off downhill with an utter disregard of personal safety that no one could fathom, and of which in 1998 I knew nothing. What he had most wanted to see at the 1994 Winter Olympics was the ski jumping from the large hill, but then something came up, so there was no trip to Lillehammer on that occasion. But at least he had the jacket, and when he saw the televised pictures of Espen Bredesen taking off in slow motion and flattening out in the air, and when he saw the mass of spectators and all the flags and heard the roar from the landing area, Pappa probably felt he had almost been there anyway.

I folded up the wheelchair and deposited it on the empty flatbed of the truck while Pappa got onto the passenger seat.

'First we have to go to the shop,' he said. 'I have to hand these in before six o'clock.' It was only now that I saw he was holding two lottery coupons in his hand.

'Are you still doing the lottery?' I asked.

'This time I know I've got a row of winners,' he said without looking at me. 'It's now or never,' he added, and we could both hear how sinister this sounded.

I stopped outside the shop by the roundabout, went in and handed over the two coupons while Pappa waited in the car. I saw all the scratchy crosses he had drawn, how they seemed to form a simple pattern that I couldn't understand, but which was simple nonetheless. They were seven well-considered numbers, I knew, because my father had been doing the lottery for as long as I could remember, he had even acquired books about probability theory. I stood there with the two coupons in my hand remembering that I had laughed at him when I heard about the books, I had laughed at the naive belief that he would win, or that he had a row of winners, as he put it, and now there I was, paying, without a hint of irony, for his two very last coupons.

'It's now or never,' I said to the man behind the till.

'That's what they all say,' he said with a smile.

'Where shall we go?' I asked my father as I got back into the car.

'You decide,' he replied.

'To town?' I suggested.

'To town,' he said.

He had become a kind of annoying echo, and I didn't say anything for a long while. I felt empty, outside myself; we picked up speed, turned left onto the E18, and soon we were motoring along towards Kristiansand with the wheelchair sliding to and fro and banging around at the back. We drove alongside the glistening Lake Farvannet and passed the place where the man who had played the role of Sørlandet in the children's stories about *Stompa & Co* died in a car accident. Pappa had once told me that as we drove by the lake a long time ago, and since then I had always remembered this fact, both because I loved listening to *Stompa* on Saturday morning radio and because I felt that the entire *Stompa* series – Tørrdal, the confused teacher, Brandt the reflective teacher and the cheery music – harked back to my father's carefree childhood.

'I thought we could watch the boats coming in,' I said,

traversing Vesterveien. He didn't respond, which I took as assent. I turned right under the high bridge and parked by the statue of Vilhelm Krag. I pushed the wheelchair up the little hill, and soon we were sitting in front of Krag and looking across the fjord and the still, black Vestergap waters to the lighthouse on Oksøy Island in the distance. We didn't say a great deal; actually, I don't remember us talking at all. We just sat there beside each other. He was in the wheelchair, I was on a bench, and behind us was the huge bronze statue of Krag, who was staring out as well, the way he had for all my life and long before. The sun was still and hot on my chest and face. Pappa had folded his hands in his lap. I had never seen him in this pose before, as though he were old and tired of living and not just fifty-five, which was what he was. He sat there serenely, watching the lethargic September flies sucking the juice from the rotting apple cores. He just sat there, and I just sat there, and everything was still even though we had the E18 twenty metres behind us and the whole of the harbour and the seaward approach before us. Everything was still and we just sat there as boats left white wakes across the fjord, long stripes that were sharp at first, then widened and disintegrated, we just sat there as the Stavanger train clanked into the railway station fifteen minutes late, we just sat there observing the blackbirds as they waited inside the rose-hip bushes, not moving, keeping a watch on us with eyes like diamonds.

'You didn't say how the exams went,' he said out of nowhere. My blood froze for an instant and I licked my lips.

'They went fine,' I said, somewhat distractedly.

'What did you get, then?' he asked, regarding me for the

first time since we had left the rest home.

'What did I get?'

'Yes.'

'Do you mean the grade?'

'Yes.'

'I got a distinction,' I said.

'You got a distinction?'

'Yes,' I said.

'Why didn't you tell me before?'

'I don't know,' I said.

'Imagine you getting a distinction,' he said, staring across the water. I didn't answer, staring across as well.

'Now I can relax, now I know you are set fair,' he said, and at that moment I felt I would have to cry whether I wanted to or not. I sprang to my feet and said over my shoulder that I had left my wallet in the pickup. I walked down the path with fast, thumping strides as I tried to quell the sobs bubbling up in my stomach. I leaned over the hot bonnet until I had regained control, then I walked back to him.

At that moment I made a decision. Or something inside me did, I don't know what. Nor do I know exactly *what* I decided, or why. All I knew was how it would happen.

After perhaps a quarter of an hour in the sun with the sea in front of us and Krag at our backs we trundled back to the car. We then drove the ten kilometres or so to the rest home in Nodeland with the radio on low. We didn't talk about exams any more, or the future, or anything at all. I only noticed that he was reassured, he had relaxed.

I pushed Pappa across the car park as small birds played in the fountain, splashing water everywhere, but when we went too close they took to the wing and sat in the trees waiting for us to go. We rolled through the doors and along the shiny floor without a sound. A piece of paper with his name written by hand hung outside his room, stuck to his door with a bit of tape and fluttered whenever anyone went in or out. It could come unstuck at any moment, or simply be torn off and replaced with another name, which was probably the idea.

Pappa was tired after the trip, worn out. I had to stand behind and support him as he tried to get up. I shuddered when I felt how light he was. It was like lifting nothing at all. I could feel his hard ribs through the Olympic Games jacket as I managed to manoeuvre him onto the bed, and once there he lay back against the pillow and closed his eyes. I had lied to him, the last thing I did for my father was to lie to him, and the lie gave him peace. That was how it was. Now he was lying there motionless, only his large eyeballs moved, he lay there stretched out on the bed in the jacket that was far too big for him, the zip was open and I could see the red tracksuit, with the white puma poised to leap from his chest into thin air. It was as if he were floating, he was stretched out in the air, he had taken off from the ramp and lay flat, and he was floating, he had the air and the darkness roaring in his face.

V.

FROM THE AFTERNOON OF Saturday, 3 June 1978, the community centre in Brandsvoll was converted into a police station. Police were brought in from Søgne, Marnardal, Audnedal and

Vennesla, plus Lensmann Knut Koland and two forensics officers from Kristiansand, in all around twenty-five people. Extra tables and chairs had to be transported from the cellar and placed in the old council room, where there was an antique wood burner with a black elk embossed in the cast iron, and pictures of the region's former chairmen hanging on the northern wall, between the two doors.

The police had almost nothing to go on. The most tangible evidence was the descriptions of the two cars. There was talk of a dark VW Beetle (probably), while the other was a large American-style car (possibly a Ford Granada). Both had been observed in the area during the relevant period. Two cars. Basically that was all they had.

On Saturday morning everyone living in the west of the region had woken up to dead telephones. It transpired that the cable had snapped above Hans Aasland's outhouse in Lauvslandsmoen, which was the sixth fire. As the flames soared and the heat intensified, the cable had melted and fallen to the ground. It was just a stroke of good fortune that the alarm calls got through, it turned out, but they were made before the cable went up in smoke and the telephones fell silent. On Saturday afternoon, workers from Televerket were out repairing the damage. Two men hung from poles, and a new wire was hoisted over the blackened site of the fire.

By five o'clock everyone had the dial tone back.

It was agreed that there would be a kind of organised neighbourhood-watch scheme. Those with cars met in the square between the chapel and the community centre, and arrangements were made as to who would drive where. Emphasis was placed on the remotest farms and any uninhabited buildings. That was where the pyromaniac would probably strike. People drove around, keeping houses under surveillance. Now and then they stopped, walked around a house or barn looking for suspicious trails and listening, even though they had no idea exactly what they were looking or listening for.

Dag was also among them.

He indicated on a map where he would drive, it was a farm in a very isolated location, and it became his responsibility. It was Peder's farm in Skogen, which was only a kilometre as the crow flies from my home at Kleveland, but to get there he had to approach from Breivoll. And that was what he did. He passed Harbakk and continued along the narrow gravel road until he reached the farm. There he got out of the car, leaving the door open, strolled around the yard and tried the door of the house, which was locked. So he went over to the barn and eventually sat down on the stone steps at the front. The grass in the garden was already ankle height. The trees in the garden were old and twisted. Birds flew to and from the barn gable. Black ants crawled out from between the cracks in the step and went back in. Pale yellow narcissi swayed by the house wall. He leaned back and rested his head heavily against the top step. Feeling strangely dizzy and tired, with the sun beating down on his face, he thought to himself that like this, just like this, was how he would like to lie, for a long, long time.

It was on his way back down that the accident happened. Maintaining a high speed on the descent, he failed to negotiate a bend and careered off the road into a tree. That was when he received a bang to the skull. This came up during the trial. In his opinion it could have been a contributory factor in the events of the next two days. He explained that something happened in his head, and it was beyond his control. A doctor's certificate confirmed that he had received some cuts and scratches to his face, presumably from a car accident, but no signs of any organic brain damage were found.

Well, anyway.

The bang to his head wasn't so bad that he couldn't call people, and half an hour later his car was hauled onto the road by a neighbour's tractor. It turned out there was only minor damage. The front was a little squashed. The glass of one headlamp was broken, the other pointed straight up into the air. Otherwise the car was intact and in drivable condition. In fact, he had been lucky. The neighbour appeared concerned, laid a hand on his shoulder and looked him intently in the eye, but Dag assured him several times that he was fine. A bang on the head, a few scratches to his forehead, that was all. That was before he looked in the mirror and saw all the blood. He got into his car and asked the neighbour to keep his eyes peeled and report anything suspicious. Then he drove off with one headlamp pointing up towards the clear sky.

The afternoon passed, the evening came. The sun sank.

At Skinnsnes, Dag was sitting on a chair in the middle of the kitchen while Alma tended to the cuts on his face. She washed them first with lukewarm water, then cleaned them with cotton and Pyrisept, which made him jump.

'Mamma, that hurts!'

'It's supposed to hurt,' she said with a smile. 'That tells you it's working.'

Then she wiped away the last remnants of blood from his cheek and down his neck.

'Now you're done,' she said.

He got up, gingerly touched his face and smiled the smile that made her heart melt.

From midnight onwards all vehicles driving through the region on route 461 were stopped by the police. A patrol car was stationed in Fjeldsgårdsletta. An officer stood waiting by the roadside, every time a car approached he stepped out, the headlamps picked him out and made the reflectors on his jacket flash. The car slowed down. Stopped. A torch was shone. A brief conversation. Registration number noted. Allowed to continue. Nothing suspicious observed. People were awake all night. It was Saturday evening and the World Cup match between Argentina and Hungary was being shown on TV, and there was always that to watch. People didn't dare turn off lights. Some sat outside on doorsteps listening to the darkness, until it was so chilly they had to go in and put on more clothes. Or, eventually, they succumbed and went to bed. One o'clock and nothing had happened. No fire alarm. No sirens. The sky was dark and still. The mist gathered and hung over the fields like weightless, discarded items of clothing. The moon came out, rose slowly over the forest and made the mist glow as though filled with a tranquil inner luminosity.

Day broke. At four o'clock it was light. Birds were singing. The sun climbed clear of the forests to the east. It was the morning of 4 June 1978.

VI.

FROM GRANDMA'S DIARY:

4 JUNE
Gaute's christening. Weather, nice and warm. Got up early. After church walked round Dynestøl. Saw where the house had stood. A strange atmosphere in the region. Met Knut on the way. He was convinced a pyromaniac was on the loose. A pyromaniac? Here?

The service started at eleven. Slowly the church began to fill. People entered the chilly vestibule, found themselves a seat in the pews, coughed a bit, flicked through the hymn book, looked up. The church was soon alive with a low buzz of whispers. The fires were the subject of the day, the four last ones. The one in Skogen, the two storehouses in Lauvslandsmoen and Olga's house, the tractor and the four explosions that were heard over almost the whole of Finsland. And then there was the sea of flames that many had seen. A number of people had been woken up and had gone outside, and then they had seen it.

The organ started up, with Teresa at the keyboard.

My entire family was there: grandparents from both sides. My godparents, Mamma and Pappa. Everyone sat on the left close to the choir leader's seat, where the wind would sweep through the two-hundred-year-old timbers. It wasn't cold outside, yet the church was still cool as it always is, even if the sun is baking outside. I lay in Mamma's lap while everyone sang. The hymn was '*Måne og sol, skyer og vind*'. Moon and Sun, Clouds and Wind. She didn't dare sing herself for fear I would wake. Mamma was thinking about the fires; recently she had slept badly, lying in the narrow bed that her father had made, wondering what sort of crazy world she had brought her child into. That was what she was thinking now as well, while everyone around her was singing. Then the Word of the Lord was read aloud and everyone rose. At this point I had woken up and was fidgety, and Mamma put the knuckle of her little finger in my mouth. Then I quietened down. I sucked her finger for the whole of the sermon.

It was a discussion of verses 26 to 31 from the First Letter to the Corinthians. Then there was more singing, and then it was time for the christening.

Pappa carried me to the font, the one made with hammered brass of unknown origin, but presumably it must have been in the old church, the one that slowly began to sink in the soft clay at the end of the eighteenth century, before it was demolished and the foundation wall moved a smidgen to the south. Mamma untied the knot under my chin and removed my bonnet with care, then Pappa lowered me and held me hovering over the water, in the exact same way that I held *my* son in the exact same place almost thirty years later. The priest judiciously splashed water over my head, made the sign of the cross and prayed for me and my life, with his hand resting lightly on my forehead.

I was serenity itself.

Once the christening was over, the whole congregation went to inspect Olga Dynestøl's fire-ravaged house. Perhaps it was an automatic reaction. I was with them. Lying in the travel bag on the back seat of the car, asleep.

From that day onwards, people began to make pilgrimages to the sites of the blazes. News spread by word of mouth, and the ruins became a kind of attraction. People drove from far and wide to see them. On this Sunday, people drove straight from the church and the christening. It appeared to be part of the experience: first the church service, then the charred remains. It was a strange sight, everyone dressed in their Sunday best assembled around the black chimney and the gutted tractor. They stood there for a short while, talking in hushed tones, gently shaking their heads, then, one by one, they turned and walked back to their cars. They had seen it with their own eyes and could confirm that it hadn't been a dream.

Afterwards the whole christening party returned home to Kleveland. The sun stood high above the house. People ate and drank, and half-way through the meal Pappa tapped a fork against his glass and stood up. He held a short speech. I have asked everyone who was there and is still alive what he said, but no one remembers with any degree of accuracy. Only that it was a wonderful speech.

It was a short but wonderful speech. The only one.

Then they all went home, as the shadows lengthened and the sun passed slowly over the ridges in the west. Evening came; the lilacs were heavy with blossom, the dusk was heavy with their fragrance. Slightly before half past ten the sun sank with a glow behind the pine trees in Skrefjellet, and the trees became dark and distinct as if they were branded into the very sky.

My parents sat in front of the TV all evening. Occasionally Pappa got up and went out onto the steps, listened for a while, then returned without saying a word. They were watching *Sportsrevyen* even though neither of them was particularly interested in sport. If either of them had been it would have been Pappa, but for him ski jumping was what counted and this evening everything was about World Cup football in Argentina. Instead they chatted in low voices about the christening. About the priest's sermon. About all the guests, about visiting the burned-out remains of Dynestøl, and about me, how quiet I had been, and how well everything had gone.

They sat watching the flickering screen with the sound down low. Pappa got up again, went over to the window and stood staring for a long time.

'Can you see anything?' Mamma asked.

'No,' he said. 'Nothing.'

Then he went out to the front steps and walked around the house. Darkness had long since fallen and the dew had settled on the grass. When he came back in he slapped his arms around his body a few times to warm up.

A televised concert by the Alberni string quartet had started at ten o'clock. By midnight transmission was finished, and Mamma switched on the radio and listened to the news. No new fires.

I had already been asleep for several hours when Mamma went to bed. She was hoping it would be an uneventful night, since the previous night had been quiet, and since Omland had prayed for them all a few hours before. I slept soundly and soundlessly in the deep cradle. Pappa sat up for a few more hours. He kept going to the steps to listen. Just after twelve he joined us in the bedroom.

'There'll be no fires tonight,' he whispered to Mamma. 'It's over now. I can feel it in my bones. It's over.'

Then he turned out the light, and fell asleep almost at once, while Mamma lay awake listening to the baby's regular breathing, which seemed to issue from the darkness.

At half past twelve they were both woken by a voice.

Someone was whispering outside the window. It was John. Pappa dressed and was out of the door in seconds. The two of them spoke for some minutes in the yard, then Pappa came back and said he had to go. It had happened again. Two houses had been torched in Vatneli, but it wasn't yet known if they were occupied or whether there were other fires. The pyromaniac was on the rampage again. Or pyromaniacs. The situation was now so fraught that all the men in Finsland had to lend a hand. People were needed to keep watch and patrol the roads.

Before he left, Mamma got up and switched on all the lights in the house. She checked that all the doors were locked, then ensconced herself in the kitchen, with a clear view into the bedroom, and watched the car's red tail lamps as Pappa set off.

He drove round all the sharp bends in Vollan, downhill onto the flat and past Aasta's house. In Lauvslandsmoen the windows in the old school building by the road were lit. Passing Lake Bordvannet, he saw the lights from the houses in the water as long, shimmering pillars. Lights were on in Solås, lights were on in Knut Frigstad's place, and in

Brandsvoll the lights were on in the large assembly room in the chapel. He saw the six glass domes shining beneath the ceiling. He saw the lectern, the one that gave the impression of being heavy and solid but that could be moved with ease, and he glimpsed the picture of the man with the hoe. There was quite a gathering of people in the car park. They stood in darkened huddles by their cars, and he couldn't identify any of them. The community centre was also lit up, several police cars were parked outside, and inside the old boardroom he saw long shadows. He gripped the steering wheel of the blue Datsun tighter and continued down through the bends in Fossan, onto Fjeldsgårdsletta, where the mist hung in great clumps a few metres above the ground. There, he was stopped by the police. He rolled down the window and an officer shone a torch into his face, then swept the beam over the rear seat; he had to state his name, where he had come from and where he was going, whereupon his name and registration number were noted and he was allowed to pass.

Rounding the bend before Lake Livannet, he immediately saw the gleam of the two fires. Even though the mist was denser here he could clearly make out the billowing flames across the sky. This was the scene he described to me so many years later, the unreality of it, yet the strange reality. As he passed Kaddeberg's and climbed he drew clear of the mist, and that was when he saw the black smoke rolling upwards and drifting across the sky like ink. Finally he arrived. He strangled the engine, got out of the car, left the door open and slowly approached the blaze. Quite a number of people had collected, but everything was strangely quiet; there was only the loud crackling of the flames and the roar of the pumps. Every so often there would be tiny sighs as something gave way and collapsed into the centre of the fire. He watched as Olav and Johanna's house was gradually swallowed up by the flames, and perhaps he thought of cheerful, blond-haired Kåre, with whom he had been confirmed in the autumn more than twenty years ago. He also saw the glow from the Knutsens' house, which was alight a couple of hundred metres along the Mæsel road. Two houses burning at the same time, only a couple of hundred metres apart. It was scarcely credible. But it was true. The police were there, and several journalists. A photographer advanced into the garden, knelt down in the high grass and snapped a shot. This was the one that on Tuesday featured on the front page of *Sørlandet*, in which the house is surrounded by a halo. Minutes later another patrol car arrived. A bit bigger than the others, it stopped beside the outhouse that had been rescued from the flames. The back door opened and Pappa saw the black shadow that stormed out. It was an Alsatian. At first the dog ran around the legs of all those present. Smelt shoes, sniffed trouser legs, then trotted on to the next person. The dog stopped at Pappa, raised its head and sniffed his hands. It stared up at him. The fire shone in the animal's small eyes. It was as if they saw everything and knew everything, yet were still enclosed in their own knowing darkness. Then it went from person to person. Scurrying here and there, between shoes and boots and trousers, until the police officer whistled, and then it took off down the Mæsel road.

After a while the order was given for everyone who could to go away and look for more fires. For all they knew, at this very moment other houses in Finsland could be alight, fires that had gone unreported, and which had to be located promptly at all costs and stopped if at all possible. No one had any kind of overview. No one knew anything. Everyone had to be on the lookout, in their own allotted area, and it had to happen right now. At roughly the same time as Pappa got into his car, a motorbike started up in the semi-gloom. Two young lads clambered on, and then they roared away. Pappa drove slowly down the hill to Kilen while scanning the darkness above Lake Livannet. He passed Konrad's green house, where he would be in the cellar extracting honey from his beehives, then passed the post office and Kaddeberg's, where all the windows were lit; even above the shelves there was a warm, yellow light. Outside the neighbouring house he could discern two or three static seated figures keeping watch. Ditto outside the Shell petrol station, and the priest's house and the old sand foundry, and by the slaughterhouse, where there was no longer any slaughtering. Halland's house was illuminated from cellar to loft, and outside the old telephone exchange he could make out two dark figures on the doorsteps. There were people everywhere, yet everything seemed so still and abandoned. Mist hung above Lake Livannet, lent a strange orange reflection by the two blazes in Vatneli, and the sea of fire and this light were the last things my father saw before there was a crash somewhere ahead of him on the road.

He managed to brake in time, and got out. He saw the overturned motorbike and the car with which it had collided, but could see neither of the two young men. Soon afterwards he spotted the police officer who had stopped the first car. He was still walking around with the red and white STOP sign in his hands. For the first seconds all was quiet. Then someone began to shout and scream. The car involved in the collision had several occupants, the doors opened and some of them got out. They weren't injured, but the two on the motorbike had been ejected in an arc over the car and lay some metres apart, on either side of the road, one with no signs of life. The other was the one who had screamed. Pappa ran over to the apparently lifeless body. Knelt down, felt his neck with one finger. The boy's heart was beating. Another car arrived from Brandsvoll and the headlamps dazzled Pappa where he knelt. In the strong glare he saw something greyish and viscous running from the boy's right ear. After that he didn't dare touch him.

More people came. The first boy was gradually calming down. A young man ran over and crouched beside Pappa. He was wearing only a thin white shirt, but he didn't seem to feel the cold. He had blond hair and was talking in low tones to the motionless boy. He bent down and laid his ear against the boy's chest, took his limp hand and squeezed it. He remained in that position for a considerable time, as though he could hear something in the chest that rendered him incapable of doing anything else. Then he got up and went over to the car that had collided with the motorbike. The driver was clearly in a state of shock, still sitting behind the wheel with his head in his hands. The man in the shirt crouched down beside him and spoke softly to him as though explaining directions. Eventually he straightened up and went to the pillion rider who had been injured, sat with him too, then returned to kneel by Pappa, who kept checking that the boy was breathing. He was like an angel, I remember my father telling me; at that juncture Pappa didn't know who this person was, of course. In the minutes following the accident he went around giving solace and help to those affected. He ensured that the driver in shock wasn't left on his own, he ensured that the injured pillion rider was being attended to and, on the carriageway, in the light of car headlamps, he knelt beside the body with the outstretched arms. He spoke to the boy in a low, insistent voice. It was like a kind of conversation even though the boy was lying mute on the tarmac without any visible sign of life. *My lad, my poor, poor lad,* he whispered. Whom he was addressing was not clear. But he whispered it again and again while Pappa sat watching, unable to do anything. There seemed to be a large silent space opening up around them, it was unreal and frightening, as though the whispering voice came from somewhere they couldn't see, and that was how they sat until the ambulance arrived. The boy was taken care of, a mask was placed over his mouth and nose, the blue lights flashed across their faces, the dark space dissolved and the angel in the white shirt was gone.

VII.

THE LAST THING I DID for my father was to lie to him. I stood in his room at the rest home and promised to drive his pickup back to Kleveland where Mamma was waiting. The idea was that she would drive to the home later in the evening and spend the night with him. I had promised to park the pickup under the old ash tree in the yard, and spread the tarpaulin over the back so that it wouldn't fill up with leaves. But I didn't. I sat behind the wheel, twisted the ignition key, drove out of the car park and turned left instead of right. Rather than going home to Finsland I headed for Kristiansand. I drove the way we had just come, continued eastwards on the E18 in the sporadic traffic, bore right after passing under the high bridge in Vesterveien, just below the ever-staring bronze giant, Krag, where we had just sat staring as well, then I swung down towards the ferry terminal and all the juggernauts and motorhomes already queueing in the numbered lanes with the sea as a dead end. I joined them and bought a ticket for the crossing, for the next ferry due into the harbour and departing at a quarter past eight, the one taking all the lorries and motorhomes to Hirtshals in Northern Jutland. I drove on, following the line of vehicles winding slowly into the gaping bow gate. There were parents with children in overloaded cars, or elderly couples sitting quietly beside each other. And then there was me, twenty years old, alone in a red pickup, 1984 model, with old leaves stuck to the flatbed floor. I followed the slow-moving queue into the boat, and for the first time in my life it felt as if I was really *doing something*, that I was performing an action that would have some significance later. I sat behind the wheel feeling that what I was doing now would come to characterise who I was, though I didn't know how. I was beckoned deeper into the ship, drove up a floor and finally came to a halt in the middle of a bend behind a German motorhome, where I yanked on the handbrake. I had driven on board the ferry to Denmark, and frankly I had no idea what I was doing there, or where I was going, apart from across the sea. I was crossing the sea. I had lied to my father, and Mamma was sitting at home waiting for me while I would soon be on my way across the Skagerrak. I locked the doors of the pickup and walked up the soft, carpeted stairs from the car deck. There were already quite a few passengers strolling around the boat, older people on shopping trips or youngsters out for some fun, and everyone was walking around orientating themselves. On the top deck I found a bar, ordered a half-litre as if it were nothing special and sat there with the ice-cold glass, waiting for the ship to set sail. I felt the rumble of the engines and a slight tremor went through the chair I was sitting in and up to my fingers holding the glass. Gazing out of the window, I saw that at last the ferry was moving. I saw the pine-clad headlands and the dark crags on the western side of town glide by. I drained the glass. Then I ordered another, without any shame or fear that someone from home might see me, although the odds of this happening on the Danish ferry leaving Kristiansand were, of course, higher than if I had been drinking in an obscure Oslo pub. I was alone in the bar and the ship was not yet out of the fjord. I thought about Pappa's car locked somewhere beneath me; I saw Oksøy lighthouse glide serenely past, and straight afterwards the boat began to rock and I knew we had reached the open sea.

I think it was the thought of his pickup, and the alcohol beginning to seep into my veins, that reminded me of one autumn day in the eighties when I went hunting with Pappa.

That day was as clear as crystal in my mind and it still is.

Early one morning in late autumn we had breakfast together at the round table in the kitchen. Just him and me, the gurgle of the coffee machine and the pan of milk crackling on the stove. Just him and me, the knife cutting into the tenth slice of whole-wheat bread, the fifth slice with cervelat, the fourth piece of greaseproof paper and the third hard-boiled egg. Just him and me, and the golden autumn morning and the first frost on the grass beneath the window.

We each had a combination rucksack with a collapsible stool. Pappa took the packed lunches, the two thermos flasks of coffee and cocoa, and last of all a bar of Freia's dark chocolate, the one with the picture of a stork standing on one leg with its head down as though it were sleeping or didn't want to see. Next he grabbed the rifle in the hall, the wooden buttstock with the grain undulating like waves towards a beach, the long, black barrel with the hole at the end into which I could just poke the tip of my little finger.

Then we went outside, and it was a lot colder than I had anticipated. My face smarted and my boots made dark tracks in the rimy grass, but that was how it should be. My face should smart, and my rucksack should bang and chafe against my hipbone with every step that I took. Everything was as it should be after there had been a frost and the morning was hazy and milky-white like the film of ice on the windscreen of the pickup, which I remember was then quite new.

I remember nothing else until we were sitting alone in the forest. We were somewhere up on Hundershei, because I can remember looking down on Lake Hessvannet, which lay black and still between the pine-clad promontories. The day hadn't grown any warmer, but the sun had risen clear of the mountain ridges in the south, and the hoar frost on the grass had almost melted. The long, green blades of grass in front of my boots sparkled. I was sitting right behind Pappa, and my knees were frozen. I sat as I had been told without a murmur or a movement. I stole furtive glances at Pappa, at him and the rifle, and I couldn't quite make it fit that he and I were waiting in the forest with a loaded gun. That wasn't how it should be. We should have been somewhere very different. I should have been at home in my room, lying on my bed with a book, and Pappa should have been in the living room leafing through a local history book, *Finsland: Gard og Ætt*, or Trygve Gulbranssen's trilogy, or simply sitting in the kitchen and looking out of the window. Anything, but not here, in the middle of the forest with a loaded rifle across his lap. I don't remember how long we sat there, it couldn't have been that long, when suddenly two large creatures leaped through the brushwood not far away. At first they were silent and glided past the tree trunks at great speed like two boats, but as they came closer I heard twigs snapping and heather and juniper being swept aside and birch saplings being knocked to the ground. Pappa raised his gun and whistled a long note. The whistle brought them to a halt. I don't think I had ever heard him whistle before, and I was so surprised that I quite forgot to cover my ears. Then he took aim. I had never believed that any animals would appear, and when they did I had never thought they would stop. But they did. They had come from nowhere, and stopped, and Pappa took aim, and everything was unreal. I didn't look at the animals, but I knew they were standing still. I was looking at him. At the neck, at the ear, at the cheek resting gently against the surging waves. Then he fired. The two animals set off again and disappeared behind a small copse. I was sure he had missed, and that furthermore I had lost my hearing, for there was a ringing sound in my ears or from somewhere deep inside my head, and my first thought was that I would have this whine in my head for the rest of my life. Then he got up calmly from the folding stool, re-loaded and said: 'Now you go and have a look.'

'But they ran off, didn't they?' I said.

'Go and have a look,' he repeated.

'Where?' I asked.

'Just go,' he said. 'Follow them.'

He flicked on the safety catch as I ambled hesitantly through the long grass, jumped over a ditch and stood on a rock covered with thick moss some way in between the trees.

'I can't see anything,' I shouted.

'A bit further,' Pappa said.

I walked a little further into the trackless terrain, crossed some soft boggy ground and mounted flat rock from which I could see far and wide.

The elk lay no more than a few metres from me. In a little marsh. Not moving. Eyes wide open. As clear as glass.

'It's dead!' I shouted.

He didn't answer, and I couldn't see him from where I was.

I still couldn't understand how it had happened. One shot. Just one shot. The two animals ran off effortlessly, and now one was lying here. Some light red, almost pink, blood flowed from its nostrils. Otherwise there were no visible marks. I approached with caution. It felt as if the animal was following me with its dark, wide-open eye. As if it was waiting for me to get closer, and when eventually I stood beside it, it said:

So there you are.

Pappa seemed quite unmoved when eventually he came over. It was as if he had done this sort of thing many times before, even though I knew it was his first kill. He came towards me through the brown grass with the rifle over his shoulder. He looked like a genuine hunter, it struck me: he went over, drew his knife and stood for a while regarding the elk. It was the blue Mora knife, the one with a thumb shield, that had been bought from Kaddeberg's a few days before. I had been allowed to select it. The choice had been between the red ones and the blue ones. I had gone for a blue one, but I hadn't imagined that this was what it would be used for. Pappa resolutely drew it from its sheath and then stabbed it into the soft neck, with no reaction from the animal.

As I sat in the bar feeling the shaking of the ferry right through to my fingertips, I visualised the knife being plunged into the neck and withdrawn. He pulled out the knife, and it was followed by a little spout of dark, frothy blood, which quickly dwindled and dried up. I could see it all. The knife. The blood. The knife. The blood. Soon I had downed the fourth beer, I got up, paid and left. The sea was quite rough so no one paid any attention to me even though I was staggering a little. I walked around the ferry without knowing where I was going. I remember vague faces, bubbling sounds from the game machines, the crush in the shops, the pleasant silence in the corridors. I remember the smell of vomit, alcohol and perfume. I had no idea how long we had been at sea or how far it was to land. At length I found myself in another bar, or maybe it was a kind of discotheque. I didn't know what the time was, but it must have been night because

I saw the moon through one of the solid plastic windows. I was sitting at a table screwed to the floor, something stronger than beer in front of me, and the music was deafening. My mind moved slowly and sluggishly as if it were living its own life, independent of me. I sat there, and I wasn't there. I saw my hands gripping the glass, I felt my lips meet the smooth rim and I felt the liquid burn my mouth and throat. In fleeting glimpses I saw Pappa floating in bed with the puma leaping from his chest, I saw Mamma sitting at home and waiting, I saw her getting up from the kitchen chair, going to the window, then the front door, I saw her opening it, going onto the steps and listening.

There were lots of people in the bar and I had the feeling they were watching me on the sly. I remember finishing the drink. I stood up and pointed to the person sitting closest to me.

'What are you goggling at?!' I shouted. I can't remember what he answered, or even *if* he answered, I only remember that the next thing I did was to smash the glass on the edge of the table. It was unbelievably easy, and I stood there holding the stem like a broken bone, and the table glittered with tiny shards. I vaguely remember several people jumping to their feet and stretching out their hands in defence. I remember that everyone's attention was suddenly focused on me; at least it was for those who were nearest and had seen my performance. Then I grabbed one of the small pieces of glass, held it up triumphantly, and made a show of putting it into my mouth as if it were a pill. I remember with amazing clarity what the glass felt like on my tongue, I remember thinking it could have been a sweet to crunch between my teeth or dissolve, and I remember the ice-cold yet liberating feeling I had when I started to knead the glass with my tongue. I remember standing beside myself and observing. I remember understanding and not understanding what I was doing. I remember the taste of blood in my mouth. Not feeling any pain, just the sticky taste of blood. I remember thinking: if I open my mouth the blood will gush out. But I didn't open my mouth. Instead I turned and left the bar with unsteady but rapid strides. I went down a quiet corridor, still with the glass in my mouth. I continued up a staircase where I met some other night birds without seeing their faces clearly or hearing what they said. Somewhere far away I thought: 'Now they're coming to get you.' Now someone will come running from the bar, or two security guards will clap you in irons, and then you will be incarcerated in a place below the waterline for the rest of the journey. But no one came. I was alone on the boat. I made my way back up to the top deck, and everything was utterly still, just a regular, sombre rumble, and that was the rumble from the engines deep beneath me. I stood there while the whole world lurched. I felt as if I had an ocean of blood in my mouth. Then I found the door that led outside onto the deck. It was as heavy as lead. I remember the howl through the crack in the door, and the wind pressure that seemed to resist all my strength. Somehow I managed to open the door. I struggled onto the deck and the night air washed over me like rain. I stumbled along holding the railing, beneath the three lifeboats that rocked above me in the darkness. There was no one else outside. It must have been the middle of the night. I looked around for the moon, but it was gone, apparently sunk into the sea. I went astern, where sudden bursts of wind blew the ship's smoke over me. I closed my eyes, and I saw the dead elk before me again, it lay in the grass staring at me, and I remembered what happened afterwards.

We were still alone. The other hunters were probably making their way towards us – they must have heard the shot and known approximately where we were – but there was no time to wait. We had to remove the intestines as fast as possible: that much he did know. At first I watched while Pappa tried to tip the elk onto its back. The animal was both limp and heavy, and it toppled onto one side. It was the head that was causing the problem. It fell to one side and dragged the rest of the body with it. Someone had to hold the head. I scrambled forwards on my knees until I had the elk's head between my thighs. Still that was not enough. I had to inch even closer and get a better grip; I had to lift its whole head so that I sat with the weight of it in my lap. It was much heavier than I could have imagined, and I could feel its heat. Minutes ago this head had been somewhere in the forest listening carefully, turning into the wind as its ears twitched. It had been listening and keeping a lookout, and perhaps it had had our scent in its nostrils, but by then it had been too late. At the moment of impact the bullet had penetrated its body and opened like a flower.

Initially Pappa seemed a bit unsure of himself. He stood with the Mora knife in his hand, the blade dark with blood after the stab to the neck. Then he pushed the point into the belly, quite a long way down, where the hide was soft and the hair thin and very fair. He mumbled something as he carefully pressed it in and hacked away from him with tiny jerking motions. The skin parted and a greyish-white sac immediately pushed up against the aperture. I thought I detected an instant twitch of the elk's head, or a shudder running through the colourless eye, but that was all. As the cut grew, the sac grew too; it had a fine network of veins coiled round the outside. Later the ribbed dark blue intestines came into view, in the end everything tumbled out of the opening, steaming and soft like foam, like silk. The acrid smell rose to meet me. I tried to swallow, but couldn't. I wanted to look away, but I couldn't even do that. I sat there with the limp, heavy head in my lap and stared at the knife slowly slicing open the belly. Pappa had to throw off his jacket and roll up his sleeves. He took hold of the stomach and the intestines, tried to drag them out of the elk carcass, there was a squelching sound, unlike anything I had heard before, followed by a deep sigh as something loosened and the whole mess poured out over the ground and his boots. I don't know how long we were there on our own, but we were almost finished by the time the other hunters appeared at the edge of the forest.

The next thing I remember is when the heart was cut out. Kasper did that, because he knew exactly where the heart was positioned and how to cut so as to remove it in one piece. He too had to strip off his jacket, roll up his sleeves and lean forwards over the empty elk. By then Pappa was hunkered down by a stream rinsing his arms and hands. I remember watching him and the blood being rinsed off into the cold marshy water, and thinking it was his own blood. Kasper lunged into the cavernous animal and was soon covered with blood right up to his elbows. All of a sudden he jumped to his feet, holding the lead bullet between his fingers, the one that had opened like a flower, and in the end there he was, holding the dark heart in his hands, holding it up so that everyone could see the perfect hole right through.

I was somewhere in the middle of the Skagerrak. I leaned over the railing and stared down into the turbid wake which followed behind us and disappeared into the darkness. The wind tousled my hair, the diesel smoke whirled and the sea foamed and frothed beneath me. I opened my mouth, spat out the glass shard and felt blood oozing over my lip. I stood like that for a long time, until there was no more blood, until it was gone, until everything was gone. Then I clambered onto the rail, closed my eyes, held tight, and let go.

VIII.

IT WAS HALF PAST TWO in the morning of Monday, 5 June 1978. The road had been cleared after the accident. The two boys on the motorbike had been transported to Kristiansand in separate ambulances. The condition of one was said to be serious but stable. The other had only minor injuries. He was the one who had been wearing a helmet. Vatneli was still burning, but Olav and Johanna's house was now a pile of glowing embers. Pappa had driven home. After sitting for a while on the front steps with his gun he went back indoors. He sat in the living room at first, but as day began to break he finally headed for bed. Cars were still criss-crossing the length and breadth of Finsland, but no new fires were found.

There was a sense of quiet conviction that the two

houses in Vatneli were the sum of the night's activities. Two residential houses destroyed. A married couple who had lost everything, and on top of that a serious motorcycle accident.

Surely that was enough, wasn't it?

Dag drove slowly past the scene of the accident in Fjeldsgård on the Brandsvoll road. The cuts to his forehead were throbbing, but they no longer hurt, and he wrapped his hands around the wheel. Then he switched on the radio. Edited highlights of the match between Austria and West Germany were being broadcast. On the Fjeldsgård Plain he was waved into the roadside.

The police officer shone a torch into his face.

'Who are you?'

'I'm the fire chief's son,' he answered.

'And where are you going?'

'Home.'

The officer hesitated, then switched off the torch.

'Get your headlamps fixed,' he said. 'Light's going in all directions.'

Then he was allowed to drive on.

The score was 2–2 as he passed Brandsvoll Community Centre. He came to the crossroads by the shop, but did not turn right for Skinnsnes. Instead he carried on past the old doctor's surgery on the bend opposite Knut Frigstad's house, the one with only two rooms and walls that were so thin everyone in the waiting room could hear what was going on inside. That was where Kåre Vatneli had sat with Johanna while Dr Rosenvold examined his leg that time in the fifties.

At the top of the hill he extinguished the headlamps. It

made no difference, he could see just as well without them, after all, it was light enough everywhere now. He felt a tingling sense of well-being spread from his stomach out to his arms. He had warmed up in the car and now he drummed his fingers on the wheel. In Argentina, Hans Krankl had the ball. Only a few minutes of the match were left now. Krankl surged forwards to the right, found himself without support and ran across towards the penalty box. The roar in the stadium grew louder. The reception went fuzzy, he tried to adjust it, but lost the station altogether. Now there was just low white noise, and with this in the background he kept driving. He felt light-bodied, felt the blood throbbing in his temples and the cuts on his forehead. He was tired no longer; he just felt light. Light and strangely excited. He reduced his speed, humming a song with neither a beginning nor an end.

He turned right, below Anders Fjeldsgård's house, stopped the car, twisted the dial backwards and forwards until he found another, a better frequency. Krankl had dribbled past Müller and Rummenigge, suddenly he had space, he hit a superb shot and the stadium exploded.

Dag got out of the car. The house was situated high up on rock by the roadside, and it was unlit. The windows were black and shiny. On each side of the front steps there were two trees, dark with thick foliage. He sauntered to the rear of the house, where he knew the main entrance was, and cautiously pressed the door. Locked. Then he returned to the car, got in, and was about to turn the ignition key, but changed his mind. He darted soundlessly from the car to the front door. There was a kind of staircase in the lawn, small steps cut into the ground. He took these stone steps in three strides. Then he was at the top. An old door with eight inlaid glass panes. He carefully tested the handle. Also locked. Then he scampered back to the car, pulled the jerrycan out from under the pile of clothes and within seconds he was back on the front steps, listening. Mist lay over the fields, just as it did down in Kilen, still, white and pure. He noticed the stars above, pale, distant, in another universe. Then he thrust the corner of the can into the lowest pane in the door. The glass, old and brittle, smashed easily. He held his breath, his heart thundering in his ears. The cap on the jerry can was stuck, and he tussled with it until he managed to get it loose. He waited a few more seconds before going into action. Not a sound anywhere. No shouts from inside, no quickened steps. Nothing. Just the sound of gushing petrol. His hands and arms went numb as he emptied the rest of the can into the dark hallway.

Meanwhile, inside the house, Agnes Fjeldsgård was trying to rouse her husband, who lay fast asleep beside her. Anders, a solid rock of a man, was then seventy-seven years old. She had to shake him hard before he exhibited any signs of life.

'He's here,' she whispered in the darkness.

'No, he isn't,' he mumbled.

'Yes, he is,' Agnes said. 'I saw him through the kitchen window. He's outside.'

She didn't have a moment to waste, donned her dressing gown and hurried out of the bedroom, through the kitchen and into the living room.

There, she saw the black figure outside the glass veranda

door. The man was bent over in an odd pose, silent and unmoving. She detected the distinctive smell and heard the equally distinctive sound of petrol being poured through the smashed glass and over the wooden floor. Everything ground to a halt. Everything except her heart. She didn't think. She wasn't even frightened. She just stood there rooted to the spot, just as Johanna Vatneli had stood some hours earlier, staring through the mass of flames at the shadow on the other side. Except that now there were no flames, there was only a shadow. For seconds they stood face to face. With only a few metres separating them. At last she filled her lungs and screamed, and then he struck the match, held it in his hand with part of his face visible in the sudden flare: some of the chin, the corner of the mouth, the nose, the eye.

Then he threw the match towards her.

It was getting light, but the birds were still silent. In the large house in Brandsvoll, Else had been sitting awake ever since Alfred left shortly after twelve. She didn't know what was happening, only that there was a fire in the east of the region. When the alarm had gone off at around midnight she had seen the blue lights flashing behind the bedroom curtains. She had dashed to the window, looking for the fire engine.

'It's going towards Kilen,' she had shouted.

When Alfred got up she hadn't dared to go back to bed; after all she had three children sleeping in the loft, the youngest of whom was only ten. She switched on the TV, but lowered the sound. For a long time she sat at the far end of the sofa watching the players running around on the pitch as if following a pattern she couldn't comprehend. Now and again she went to the stairs and stood listening. She saw nothing, heard nothing. Had she walked around to the eastern side of the house, she would presumably have seen the flames billowing across the sky. But she hadn't; she didn't dare venture outside the house. The furthest she went was to the door, and it faced west. From there she could see the light in Teresa's windows, while Alma and Ingemann's house lay hidden behind a pine-clad hill.

In the end she sat on the sofa under a blanket. She began to feel drowsy, but was determined not to fall asleep. She sat in this state for quite a while. Then she fell asleep.

She woke with a start at a little after half past three.

In seconds she was in the porch, where she grabbed a jacket and ran to the front steps. She just caught sight of the car headlamps turning off the main road, they dazzled her for a brief instant, before they were dipped and the car drove into the yard. One of them was obviously broken because it was pointing up into the sky. She didn't know who it was until the door opened and he got out. She was at once reassured.

'Ah, it's you,' she said. 'I thought you were driving the fire engine.'

'It's in Vatneli,' he answered. 'We need it to put out the fire, so I had to use my own car.' He approached her, rubbing his hands. It was obvious he was cold.

'I thought you might want to hear the latest,' he said.

'The latest?'

'Yes,' he said, coming closer.

'Well then?'

'The pyromaniac has struck in Solås.'

'In Solås? Where in Solås?'

'Agnes and Anders's house,' he replied in a quiet voice.

She froze, the blood turning to ice in her veins, until it slowly thawed again.

'Anders and Agnes,' she repeated, as though she didn't believe what he had said. 'That's not far from here, is it.'

'He poured petrol through a window and lit it,' he said.

'And there's me sleeping on the sofa,' she muttered.

'It's dangerous to sleep tonight,' he said.

'But this is just sheer madness,' she whispered. 'This is the work of a madman.'

'Yes,' he said, coming even closer. 'This is the work of a madman.'

She saw his face clearly in the light from the outside lamp. His eyes were shiny and bright. His hair was dishevelled. He had soot over his face and on his shirt. It struck her that he looked much as he did when he was a child. She remembered him, of course, from the days when he used to run across the field and she would give him juice in the kitchen. Alma and Ingemann's well-behaved, clever son.

'Have you hurt yourself?' she asked.

'It's nothing,' he answered. 'Just a few scratches.'

'Wouldn't you like to come in and warm yourself?'

He gave a slight shake of his head.

'The person behind this,' he started, 'the, the . . . We'll catch him sooner or later. He won't escape.'

'It's hard to believe, all these things going on,' she said.

She pulled her jacket tighter around her and looked up at the unlit windows where the children were asleep. When she turned back he was staring at her; it was as if he had changed in the few seconds she had looked away.

'The worst thing that can happen now, do you know what that is, Else?'

'No,' she quavered.

'It's a fire breaking out here.'

'Here?'

'Yes,' he said. 'Here.'

'Don't say things like that, Dag,' she said.

'Now that all our equipment's in Vatneli,' he continued. 'So if something were to happen, then . . . it would take ages to move it all.'

'Let's hope there are no more fires tonight,' she said.

'Right,' he said, without averting his eyes.

'I can't take any more fires,' she said.

'Well,' he said nonchalantly. 'We've had enough of them now.'

'I pray to God that nothing will happen.'

'Yes,' he said slowly, before turning and walking to his car. 'That's the best thing you can do, Else. Pray to God.'

Alma was sitting by the kitchen window, fully clothed; the coffee pot stood on the stove, cold and gleaming. She had sliced a whole fresh loaf, one of those she had baked on Sunday morning while all had been peaceful. She had set out jam and cured sausage and some Prim cheese spread in case Dag had time to sit and have a bite, if he came home at all.

Ingemann had stayed with her in the living room for a few hours, but then he had gone upstairs to bed. Shortly afterwards the alarm had gone off. He had sat there, fully dressed, in the dark blue overalls that still smelt of fire, but as he was about to go he had experienced stabbing pains in his chest.

'It's my heart, Dag,' he had said. 'It's my heart.'

Dag set off in the fire engine. Alma and Ingemann sat in silence, listening to the sirens wailing past the house, watching the blue lights flashing across the living room walls, over the piano and the trophy shelves. They sat there as the sirens slowly became fainter, but neither of them had said anything, not a word, and in the end Ingemann had gone upstairs, leaving the entire living room smelling of fire.

A few hours later Dag returned home. He stood for some seconds in the hall, telling them between gasps about the two fires in Vatneli, and about the motorbike accident in Fjeldsgård, then ran to the door and Alma was left in the hall with the blood pounding in her temples.

That was when she realised: he smells of petrol.

Now she got up from her chair, crossed to the window, but there was nothing to see, only the hazy reflection of her own face. Went to the front steps. The mist hung like soft silk above the fields, and little by little day was breaking, but it wasn't possible to see the main road yet. She was about to go in when she heard the car. It was coming from Brandsvoll, getting closer, moving slowly, changing gear, and turned into the drive. The headlamps caused the mist to gleam curiously. She saw who it was, but the car didn't stop in the yard, it continued slowly up the hill to the fire station.

She made a sudden decision. She went and put on Ingemann's windbreaker, the one with pockets and zips on both arms, then she went outside into the grey morning light, crossed the yard and scampered up the hill. When she saw the car outside the fire station she was neither relieved nor surprised. As she approached she slowed down so she was walking at normal speed. The car was there, the door was wide open, but Dag was nowhere to be seen. The hot engine was ticking. There was a smell of exhaust and wet earth, forest and summer darkness. The fire station door was locked. There was no light apart from the single bulb above the gateway. He wasn't there. She stood weighing up the pros and cons, but then continued up the road anyway. It wasn't far up to Nerbø, where Sløgedal's house was. She had the constant sensation that Dag was walking ahead of her in the grey dawn. She visualised it: he was ahead of her, and she was following. Or vice versa: he was walking behind her, he could catch her up at any moment, and put his hands over her eyes as he had done in the kitchen that time. She thought she heard footsteps, but whenever she stopped there was complete silence. She pictured his face and she heard him talking to himself upstairs in the house. His voice was much higher than usual, as though he were a child again. She pictured the weird, stiff face that he had put on over his old one, that stayed for fleeting seconds, then cracked and was gone.

She walked faster and faster until she was running, all the jacket zips jingling. Then she caught sight of the house. It was completely isolated. All the windows were black. The walls grey. Slightly to the left was the barn, also grey with hazy contours, like an ancient ship on a foggy sea. She slowed down again. She wasn't used to running; her heart was beating painfully and she had a taste of iron in her mouth. Clambering down from the road, into Sløgedal's garden, she stopped under the old fruit trees and listened. Nothing, just her heart racing in her chest. She held onto a tree until her breathing steadied. Then she moved a few steps closer to the barn, and that was when she saw him. There were no more than ten, perhaps fifteen, metres between them. She gave a little start, even though, deep down, she had always known he would be here. He was bent over in a strange position as though studying something on the ground by the barn wall. Then he put the white can down on the grass. She both heard and saw everything with total clarity. She seemed to have acquired an animal's hearing. It was like the first days after she had given birth: all of a sudden her senses had been heightened. For several months she saw and heard with greater precision than at any other time in her life. Now it was occurring again. She half-opened her mouth, her lips moved, but no sound came out. It was like a large flower opening somewhere in her chest. It thrust out petals, it hurt so much she wanted to scream, but the scream wouldn't come, her lips moved, but still there was no sound. She heard the last drops of petrol slopping around in the can. She heard the rasping of the matchsticks. She heard the flare of the matchsticks. Then his face was lit up. She thought of all the times she had sat at his bedside while he was asleep. She had never said a word to anyone, but she had often sat at his bedside crying soundlessly. She hadn't been able to help herself. It just came. He had been lying there so peacefully, his face both open and closed; he was very near and he was unapproachable, and then the tears had flowed in torrents. And she hadn't known if it was with happiness or sorrow. The little boy had come to them as a miracle. They had been allowed to keep him for a while. But then they would lose him. It had hurt so much. She hadn't been able to think of anything else except that they would lose him. A wave surged up from her stomach, it rolled through her chest, hot, washed through her throat, but came to a halt in her mouth. She had learned to cry without making any noise at all. She was standing perhaps ten metres behind him, but now she was incapable of crying. She just stood there and saw his face merge into the darkness as he lowered his hand and threw the burning match. The flames burst into life. It was like an avalanche of fire. At once everywhere around them was lit up. It was a restless yellow light that made all the shadows tremble. He staggered backwards a couple of paces while she remained motionless. The flames were already licking high up the wall. She saw the closest trees, the spruce forest, strangely illuminated, like a gathering of old people – wise, mute and sombre with all they knew – a weeping birch nearby, almost rigid with terror, and the fruit trees around her with their white flowers raised high against the sky. She was numb, yet felt as if she were sinking. Her feet, ankles were sinking slowly into the earth. At first it hurt, thereafter it was no more than faint discomfort. In the end, she felt nothing. The pains in her chest vanished. The flower was there, but it no longer hurt. Within seconds the whole of one barn wall was ablaze. From it came a sort of wind that was both freezing cold and burning hot. The wind drove the flames, goaded them, not allowing them any peace. She felt the wind on her face, on her cheek, on her brow.

Then he turned.

It was as though he, too, had always known that she was

there. That they had gone up there together. That she had been standing behind him in the dark garden. That she had been sitting at his bedside and crying as he slept. He had always known. For two, perhaps three, seconds their eyes locked. He did nothing, said nothing, just looked at her with his hands hanging limply by his sides. She didn't do anything either. She saw his shadow, long and alive, stretching almost to her feet. His shadow was also full of a desire to free itself, become at one with the darkness and leave him standing alone. The wind from the fire was so strong that it made his shirt flap. A firestorm was building, it seemed to have been waiting in the barn for all these years and had now finally been let loose. Everything was being let loose. And she crumpled. And in a way this was good. In a brief glimpse she saw him catch fire, first his shirt, then his hair, then all of him. He went up in a blaze and stood before her, on fire, without turning a hair. She heard the sound of tiles cracking and falling to the ground like heavy, lifeless birds. A swarm of sparks tore itself away from the rest of the flames and soared at great velocity into the sky, which was completely lit up now. A high, singing tone arose from somewhere in the barn. She had never heard anything similar; it was a lament that was reminiscent of a song, or a song that sounded like a lament. She saw that he was smiling, and she was the only person in the world who could receive this smile. Then she turned and walked the short distance home.

5

I.

THE FIRST ICE ON LAKE LIVANNET. Suddenly one morning it is there. Sunrise: 9.22. The black water glistens. Later that morning a lighter channel stretches from the middle almost to the shore. Birds land. Seen from afar, they are entirely black, virtually impossible to tell apart; they approach the open water with caution, perch for a moment, irresolute, the boundary isn't clear, then it cracks beneath them.

The same afternoon I let myself into Finsland Church.

Inside the door I was in total darkness, I had to grope my way forwards, eventually finding a door handle, and then I was in the hall, which was light, and there was the priest's office at one end. At the other was the door that led into the church. The door was low and creaked as I opened it. I entered the church directly behind the altarpiece. There was something written, quite high up, which was illegible. I stepped forwards, stood by the altar railing and looked down the nave. It was a bit smaller than I remembered it, yet more or less the same. It was quite cold inside. I had been advised to come just after a service or a funeral because the heat lingered for a long time afterwards. I made my way down the central aisle on the soft carpet, and when I reached the door I turned and went back. Then I sat down on one of the pews. I recognised the dry creak I first heard when I was a baby, and the same smell of wood and age and grief. I tarried awhile. I saw the hole in the vaulted ceiling where the old stovepipe had exited. I looked up at the four beams forming a square under the high roof, and remembered my fantasy that all the dead were sitting there, dangling their legs while listening to the priest. That was just after Grandad had died, so I had a need for him to be there still. For him to be sitting up there, dangling his legs. Also during the prayer.

I sat there for about ten minutes. Then I got up, walked down the aisle and into the vestibule. The stairs to the church tower were on the left. There was a solitary light bulb glowing on the first landing, but the higher I ascended the darker it was. The staircase tapered, at the end it was like a steep ladder. At last I was at the top. The black bell hung above me in the darkness, black and heavy. I tapped my knuckle on it. The sound was the same. Deep, while bright and free. I recognised it from all the times I had heard it chime. From the time Grandma died, and Pappa, and Grandad, and from the June day and the nine strokes while I lay in Mamma's lap with her little finger in my mouth.

I climbed down from the tower and went up to the balcony where the organ was. It was hard to believe that the old organ still existed, but it did, it was still on the right by the north wall. I sat down at it. Placed my feet on the pedals, pressed a key. Nothing. I pulled a little peg labelled *Viola dulce*. A reedy sound was emitted, as though it was being released through a crack, and crumbled at once. I tried a peg labelled *Vox celeste.* It was silent. Sitting there, I thought about Teresa, attempted to recall something she had taught me, but at that moment it felt like a very long time ago. I couldn't remember anything except that now and then her hand would grasp my forefinger and middle finger and place them on the right keys. She had sat on this exact spot and played when Pappa was christened, and at the confirmation when Kåre first entered, straight after Holme, and later when they left to start their long lives. And she had sat on this exact spot when I was christened twenty years later, 4 June 1978, when Finsland was ablaze. I tried the peg marked *Vox humana.* It was a low, trembling note that grew and became firm and strong for as long as I kept my foot on the pedal.

Eventually I went downstairs and proceeded slowly up the central aisle. My footsteps were inaudible. I walked to the end and sat in the first row, on the left, precisely where I sat at my father's funeral. I closed my eyes, and after a while I seemed to hear the sound of people in the rows behind me. I heard them coming in, heard them walking on the soft carpet, opening the small, creaking doors to the pews, carefully taking a seat, thumbing through the hymn book and looking up. I sat there listening to the whole church slowly filling. I thought of the evening in Mantua when they had all gathered to hear me. Now they were here, I knew it was them, they were trying to be quiet, but I heard them nonetheless. I sat without moving at the very front, and they sat without moving behind me. I waited for a few minutes. It was good to sit like that, just waiting, waiting for nothing, and it felt as though those behind me were thinking the same. I let it go on for a few more seconds. Three. Two. One.

Then I turned.

II.

I CAME TO AS DAY BROKE. People were stirring, many were already standing by the exit with their shopping bags, and as I squinted into the strong, milky light I saw the ferry was docking in Hirtshals. I saw the harbour district with its rusty fishing smacks almost frozen in the water, and I saw one lonesome forklift truck on its way along the wharves with its fork raised unnaturally high. I made an attempt to get off the bench on which I had slept, but my head ached as if possessed, so I remained where I was until the last person had left and I was alone again in the corridor. Then I staggered to my feet and followed the carpeted steps below deck. I got into Pappa's freezing car, and as I closed the door, fastened the seat belt and drove towards the light, gradually what I had done came back to me. It was only when I emerged into the murky morning light that I tasted the blood in my mouth. I cast a glance in the mirror and saw I had dried blood on my lips and down my chin. My tongue was sore and swollen, and the insides of my cheeks were covered with little cuts from the glass. It felt as if I couldn't talk, but that didn't matter because I had absolutely no intention of talking to anyone. I drove around the quay area and finally turned right, into a street called Havnegade, followed it for a while, then bore left and drove along a road with netting extended above it and at last found a car park not too far from the sea, and not too far from a pub, Hirtshals Kro. I sat in the car holding my pounding head in my hands. Again I tried to unravel the last twelve hours, from the time I left Pappa at the rest home in Nodeland until boarding the ferry and finally climbing over the railing and hanging over the seething sea. Of the subsequent period until I woke on the bench in the corridor I remembered nothing. I have no idea what happened. Did someone come across me outside in the darkness, or did something inside tell me that was enough, pack it in now, pull yourself together, climb back over that railing and get yourself into the warmth?

I don't know.

I must have stayed in the deserted car park for more than an hour until I felt capable of walking erect. Then I opened the car door, wrapped my jacket tightly around me and walked down to the quay. The weather was dank and cold, the mist hung, greyish-silver, over the sea, and by the quay the water was as still and shiny as oil. I wandered around in the sea breeze until my head felt a little clearer. Then I went into Hirtshals Kro and ordered a cup of coffee. The publican did a double take when he saw me; standing in the cramped toilet a minute later, I realised why. My eyes were red and swollen and animal-like, while the blood had run down my neck and dried in long gashes. I washed with meticulous care. There was a dried-up, cracked piece of soap on the sink, I did my best to create some foam, then scrubbed my whole face even though it hurt. Afterwards, sitting with a steaming cup in front of me, I could hardly drink, for the sores in my mouth opened up immediately, making the coffee taste of rust. I sat alone in a corner while what I assumed were three local alcoholics sat in the bar, each nursing a glass of frothy beer.

The rest of the morning in Hirtshals passed in a grey, languid haze. I gradually recovered on my way to the ferry terminal and bought a ticket for the next crossing. Once that was done, I got into my car and searched the glove compartment. The only paper there was a pile of lottery coupons Pappa hadn't got round to filling in, but that was good enough for me. There were several pens as well. Fortunately, one of them worked, and sitting in the grey, utterly deserted car park in Hirtshals I wrote:

> The sky is opening. Cows are standing at the edge of the forest, gazing towards the house. The clouds are in rapid motion. I look out at the wind. I am sitting by an open window and watch the wind shaking the heavy boughs of the old ash tree. I am writing. Clouds, boughs, a hand writing.
>
> On the very margin.
>
> The scent of sweet soil reaches my face. The cows retreat into the forest. A black procession into the blackness. One by one. Gone. One by one. I am cold. A loose windowpane rattles in the loft. From the lake come dancing white bodies and heavenly music.

I read through what I had written, improving and correcting here and there, but the text remained largely as it had been. It occupied space on the back of five lottery coupons that Pappa never managed to fill in. It was the first time I had read through anything I had written without feeling ashamed. It was a slightly unreal, airy feeling. Unreal yet wonderful. I went for another wander around the quays with my head still feeling like a tender, pounding turnip. Everything was still grey and languid, the water in the harbour as thick and smooth as before, rubbish floated against the sides of boats as before, and out at sea the mist hung as soft and silvery-grey as before. Yet something had happened. I walked, thinking about what I had written. About what was now appended to lottery coupons, and which I would read through as soon as I returned to the pickup. I walked and saw all the grey around me as the sea air and diesel fumes tore at my nostrils, yet something had changed. And it could be seen on my face. If someone came over to ask me what the time was, they would notice it, I imagined, glittering like a diamond in one eye.

At three o'clock I got back into the pickup, started the engine and drove down to the ferry terminal. I queued at the head of the line, waiting for the ferry to arrive, and tried to write a bit more. I read through what I already had, and then attempted to add a few more lines. The ferry came into view an hour later, and by then I must have scribbled over ten coupons. Once on board I found myself a place on my own, and there I laid out all the coupons in front of me and read through them all. I felt the roar of the engines as the ferry set off, but I was too engrossed to look up and out of the window, I was too engrossed to see the grey town disappear in the matt silver mist. I was somewhere else entirely. I sat bent over the papers, reading, adding, rewriting. However, I was only satisfied with the first text I'd written. It stood apart, it had some of my native countryside residing in it, while the other bits were more run of the mill.

As the crossing continued I stared out of the discoloured window. I felt totally drained, but was unable to sleep; I just sat there, letting the vibrations of the boat ripple through me. My head was on the mend – it was as if my skull had been opened and my brain reinstalled – and when I drank coffee it no longer tasted of rust. Seeing the lights of Randesund glide past I felt almost as before. I was in my pickup even before the ferry had docked. The bow gate opened, and I saw the harbour lights and the smoke from the ferry being swept across town. I put the pickup into first, I was as before, but I had become someone else, and no one saw that as I drove out of the boat into the autumn evening and all the way home.

The following night, at a little after four, my father died. The last thing he said was: *Mm, that's heaven.* Just as Grandma had noted down. That was after the last dose of morphine, while he was smoking his last cigarette and ash was fluttering down on the sheet. The last thing I did was to lie to him, and I didn't even have time to tell him I had become a writer.

III.

IN *FÆDRELANDSVENNEN* ON Monday, 5 June, the whole of the first and last pages are devoted to the three most recent fires, and the failed attempt at the house of Anders and Agnes Fjeldsgård.

Headline: *Finsland, Region In Panic.*

There are two photographs on the front page. One shows Johanna sitting in Knut Karlsen's cellar. She is wearing a dressing gown and staring into the middle distance with her head resting on her hands. She has already given up. The second photograph shows her almost burned-out house. In the foreground are the contours of five people. I don't recognise any of them.

The back page shows the wrecked motorbike on its side, right behind the car with which it collided. The picture was taken as the ambulance was leaving the scene of the accident. Dag isn't there. Nor Pappa.

On the last page there is also a picture of two police officers taking shots of the steps down from Anders and Agnes Fjeldsgård's house. It is still dark. One is holding a torch while the other is leaning over with an outmoded camera, the kind you see in old films with a large dish-shaped flash lamp on top.

At the bottom of the page Lensmann Koland is pictured in conversation with Anders Fjeldsgård and police officer Tellef Uldal. It was Uldal who had brought the Alsatian. The dog had set off down the Mæsel road but came back after a few minutes. Next, he let it loose outside Anders and Agnes's house. It had wandered around the steps sniffing the matches on the ground. Then it had run down the steps, across the road and into the darkness towards Lake Bordvannet. It had been gone a long time and then began to bark somewhere by Duehei, on the eastern side of the lake. There was a clear and distinct echo. The dog barked, and another dog answered. Then it was back, no further developments.

Later, the Alsatian was released outside the barn belonging to cathedral organist Sløgedal. This was while the barn was still burning, and the flames were reflected in the animal's small eyes. It was clearly confused at that point, and ran first in one direction, then in another. It sniffed the barn wall, the fruit trees, continued down the road to the fire station, sniffed around the building, then tore off towards Alma and Ingemann's house. It sprinted around the garden whimpering and whining, before returning. This was when all hands were required at the pump to save the organist's property; water was being directed at the west wall and roof, and men stood spraying while Sløgedal's barn wailed and finally collapsed and the flames billowed across the sea. The dog sat by the fire engine, pawing one wheel and whimpering.

In the photograph Lensmann Koland appears tired and bewildered. In the interview he says it is all very complicated. There are no leads. The sum of their knowledge is that the culprit is most likely a young man. The distance between the fires is barely ten kilometres. Petrol is used. A car with extinguished headlamps has been observed. Apart from that, nothing. It all seems so desperate. The pyromaniac seems to be taking huge risks. The last three fires were started while the police were stopping all the traffic in the area, and while almost everyone was awake or on watch. Apparently this man really wants to get caught.

It is very complicated, yet simple.

Two KRIPOS detectives were on their way from Oslo that morning, but they weren't installed at Brandsvoll Community Centre until around two o'clock in the afternoon. By then the sky had clouded over, and a vast tarpaulin was nailed over the entrance to Anders and Agnes's house in case of rain. The hall reeked of petrol, and there were fragments of glass everywhere. Anders and Agnes stood in the background watching, him with his hands thrust firmly into his pockets, her with her arms crossed. Under the circumstances they were quite composed. For some hours they became strangers in their own house. No one, themselves included, was allowed to touch or move anything. Several journalists came. Everyone wanted to speak to Agnes, the woman who had actually seen the pyromaniac. She had been standing a few metres away, with only the window separating them. She had caught a glimpse of the face in the light from the match, the one that was presumed to be match number two. Two matches had been found on the steps. One had flared up briefly before going out, the other had burned down to about halfway and snapped in the middle. They must have been struck consecutively. And tossed towards the hole in the window, one after the other. Both had missed, hit the glass and fallen outside.

They asked her to describe him.

A good-looking young man, she said to a journalist, half in jest. He took notes with alacrity, and the following day it was in print. The arsonist was not only young, he was also tall and good-looking. He appeared from the great unknown and disappeared leaving not a trace, except for flames. And a region paralysed with panic. And, indeed, two burned-out matches. He had thrown the last match at the window after discovering her presence. She had screamed, he had seen and heard her, and this notwithstanding he had thrown it. She had been a whisker away from disaster. If the match had gone through the hole she would have found herself amid a raging fire within seconds. The same could be said about Olav and

Johanna, but they got out. And in a way they found themselves amid the sea of flames all the same.

It was decided that both the couple in Vatneli and the couple in Solås would be given police protection that night. Olav, incidentally, lay for large parts of the morning in bed screaming. Johanna sat beside him, but evidently there was nothing that could quieten him. The screams came in great, harrowing waves that threatened to tear him to pieces. She tried to hold his hand, but he kept pulling it away. He screamed at her, he screamed at the wall, he screamed to God. It was as though he was being turned inside out, as though something wild and untameable was struggling to be released from his body, but he wouldn't let it happen. He wouldn't let himself be torn apart. At length the doctor came from Nodeland and administered tranquillisers. Johanna was offered some tablets as well, but she declined. Later that morning Olav fell asleep, and Johanna stayed on the bed, holding his hand and staring at his serene face. She sat like that for half an hour, perhaps even longer. She was utterly drained. She looked at her husband, saw that he was handsome, though very old: his hair was white, his cheeks hollow, eyelids red, forehead smooth and unlined. There was a thin, transparent quality to his skin now, as if he were in the process of dissolving. She wondered whether she actually knew this man. Was this the man with whom she had spent her entire life? Was this the man with whom she had had their only child? Was this the Olav who had witnessed their happy son waste and die? Was this him?

He was so far away, yet so near. His hand was warm and still. She held it in hers, closed her eyes and heard cars driving past on the road. She heard birds and low voices from the floor above. They were strange, unfamiliar sounds, even though she was a mere fifty metres from where she always used to spend her mornings. At this time she would usually put on coffee. She would switch on the radio and listen to the Sørland channel, and as she sliced the bread Olav would come in and sit down with his shirtsleeves rolled up and his hands smelling of soap though still dirty from working in the wood shed. Then they would take a seat on opposite sides of the table and eat. Olav would draw the curtain to the side, as always, and look down onto Lake Livannet or the cherry tree that was still in flower.

Eventually she reclined on the other bed that had been brought in for them. She could feel that she was bleeding, but she couldn't be bothered to get up. The blood ran and she drifted away. It didn't hurt any more. Before she fell asleep she turned her head sharply to one side and her lips moved imperceptibly. It was as though someone had quietly entered the room, sat down on the edge of the bed, placed a hand on her forehead and whispered her name.

IV.

WHAT WAS IT Aasta said about Johanna? She couldn't laugh, she couldn't cry. She couldn't do anything.

And Alma. What could she do?

She went home under her own steam. It was shortly after four o'clock in the morning. Dawn had arrived, birds were singing, but she didn't hear them. She hurried down the road from Sløgedal's house as the fire in the barn slowly grew behind her. She heard the roar of the flames, but she didn't turn. She walked past the fire station, down the hill to the house, past the workshop and across the yard. She walked up the four steps into the house. She hung Ingemann's jacket on the hook in the hallway. Proceeded into the bathroom, rinsed her face thoroughly in cold water. She didn't look up, just washed and scrubbed until her cheeks were numb. She switched off the light. Closed the door. Then she tiptoed up to the first floor and got into bed beside Ingemann. She could hear from his breathing that he was awake, but she said nothing. They both lay still as the birdsong outside became louder. They both lay still as they heard the fire engine approach. They both lay still as several cars raced past, continuing up to Sløgedal's house. They both lay still until there was a ring at the door downstairs. Then she jumped to her feet, went down and opened the door.

It was Alfred. He smelt of fire.

'Alma,' he said.

'Ah, it's you,' she answered.

'Sløgedal's barn has burned down.'

'Yes, I know,' she said.

'Alma,' he said. 'Are you alright?'

'Yes,' she said. 'I'm fine.'

Alfred hesitated.

'Is Ingemann in?'

'Of course,' she answered distractedly. She looked past Alfred, into the clear, chill morning and the first sun spreading its golden rays over the ridges to the west.

'Can I talk to him?'

She went upstairs and stood in the bedroom doorway. Ingemann was lying on his side breathing heavily, but she knew he wasn't asleep.

'Alfred's here,' she said quietly.

'Tell him I can't come,' he replied.

'Sløgedal's barn's burned down,' she said.

He didn't answer, but she noticed him stiffen. She looked at the dishevelled bed, the clothes hanging over the chair, the partly open wardrobe door with one sleeve of his best suit and her dark winter coat poking out. Ingemann still didn't move, but she could see he was listening.

'I said Sløgedal's barn has burned down.'

'Yes, I heard,' he said.

'You can't just lie there. You're the fire chief, aren't you.'

Ingemann and Alfred chatted in hushed tones while walking the few hundred metres up to the sharp bend, past the fire station and all the way to Sløgedal's farm. Alfred reported on progress with the fire, he told Ingemann they had managed to save the farmhouse: there were a couple of cracked panes, the paint was a bit blistered, some roof tiles had detached themselves, but otherwise it was intact.

'That's good,' Ingemann said. Nothing else.

Alfred then mentioned that several journalists had already turned up, and television crews had been filming.

'Soon the whole country will know about this,' he said.

Ingemann didn't reply.

By the time they reached the razed barn their conversation had long since dried up, and they stood next to each other, silent, staring. What could you say? Everything was ash, a burned-out structure, mangled corrugated iron. Even the ground was black and scorched in a wide radius around the site.

'Are you alright?' Alfred asked.

'Yep,' Ingemann answered. 'I just need to sit.'

Alfred hunkered down beside him on the steps. It was quite cramped and they sat there for a good while without saying a word. The sun rose clear of Kviheia to the east, the dew dried slowly. You could see there had been frenetic activity during the night: the grass was trampled flat, there was some rubbish, a few empty bottles and so on, hurled over by the house wall. Ingemann closed his eyes. He sat in this way and felt the sun warming his face.

'Dag has been so kind as to provide food,' Alfred said, next to him.

'Has he?'

'We never run short of fizzy drinks and chocolate,' Alfred went on. 'He's sort of become the new fire chief now.'

'Yes, he has that,' said Ingemann.

Not long afterwards a car parked in the yard. Two men got out. One was the cathedral organist Bjarne Sløgedal, the other was his father, Reinert, the old sexton and teacher. They had been notified about the fire in the early morning and had immediately jumped into a car and driven all the way from Kristiansand. Now they were here, in the first rays of the sun, staring at the devastated barn. The son strode forwards, his father followed, both seemed slightly out of place; as if they had come to the wrong address, or were lost, and now they were strolling over to Alfred and Ingemann to ask where they actually were. The four of them stood talking. Alfred told them the little they knew. The fire had started around four o'clock, at daybreak. No one had seen or heard anything. No cars. Nothing. A police patrol car had passed by only a few minutes before. It was as if the fire had started itself.

The four men then went onto the barn bridge, right to the top, where it suddenly ended in thin air. Smoke still eddied up from the ruins, grey, almost transparent, struggling to rise before dissipating of its own accord.

'Mother's loom's gone now,' Bjarne said in a low voice. 'We had put it in the barn for safe keeping,' he added, pointing to somewhere in space.

'She loved that loom.'

No one said anything for some time. They were letting the words about the loom sink in when a figure appeared on the road. It was Dag. He looked happy and loose-limbed as he walked under the fruit trees in the garden, jumped up, smacked one of the lowest branches and tore off some leaves, which he threw onto the ground at once. When he saw who was with Alfred and his father on the barn bridge he immediately turned serious. At first he appeared to be considering whether to go back, but then he continued with determined steps. He walked up to the bridge and shook hands with both of them. First Bjarne, then Reinert.

'Is it really you?' Reinert said.

'Yes indeed,' Dag said.

'You've certainly grown since I last saw you.'

'And you've certainly got older,' Dag answered.

And they laughed. Not for long, though.

'This is truly tragic,' Dag said.

'I was just saying that Mother's loom has gone,' Bjarne said.

'Yes, I remember she used to weave,' Dag replied.

Reinert said, 'I'd been hoping there would be something left.'

'It's terrible,' Dag said.

Then all five of them walked down from the bridge.

Dag broke off a branch from the partly destroyed hanging birch and began to stir the ash with it. The others watched him. No one said anything. Reinert dried his sweat. Then Ingemann began to stroll down towards the house, followed by Alfred and finally Sløgedal Father and Son, all heading for the parked car. Dag soon caught up and stood beside them with the branch as if it were a present he wanted to hand over, given a suitable opportunity.

'The police will have to make sure they catch the nutter who did this,' he said. 'You can't have a man running around terrorising everyone.'

'No, you can't,' Alfred agreed.

'He's a madman.'

'Yes, he is,' Reinert affirmed.

'It must be someone who . . .' Bjarne trailed off. 'It's so heartless.'

'And there's nobody doing anything,' Dag exclaimed. 'No one! Why is no one doing anything? This cannot go on!'

'No, it can't,' Alfred said.

'He's a sick, sick man.'

There was a short silence.

'A sick man!'

'Yes,' Alfred said.

'Let's go home now, Dag,' Ingemann said. 'We need some food, you and I do.'

'I forgot to ask what you were doing now,' Reinert said, apropos of nothing.

'Yes, you had such great plans, you did.'

'No good has come of me,' Dag answered.

'Oh, yes, it has,' Ingemann rejoined.

But Dag interrupted him.

'No, Pappa,' he said quietly. He sent them all a heart-felt smile. 'No good has come of me.'

V.

THE PHOTOGRAPH IN *Lindesnes* on Saturday, 3 June shows Ingemann standing beside the fire tender with an expression that is hard to interpret. At this juncture he must have had his suspicions. In the interview, however, there is nothing of any interest; on the contrary, it is very factual and prosaic. The heading reads: *We have a lot of equipment for a small region.* He discusses the nearly new fire engine. The water pump at the front is a Ziegler and can discharge water twenty-five metres into the air. Moreover the hoses are 800-metres long, and there are three portable pumps, the largest of which supplies a 1,000 litres of water per minute, the others 200 and 150 respectively. No one can have a word to say against the equipment, he asserts. No one could be better equipped than this little region. Given there was a pyromaniac on the rampage, it was good he was active here, he says, puffing out his chest in a proud, manly way. He is asked about the most recent fires, and about the alarm, which last night, could be heard right up by the church. The last question in its entirety: *After dealing with so many fires over the last two days, I suppose you must be tired, aren't you?*

Answer: *Yes, we're tired. Very tired.*

It was decided that the organist, Bjarne Sløgedal, would keep watch outside his house the following night. The police thought that the arsonist might return to *complete the job*, as people said. The house was still standing, after all. Sløgedal was furnished with a gun, a Mauser rifle without a shoulder strap, and it was agreed that he would hide behind some bushes a short distance from the house. If the arsonist made an appearance he was to fire three shots in the air in rapid succession. That was the arrangement.

Then it was a question of waiting until the evening.

In Solås a patrol kept watch on Anders and Agnes Fjeldsgård's house. There was a multitude of eager spectators who in the course of the day had heard about events. Later that afternoon Dag also dropped by to have a look. That was while the KRIPOS detectives were sifting through the evidence under the tarpaulin nailed to the door. He stood on the lawn outside, chatting with Anders. Agnes walked down towards them. She was doing the rounds with a dish of pancakes. The officer down by the road already had one in his hand. Anders didn't want one, but Dag did.

'Thank you very much,' he said, looking her in the eye.

A bit later Agnes Fjeldsgård tried to get rid of the pervasive smell of petrol. It had spread and hung like a stupefying fog throughout the house. She scrubbed the floor several times, used sand and green soap, but the petrol had managed to permeate deep into the floorboards. The air quivered and a heavy vapour was released from the woodwork. The door was kept wide open, even after the KRIPOS officers had left. There wasn't a breath of wind. The heat shimmered at the end of the plain in Brandsvoll and Lauvslandsmoen; even the birds were quiet.

It was past five o'clock, Monday afternoon.

At approximately that time Alfred was summoned by the police.

Else was informed that she should tell Alfred to appear at the community centre. She was instructed to do this in a casual, inconspicuous way. So as not to arouse Alfred's suspicions. Not to alert him to the fact that he was a suspect. After all, he had been very active in the extinguishing of many of the fires.

Alfred was ushered into the old boardroom where a makeshift office had been set up with a desk, three chairs and a typewriter. He was asked to take a seat in the chair on one side. Two police officers occupied the others. Then the interrogation began. It took him a while to realise that this was actually about him.

Perhaps it wasn't quite accurate to describe it as an interrogation. The tone was relaxed in spite of everything. He was offered coffee from the huge boardroom flask, the one that used to last a whole board meeting in the old days. Then he was invited to tell them about the last three fires, the two in Vatneli and Sløgedal's barn. Meticulous notes were taken. One officer sat with his back to them, hammering the questions and answers into the typewriter. Alfred spoke quietly, pausing occasionally, leaning forwards to drink from the steaming cup and coughing, at which both looked up attentively from their papers. He was asked how much he had slept in the last seventy-two hours. He replied that he had no idea, as indeed was the truth. It was suggested that he must be dead on his feet, which he confirmed. He was asked about the Skogen fire, why he thought it had been started in the morning and not in the middle of the night, as had been the pattern with the others. He said he had no idea. He was asked if he believed there was a pattern, but to that question he had no answer. He was asked why he had joined the fire service. To which he answered that he had been recruited, and that furthermore his experience was that it was a meaningful job. The word *meaningful* elicited more questions. Could he expand? He made an attempt. Finally, he was asked what his experience of the last few days had been. He considered the question for a while, leaned forwards and answered: *Unreal. Unreal. Absolutely unreal.*

After roughly twenty minutes he was allowed to leave. Before getting up, he asked:

'Why are you actually questioning me?'

'It's part of the investigation,' came the answer.

'Does it mean that I'm a suspect?'

'It means neither one thing nor another.'

Then he left.

When he arrived home, Else had a meal on the table, and he told her about the interview while they ate. He said that the police might be working on the possibility he was the arsonist. She looked up. She looked at his hands, his mouth and the whole of his face. She saw the steam from the coffee cup rising in front of his eyes.

Then she laughed.

They listened to the six o'clock news. The fires were the second item. The first was a terrible train accident outside Lyon, in which eight people had been confirmed dead so far. Then about the four latest blazes in Finsland. Two arson attacks with intent to kill. Four elderly people who had come within an inch of death. Lensmann Koland was interviewed; his voice was firm and assured. He said the police still had no definite leads. The two cars were mentioned. Followed by Agnes Fjeldsgård's sighting: a thin, young man. That was all they had for the moment. Finally the lensmann urged everyone to be vigilant at night. That was all there was about the Finsland fires. Next there was a brief mention of the World Cup. Austria had been knocked out, as had France, Spain and Sweden.

Else got up to switch off the radio, while Alfred drained the last drop of coffee and was on his way towards the living room for a lie-down.

That was when Else caught sight of a man walking across the field. She immediately recognised who it was, but was taken aback by how old he looked. Ingemann was walking across the field alone. It was the shortest route between the two houses, although it was seldom used. The sun was behind him and he cast a long, thin shadow, which must have been four times his height. It was as if ten years had passed before Else's eyes without her noticing. Ten years had passed and Ingemann had become well over seventy within a few days. There was something about the way he was walking, or there was something about his back, the bent neck, perhaps the arms, the way they swung as he walked. This was an old man walking towards them.

Alfred and Else sat quietly in the kitchen waiting for the bell to ring in the hallway. Then Alfred got to his feet, went into the porch and opened the door.

'So it's you, is it?' he said.

At first Ingemann was unable to utter a word. He just stood there in his dark overalls, the ones he usually wore for emergency call-outs, the ones that smelt of old fires and had the vague semblance of a uniform. Seconds passed, then he stretched out his hand.

'Look at this,' he said.

At once Alfred recognised the cap from one of the fire service's white jerrycans. Only a few hours ago he had refilled some of the jerrycans with petrol. Ingemann's hands were black with soot; the cap was white.

'I've . . . I've found this,' Ingemann said.

'Uhuh,' Alfred replied.

'And I've come to tell you.'

'You've come to tell me what?' Alfred queried, looking down at his old neighbour standing in the warm evening sun.

'That I know who it is.'

Alfred had to support him into the chair under the clock. Else took him a glass of water. He sipped a little, but left most of it. There was an acrid smell of ash and soot about him. The petrol cap had been left outside on the steps, and Alfred went to fetch it. Ingemann sat in the chair under the clock twisting the lid between his fingers. There was a long silence, only the sound of the lid turning; then he began to talk.

He had walked up to Sløgedal's razed barn and mooched around on his own. He had stood on top of the barn bridge and surveyed the ruins, just as they had stood with Reinert and Bjarne a few hours earlier. That was when he had suddenly spotted it, he said. He couldn't understand why no one had seen the cap before. It was lying in the grass by the barn for all to see. He had been standing precisely where the bridge should have continued upwards, and he couldn't understand why the petrol cap should be lying there in the grass. He stood there feeling the light summer breeze on his face, then raised his eyes and stared at the birch that had stood next to the barn. The closest branches were burned off, elsewhere only blackened stumps resembling bones protruded. The little foliage remaining was brown and withered and rustled drily in the wind.

Then, all of a sudden, he understood.

That is, he both understood and he did not, but it made no difference.

That was what he told Alfred and Else. He leaned back and rested his head on the wall beneath the clock. He closed his eyes, then opened them, and in the interim they had become narrow and dark and wise, yet they were quite alone in what they knew.

'Now I've told you, Alfred, would you be so kind as to notify the police? I don't think I'm capable of doing it myself.'

VI.

IT WAS TERESA WHO FOUND HER. She'd had an inkling that something was wrong, and she was sure Alma was at home – from her window she had seen her go in – yet no one answered the door when she rang. In the end, she pushed the door. It was unlocked. In the hallway, she called out. Still no answer. She took a few cautious steps inside. There was no one in the kitchen. Just the wall clock ticking blithely away, a solitary cup of coffee on the table, some washing-up on the drainer, the kitchen cloth over the tap, a bumblebee banging its head against the windowpane. Teresa was about to leave when she heard something on the floor above. She ascended the stairs and peeped through the one door that was open. Alma was lying on the duvet fully clothed. Her coat was buttoned up halfway. She was even wearing shoes.

'Alma?' Teresa whispered.

She wasn't quite sure why she was whispering; perhaps it was the sight of the shoes on the duvet, perhaps the blank, staring eyes. Alma didn't move, but she had called out, Teresa was sure of that.

'Alma,' she whispered again. This time it was not a question but a statement of fact. Alma lay stretched out and stiff like a damaged statue, but with her hair cascading attractively over the pillow. She was breathing through an open mouth, her eyes were staring up at the extinguished ceiling lamp and her chest was heaving.

'It's him,' she whispered. 'It's him.'

Teresa stood at her bedside, but Alma wasn't looking at her.

'It's all over,' she whispered.

She turned her head towards Teresa, as though she had suddenly become aware that someone had entered. Her lips moved. Teresa bent down to hear. Her voice was hoarse and slightly ragged, sounding as if it was coming through a thin crack.

'I can't move.'

She didn't say another word.

Teresa writes about how she took off Alma's shoes. First the left one, then the right. Some sand and earth fell onto the duvet. She brushed it onto the floor and placed the shoes neatly beside each other by the door. Thereafter she unbuttoned the coat, opened it and folded it to the side. Took out her right arm, then her left. It was like undressing a sleeping child. But Alma wasn't asleep; she was staring up at the lamp under the ceiling, and was beyond reach. Teresa removed all her outer clothing, then she spread Ingemann's duvet over her.

'Have a little rest,' she whispered. She thought she saw a slight movement of Alma's head, but she said nothing, just lay with her eyes open.

That was when Teresa heard the strains of music below. It was piano music, and she immediately recognised the piece that was being played. She looked at Alma, who had closed her eyes. Lying there, still and serene, her forehead smooth, some fir needles and other bits in her hair, she looked a great deal younger than she was in reality. It was as if she had been lifted and was floating off on the music pouring into the room beneath them.

Teresa rose to her feet and went downstairs. The music

became louder. She went into the living room and looked at the figure sitting at the piano.

'You play well,' she said.

He gave a start, removing his fingers from the keys as though they were red-hot. The notes lingered in the air, merged into each other, sank and were gone.

'Do you think so?' he asked.

She nodded.

'It's a long time since you taught me this one,' he said.

She nodded again.

'Would you like me to play a bit more?'

He didn't wait for an answer but turned back to the keys. Struck some chords. It was only now she noticed the acrid smell of fire pervading the room. He was wearing a white shirt that was stained down the back and sleeves, there was a long tear over the shoulder where she could see the pale skin beneath, his hair was unkempt, his hands dirty. She forgot to listen; it was unlike her, she usually listened to her music pupils. She forgot everything to do with technique or expression or presentation. Instead she seemed to sink into the music, or it sank into her. She just stood staring at Dag as he played, staring at his dirty fingers, which left not one mark on the white keys.

She didn't hear the knock at the door, barely noticed the people entering the hall, the shout, neither she nor Dag noticed anything until a police officer entered the living room. Followed by Alfred. And last of all Ingemann. Only then did he take his fingers off the keys, and there was silence. He looked at each and every one of them. No one said anything. Ingemann's face was ashen; Teresa couldn't remember having ever seen him like that before. He was leaning against the door frame, and for a moment she thought he was going to lose balance and fall over, but he didn't, he remained upright. He stepped forwards, into the middle of the room, and he seemed to be carrying the whole house on his shoulders.

'Dag,' he said. That was all he managed to utter.

'You have to come with us,' the policeman said.

'Where to?' Dag asked.

'It's best you go along,' Alfred said quietly.

Dag carefully lowered the lid over the keys, then let it go with a sudden bang. A mournful, barely audible swell of notes came from the instrument's dark innards. Then he got up and the officer held him warily by the arm, and as he left the room he turned to Teresa and smiled.

6

I.

LAKE LIVANNET, WHITE AND STILL. No birds. Just sky. Wind and ice. At some point the thermometer creeps down to minus twenty-five degrees. Can only write for short periods before my fingers go stiff. Later the weather brightens, February and March come, westerlies arrive and slowly it becomes milder.

I try to gather everything together.

Grandma writes in her diary on 22 January 1998, the day after Pappa's lungs were drained of four and a half litres of fluid: *I have been buried.*

Just that. He was still her child, of course.

And I was still his son.

I remember going to Olga Dynestøl's barn. When I went there with Pappa all the animals were still hanging from the ceiling. There were three in all, and one was the elk Pappa had felled with a single shot, but I didn't know which. Hanging from their rear legs, all three looked alike: dark red, skinned, laid bare. Then, one by one, they were slowly lowered. Three men held the rope; two others sliced the carcass into ever smaller parts. A compass saw was used to cut the throat, and out shot a tidal wave of blood that had collected inside the animal. An extra feed sack was found and placed underneath. There was a sweet-acrid smell of tobacco smoke. The pulley on the tackle in the ceiling groaned as the carcass was lowered even further. A man held it as a large piece was sawn off. In this way the carcass decreased in size, and in the end it could be sawn into two equal halves. Two men held a thigh each, and as the carcass was parted they both reeled under the weight. Pieces of meat were cut off the carcass and carried over to the bandsaw where they were sliced into even smaller portions. The saw sang through the meat, groaned through the big thigh bones and stuttered through the ribs while one man kept squirting water so that the operation ran as smoothly as possible. I remember the spicy smell of sawn leg, and I wasn't sure whether I liked it or it made me feel nauseous. Finally the portions were thrown onto the slaughter table where bone, sinew and bloody shreds were cut off. The bullets were also dug out and placed beside each other on the edge of the table. After penetrating the bodies they had been transformed beyond recognition. Some had become little flowers with torn petals, others tiny bleeding birds. All were lined up as though in some way or other they had value, even though no one wanted them and ultimately they were discarded.

I was in Olga Dynestøl's barn watching the meat being cut up and apportioned in unequal heaps. Some were larger, some smaller. One heap consisted of a single piece of meat and some bits of bone that were nothing but dog food, others were so large that they needed several people to carry them.

Then the names were read out and the heaps distributed among those present. The men had tubs and carrier bags and black bin bags, which they filled. Then they left down the barn bridge and disappeared into the darkness. That was how Kasper left, that was how Sigurd left, and John, and all the others whose names I can't remember. They scooped up the meat and left through the barn door. That was how Pappa and I left. His name was called, and we went over to the heap that was ours. I helped to put the meat into the tub; it was strangely smooth and freezing to touch. There were bloody pieces of meat mixed with knuckles and hollow bones. We painstakingly collected it, filled the tub, Pappa lifted it, and it was very heavy, I could see that. I had to give him a hand as we walked down the slippery barn bridge, then we were in the darkness where the elk heads and the skin and all the bones were dumped. The head of the elk that Pappa had shot was there, too. The eye was still staring at me, but it had lost its gleam. Now it was all black. We continued down to the pickup, and on the way there it felt as if the black eye was following us and it saw who we really were.

Who do we see when we see ourselves?

Three, maybe four, seconds pass.

II.

SOME TIME AFTER PAPPA DIED I visited Grandma, and I told her about the autumn day he shot the elk. We both needed to talk about him, about what we could remember, how he had been, what he had said and done, who he actually was.

I talked about the strange feeling of being involved in something neither of us quite understood, but which we still mastered. As I mentioned, Pappa had never shot an elk before, and he never did again. But the one time he did, it was with a single bullet, right through the heart.

When I was finished she sat quite motionless with the diamond in her eye glittering. Then she said:

'I've never heard that before.'

'Well,' I said, 'now you know.'

When I was about to go, I said:

'By the way, I've begun to write.'

'Write?' she queried.

'Yes. I'm going to be a writer.'

She went quiet for a moment, then said:

'You mustn't ruin your life, even if your father is dead.'

I felt an immense fury bubble up, but I managed to retain a clear head.

'I am not ruining my life,' I declared coldly.

'No one can live from writing,' she said.

I didn't answer. I stood there in her chilly hallway at Heivollen thinking she had understood. After all, that was why I had told her. She wrote herself.

'You're going to be a lawyer,' she said in a cheerful tone, as if to put me on the right track.

'I am not going to be a lawyer,' I said undeterred, fixing my eyes on her, and at that point I think she realised I was serious.

'Can you write, then?' she asked in some confusion.

I took out an envelope and passed it to her. Inside was the text I had written that grey morning in my father's pickup. I had typed a fair copy and folded the sheet several times. Now she was holding the sheet in her hand as I walked towards the door. She followed me to the front steps and stood there as I started the car and reversed onto the road, and as I was driving away I turned and saw that she still hadn't gone in.

From that day henceforth she never mentioned the text once, but while tidying the house after she died I found the envelope among all her papers. It was open and the sheet unfolded. She had read it, and perhaps she had understood. But she hadn't said anything.

Yes, she had understood.

III.

AT FIRST HE DENIED EVERYTHING. He sat on the same chair that Alfred had occupied a few hours earlier and explained in detail how he had tackled fires. The telephone rang. Next was the alarm. Then the fire engine. Pumps, hoses, water, flames, house, all the people congregating, all the faces lit up by an intense glare and somehow losing their features. Or was it the opposite? Were all the features sharpened? *Did he know any of the people?* No. Yes. Maybe. He didn't have time to check. *Did he know any of those whose houses had been set on fire?* No. *Did he know Olav and Johanna Vatneli?* No. *Anders and Agnes Fjeldsgård?* No. That is, he knew who they were – Alma used to clean their house every fortnight. Besides, Finsland was a small community, everyone knew everyone else.

He was asked why he had joined the fire service. He leaned forwards. *Why?*

He told them there had never been a particular point when he had made up his mind to join. It was how it had always been. It had happened naturally. Ingemann had taken him along on the fire engine when he was a small boy. He told them about the two houses he had seen burn down, and how even then he had felt a deep desire to be a firefighter one day. To rescue burning houses from flames. Nevertheless, he told them nothing about the dog. Nothing about the wailing, which was like a sort of singing. *A deep desire?* Yes, he answered. A deep desire.

He was asked about his job at Kjevik. *Why had he applied to work there? Why?* He was a firefighter, wasn't he, and he needed a job. And then, of course, there were planes landing and taking off as well. *What was it about planes?* He couldn't say. But he liked planes. *But it was a lonely job, wasn't it?* Yes, it was. *And he was happy in his work?* Yes. *He liked being alone?* Yes. *Always?* No, not always, of course. *But often?* Yes. He was asked about his military service at the garrison in Porsanger. At this he went rigid for a second, but quickly relaxed again. He was asked why he had returned early. He had been discharged, he answered, sitting forwards in his chair. Drank some coffee from the cup that had been set down in front of him. *And what are your plans for the future?* He shrugged. Time would tell. That was noted down. Next, he was asked about the scars on his forehead. He told them about the accident but nothing about the bang to the head which he later maintained had changed his personality. Then they talked a bit about the football World Cup. *Was he following it?* Yes. *And his favourite team?* He didn't have one. Everything was noted down. Then he was asked about the fire in Skogen; why did he think it had been started in the morning and not at night? He had no idea. Then there was the fire at Dynestøl. And the two in Vatneli, and Sløgedal's barn. And the attempt in Solås. *Agnes Fjeldsgård saw the pyromaniac with her own eyes, didn't she?* Yes, he said. *She said it was a young man. Your age, perhaps?* Yes, he answered. Who could that be? *Who do you think?* A madman, he said. *A madman? How do you mean mad?* Someone who needs help. *Help?* Yes. Someone who needs help.

They took a break after the sun had gone down, and he joined two officers on the steps for a cigarette. It was still nice and warm; the air was sharp and clean after the short but intense downpours earlier in the afternoon. There was almost no traffic on the road, and there wasn't a soul to be seen. Dag was offered a light by one officer; he leaned forwards, cupped his hand around the flame for a brief instant before inhaling the smoke deep into his lungs and letting it out through his nose as his eyes narrowed. They stood outside for five minutes, maybe longer. No one said much. They smoked. The officers didn't seem to consider the possibility that he could leg it at any moment and disappear into the dense forest opposite the community centre. They smoked their cigarettes to the end, tossed them down and ground them into the gravel with the tips of their shoes. Then they all went back inside and resumed the interview.

At just after half past seven there was a three-minute item on NRK news from the very south of Norway, the small region of Finsland, which in recent weeks had been beset by an arsonist. Tranquil images flickered across the screen. Viewers saw a peaceful wooded hamlet, the sun was shining, it was summer, there was a burned-out house in Vatneli, there was the house with a cracked window belonging to Anders and Agnes in Solås, and there was Sløgedal's barn, with Alfred hosing it down.

The whole business was incomprehensible.

At approximately the same time, Bjarne Sløgedal went into hiding behind some bushes opposite his house at Nerbø. He carefully placed his rifle in the heather while he sat down. The rifle was loaded and he had taught himself how to flick off the safety catch. The sun was singeing the tops of the trees in the west, the air was full of insects, buzzing across the sky in all manner of unfathomable patterns. He had brought along a book, and settled down to read while it was still light; however, it was difficult to focus. The situation was too absurd. He, the cantor at Kristiansand Cathedral, trained at Oslo conservatory, the Juilliard School of Music in New York and the conservatory in The Hague, Holland, sitting hidden behind a bush facing his own home with a loaded rifle at his side. He, the man who, some days previously, had opened the International Church Music Festival in Kristiansand Cathedral with no less than Ingrid Bjoner, who sang Pergolesi's heavenly 'Stabat Mater' with her sister to a packed audience, he was sitting here now and listening for God knows what. The evening before he had been in the cathedral, now he was here, in the heather and grass, not knowing what was going to happen. If a stranger appeared down by the house, what would he do? Oh yes, he would fire three shots in the air. Three shots. And what if no one heard them? That possibility hadn't been discussed. It had been regarded as highly improbable that no one would hear the shots. And, anyway, the pyromaniac would be frightened and take to his heels. That was the plan. And there was a sheen of unreality over everything. It had turned cooler, and he pulled the anorak tighter around him. Every so often he raised his head. Was that a noise? A twig breaking? Someone coming down the road? No. Nothing. He looked down at the remains of the barn. Smoke was no longer rising from the ruins; however, small swarms of mosquitoes and other insects had collected and were dancing feverishly above the wet ash. Occasionally cars slowed and meandered past as the drivers ogled the destruction. No one saw him. No one knew he was sitting there. It was eleven and long past reading light. He had to strain his eyes to distinguish the ruins from the surrounding dark forest. He gingerly raised the rifle and placed it heavily in his lap.

At the same time Pappa was putting me to bed at Kleveland. I slept soundly after the long, hot day; he stood for a moment gazing at my tranquil face, at the closed eyes and the tiny mouth with the lips slightly apart, then he tiptoed out, leaving the door ajar. He whispered to Mamma in the kitchen, poured himself a cup of coffee, went to the front doorsteps and sat there with the steaming liquid and Grandad's rifle beside him as he listened to the night.

*

Later, as the summer darkness well and truly deepened, Olav Vatneli got out of bed in Knut Karlsen's cellar. He stood for a moment beside Johanna's bed. He had been sound asleep, dreamless. How long he didn't know to any degree of accuracy, but he remembered he had been screaming. But now he felt strangely clear-headed and perfectly calm. It was as though he had been far away, in another world, and now he had returned and saw everything through new eyes. He put on his trousers and one of the new shirts. He took the polished shoes, which were still stiff and unfamiliar on his feet, donned the new cardigan, placed the beret on his head and quietly left. He exchanged a few words with the policeman keeping watch outside. Then he continued down the slope to Odd Syvertsen's house. From there he could see the remains of his house. Walking in these new clothes, he felt like a stranger, someone who had been away for a long time, someone no one knew and who had got lost into the bargain. That was how it felt, that he had got lost or couldn't remember exactly where his house was, the house where he had lived for the last thirty-five years. He approached quietly and carefully, as if someone were slumbering in the ruins, someone who must not be awoken on any account. He made it to the road, stuffed his hands into his pockets and strolled on. Then he stopped, and there, around twenty metres away, he stood gawping. It was as if he could never have enough of the sight. He looked. And he looked. And he looked. He had said that he was going to see his fire-ravaged house, and that he was going to see it on his own, but he hadn't imagined that it would be at night. Now here he was, and he felt nothing. He was just empty and strangely clear-headed at the same time. He moved forwards, and the new, stiff shoes crunched in the gravel at every step. Then he stopped again and just looked. It was as if he could see right through everything. And indeed he could. He stood there looking right through the living room, the hall, the staircase and the kitchen. Warily, he walked into the garden, drew near the front steps strewn with charred wooden boards, ash and crushed glass. He sat down. He sat for a long time on the steps outside his house, which was now no more than air. He didn't have a thought in his head. There was dew on the grass, and mist hung over Lake Livannet, just as on the night of the fire. Then he caught sight of a hazy figure. He knew at once who it was. He rose slowly and deliberately, brushing the ash and glass off the seat of his trousers as the figure came into the garden and approached the stumps that were all that was left of the cherry tree. Olav was standing on the lowest step, but the figure didn't come any closer. They stood motionless, looking at each other, but neither of them spoke. What could they say? It was about twenty years since they had last seen each other. After two or three minutes the figure blurred, dissolved, and ultimately merged into the night air. Olav tarried on the lowest step, waiting, but nothing happened. In the end he headed for the wood shed, which was almost unscathed. He opened the door and went in. It was cold and damp inside, from all the water that had been sprayed over it. The earthen floor squelched under his shoes, it was completely black and for a second he was in the stomach of a whale. Still, he knew exactly where he was. The bell rang cheerfully as he dragged at the bicycle caught in some junk that had accumulated by the wheels. It came free and he trundled it out. The bike was as good as ever, just a bit rusty and covered with dust, and both tyres were flat. He leaned it against the shed wall, as it so often used to stand when Kåre was sitting at the kitchen table doing his homework, as if ready to whiz down the hill to Kilen. He tried the bell, and it sounded as good and clear as ever it had. Now he would have to come and take it if he needed it, he thought. And the punctured tyres wouldn't make any difference. For who needed air in tyres who himself was made of air?

IV.

THE DARKNESS LAY thick against the windows of the community centre, converting them into large, unclear mirrors. Everyone inside could look up at any moment and see a white indistinct face simultaneously peering up from another corner of the room, they could sit for a moment staring at this face that stared back with rapt attention before they realised: that's me.

The interrogation had gone on for several hours. The petrol cap was produced and placed on the table before him. It was white, and *FB* had been painted along the side in black, somewhat wobbly letters. He didn't bat an eyelid. *Do you know what this is?* he was asked. Yes, he replied. *And do you know where it was found?* No, he said. There was a silence. A car passed by on the road. He leaned forwards and had a sip from his cup. *Do you know who found it?* This time he didn't answer, just gave a casual shrug. Something was beginning to happen to his face, it was stiffening and the features were hardening. It was as if it was going to crack, but it didn't. It just got harder and harder.

And then.

Your father. It was your father who found it.

That was the moment everything came tumbling out.

It was 11.17 p.m.. The precise time was hammered in next to the confession. *Suspect confesses.* Interrogation provisionally terminated at 11.25 p.m.. Statement read and approved by the suspect. Police car requisitioned to transport prisoner to Kristiansand District Prison. There was a sudden atmosphere of departure in the council room. Officers went out for some fresh air. Dag joined them, but this time he was handcuffed and he wasn't given a cigarette. NTB, the news agency, was contacted. NRK broke the news on its late-night programme with a brief item. *This evening the arsonist recently spreading fear and panic through the small community of Finsland in Vest-Agder has been arrested by the police.* Seconds later there was an avalanche of telephone calls from every newspaper. Knut Koland sat answering all the enquiries with equanimity. There was not a great deal he could say. It was still too early. *Who is he? Who is the pyromaniac?* It's a young man from our region, he replied. Nothing else. The lad would be driven the thirty kilometres to Kristiansand, where he would be brought before the magistrates' court on a charge of arson with intent to murder. He called him 'the lad' all the way through. There was nothing else he had to say. Four words, that was all.

He has been arrested.

Slightly after half past twelve the car arrived to take him to the prison in Kristiansand. Two officers entered the council room, one gave a brief nod, then Dag got up slowly and followed them into the night. It was chilly, as the nights had been of late, and he ambled down to the waiting vehicle. He could see Alfred and Else's house at the end of the field, all the windows lit, the old shop beside the crossing dark and still, as was the chapel. The officers opened the rear door of the car; one officer placed his hand on Dag's head and carefully but firmly pushed him inside. The last he saw was the mist which also this night had appeared from nowhere, and hung so strangely white and pure and unsullied a few metres above the fields.

V.

LENSMANN KNUT KOLAND is interviewed in the Wednesday edition of *Fædrelandsvennen*, on 7 June 1978, where he informs readers that the pyromaniac has been remanded in custody for twelve weeks. He says nothing about the identity of the suspect. Or the fact that he is the fire chief's only son.

In the same newspaper, at the very bottom of the first page, a short article about the motorcycle accident: *Young Man Still Unconscious.*

Koland says in the interview that he hasn't slept for the last three days, and that he is glad it is all over. While emphasising the enormous human tragedy it masks. 'It's very sad, the whole business.'

In a way this is where everything begins.

*

Later that morning a car started at Skinnsnes. It was a dark red Ford Granada. The bumper was a bit compressed, there were remnants of earth and bark in the chipped paintwork by the Ford badge and one headlamp was slightly off-kilter. Ingemann was driving, with Alma beside him. They were both silent. She sat quite still with a bag in her lap and her hands folded over the clasp as if afraid someone would take it from her. The car turned right, passed the disused co-op building where the balcony was empty and the flagpole bare, as it had been for as long as anyone could remember. They drove downhill past the chapel, past the community centre, which was now completely deserted and quiet, continued gently down round the bends to Fjeldsgårdsletta, and there he accelerated and they raced past the old garage at the end of the plain. Soon they saw Lake Livannet, which lay there as it always had, glittering jauntily in the sun, but inshore the water was black and still. They parked in the shade outside Kaddeberg's shop, got out and mounted the five steps of the staircase you could access from both sides. They entered the chilly shop where Kaddeberg himself was behind the counter with a pencil stump behind one ear. He sent them a measured though friendly nod, and Ingemann nodded back. There was no one else inside, and Kaddeberg left them in peace. All they wanted was a card, with a picture of some flowers perhaps. Alma found a suitable one on the small stand by the till. It was plain, with a picture of a closed rose on the front and without any writing. She gave it to Ingemann and wandered back to the car while he paid. Before they set off she wrote: *In our thoughts.* Then the two names. Alma. Ingemann. That was all. Then they drove on. The car crawled up the hills past the post office. Alma gazed down at Lake Livannet glittering and quivering in the morning breeze. It was another radiant summer's day. It was going to be hot. The sun was already high in the sky, and she could feel perspiration on her back. They passed Konrad's light green house, continued past the road to Vatneli, and reaching the brow of the hill they turned right and into the yard of the little house with the splendid view of the lake and the dark blue hills to the west. The house belonged to Knut and Aslaug Karlsen. Alma felt dizzy. She put the card into her bag, then retrieved it and got out of the car. They stood for a moment in the hot sun, casting long, slender shadows. Ingemann took a comb from his rear pocket and swept it through his hair a couple of times, from the front to the back. She affected to adjust her hair, flicked some dust off her coat, checked her bag to make sure the card was there, but it wasn't, it was in her hand. Then they walked to the door together. Ingemann leaned forwards and knocked three times. They waited; neither of them had said a word since they left home. Now Alma said: 'I can't do this. I can't.'

They heard footsteps inside, a blurred figure came into sight behind the frosted glass, the door opened. It was Johanna. She had washed her face; her eyebrows were still marked by the fierce heat. She had no teeth in. She looked at Ingemann, then Alma. Her face lit up strangely when she realised who they were, as if age and sorrow were erased for an instant, as easy as anything. There was almost a kind of smile. She said: 'It's good you've both come.'

Then she opened the door wide. Inside, Olav was on his feet and waiting. They went in. Alma first, followed by

Ingemann. He closed the door gently after him. Silence, apart from the birds.

No one knows what the four of them talked about.

7

I.

IT EMERGED THAT THERE WERE three of him. It came out in all the letters he wrote to people in Finsland. He referred to himself in three ways.

There was Dag.

Then there was *the lad*.

And lastly *I*.

The lad, that was what Ingemann used to call him.

Perhaps it was *the lad* who lit the fires, and then Dag came along and put them out? I don't know. Perhaps it was the other way around: *the lad* put them out? But who in that case was *I*?

Letters streamed out of prison in the initial months. First and foremost he wrote to those people whose houses he had set alight. He wrote to Olav and Johanna Vatneli. He wrote to Kasper Kristiansen. He wrote to Bjarne Sløgedal. He wrote to Anders and Agnes Fjeldsgård.

But also to others. To Teresa. To Alfred. And to more. It has not been possible to obtain a clear overview. Most binned the letter after quickly skimming it. It was as if it were dirty, an infection they didn't want in the house. It was disposed of. Often the letters were extremely incoherent. Incoherent, yet somehow well written. When I asked Kasper what was in his letter, he had to give the question some thought.

Mm, what did he actually write?

Occasional reflections about God, about true believers and the godless. The godless, among whose number he counted himself. The days passed, and he sat writing on the top floor of the courthouse in the heart of Kristiansand. On 9 June the boy involved in the motorcycle accident in Kilen woke up in the intensive ward at the hospital. It was night. Suddenly he opened his eyes. He had survived, but some cerebral matter had of course leaked through his ears and he was a different person.

The weeks passed. On 25 June, after extra time, Argentina became the World Cup football champions at an over-crowded Mar del Plata stadium. He didn't notice. He was elsewhere. From his window he could see the sea, and the planes that flew in at a low altitude over the town. He could see above the spire and the luminous clock face on the cathedral tower, he could see down into the market square and the entrance to the Mølle pub. On Saturday evenings he knew there were people from Finsland inside, and when he saw that some were smoking outside the entrance and laughing, he opened the window a fraction and shouted down to them.

As the months went by the stream of letters slowly dwindled. In the end there were no more letters. In the end there was nothing. In the end you could wake at night and imagine it had all been a dream.

Autumn came. The sites of the fires lay like blackened wounds, but in the course of the summer, bit by bit, the grass had begun to grow through the ash. In September Kasper demolished the massive chimney at Dynestøl; at Vatneli the foundation walls were broken up and carted off; at the bottom of the Leipsland ridge there were the four corner-stones forming a perfect square. Winter came. In January Johanna died. She was a model of composure during her last days. Exactly like her son. A few days later it began to snow, at night when everyone was asleep. Large, jagged snowflakes fell over the forest, over the houses, still and white, the snow swirled right down into your dreams, and when you awoke the next day the world was new.

II.

THE COURT CASE CAME UP on Monday, 19 February 1979. The judge, Chief Justice Thor Oug, arrived in the courtrooms a few minutes before nine o'clock. Everyone was already in position: the counsel for the prosecution, detective inspector Håkon Skaugvoll, the counsel for the defence Bjørn Moldenes, as well as two psychiatric experts, Tor Sand Bekken from Eg Hospital and Karsten Nordahl from the Neurological Clinic. Dag was sitting beside the defence counsel. He seemed self-possessed, almost cheerful. Several times he leaned over to his counsel, whispered something in his ear, leaned back in his chair, stretched out his arms and smiled with contentment. Before the court sat, the door opened. In came a woman of around sixty, wearing a dark coat glittering with tiny raindrops, followed by a somewhat older man with smoothly combed hair. He was also dressed in black and was holding a lowered umbrella in one hand. They had made it. Alma stopped as she entered the room. As though her eyes had to get accustomed to the light. She adjusted her hair and brushed the raindrops off her coat. Her gaze was firm, but distant, as though she was actually somewhere else. She seemed to be looking through the seven people sitting there; she both saw them and she didn't. And perhaps that amounted to the same thing. Ingemann shook the umbrella, splashing the water all around, sent the judge a brief nod, and the prosecution counsel and the experts, without having a clue who was who. Then he sent Dag a wan smile. The usher led them past the prosecution bench, and they found seats at the very back where chairs had been set out for the public, and where only the *Fædrelandsvennen* reporter had been sitting.

Then the court was in session.

The prosecution counsel began by reading out the charges. There were ten in all. It took almost half an hour to complete this part. Dag sat intently watching the barrister. He listened with visible interest and some curiosity, as though he would discover at last what had really happened. When the prosecution counsel was finished, turning to Dag directly for the first time, he said: 'As the accused is suffering from a serious mental disorder and is therefore in terms of criminal law not responsible for his actions, I am asking you not to plead guilty or innocent but to say if it was you who performed the actions described in the list of charges.'

The response was a succinct, 'Yes'.

Dag was able, subject to minor alterations, to concur with the detective inspector's account of events.

It was him.

Thereafter followed a comprehensive description of all the fires. He was asked to state if there was any doubt regarding issues of detail. And he did that without any reluctance. He kept adding corrections and factual information, as though this were about another person, as though he had only been a witness, and in this way slowly the whole picture emerged. By the end of the morning, as the rain was replaced by sleet and finally wet, heavy snow, all the fires had been described as exhaustively as was feasible, from the striking of a match to the razing of the house. Or right from the moment he fetched the petrol can from Skinnsnes fire station until he sounded the alarm and got into the tender with sirens wailing and blue lights flashing. It was as if everything was brought back to life. All the questions and the answers that filled the gaps seemed to rekindle the flames. He was there again, he was alone in the darkness again, watching the flames grow. They crackled and wailed and soared into the sky, the sea of blaze surged, and deep inside could be heard a high-pitched note, a kind of song.

At half past eleven the court adjourned.

Alma and Ingemann, who had been silent and virtually motionless throughout, stayed where they were while the journalist, the prosecution counsel, the defence counsel and the two experts got up and disappeared down the corridor. Dag stayed put as well. For a brief period there were only the three of them in the room. Dag turned and smiled. Ingemann sat bent over, looking at the floor.

'How are things at home?' Dag asked.

'Fine,' Alma said. 'It's . . .'

'And you're in your workshop, Pappa, like before?'

Ingemann's head shot up.

'Yes, I am,' he answered. 'I have to be, of course.'

'And you, Mamma, I suppose you're still dusting my trophies?'

This time she couldn't produce an answer, she just smiled. It was a big, warm smile, the kind only she could give him and only he could receive. It lasted several seconds. Then it burst. She lurched forwards, gasping for breath as if she were being suffocated. Ingemann grabbed her by the arm as the usher bounded over; Dag got up, but didn't move from his place, and watched his mother being helped out of the room. From outside the sound of her sobbing could be heard, grossly magnified and distorted by the long corridor.

When the trial resumed, however, at just past twelve, both she and Ingemann were back. They wouldn't be deterred. She seemed to hold her head even higher than before. She looked right through everything and everyone and it was impossible to discuss or explain what she saw.

He was instructed to stand while his personal details were read out. Then he was instructed to sit down. He sat back in his chair while the prosecution counsel gave a brief résumé of his life. Born in 1957. Raised in the sixties and early seventies. A good-natured, helpful boy. Bright at school. Excellent references from everyone. Unblemished record. In short: a boy with a future.

And so.

*

The sentence was passed on Monday, 12 March. The day before my first birthday. It was a cold day with the wind coming from the north-east. The courtroom was the same as the one when the case came up a month earlier, but on this occasion neither Alma nor Ingemann was present. Alma had sent him a new, warm woolly jumper some days before and he was wearing it when he was led into the courtroom.

Chief Justice Oug didn't let the grass grow beneath his feet; as soon as court sat he delivered the judgement. Dag was sitting too, and followed with rapt attention.

There was no punishment and there were no insurance claims. Only five years' detention in a psychiatric hospital.

Then it was over. It had taken no more than a few minutes. Dag rose and walked into the corridor with his defence counsel and the two men who had accompanied him from Eg Mental Hospital. Was that all? No punishment? No prison? No compensation? Nothing. Just five years in a mental institution. He was almost elated as he crossed the newly polished courthouse floor to go out into the bitterly cold morning. Five years. What was five years? He would only be twenty-seven when he was released, and he would still have his life ahead of him. It was almost too good to be true. The car taking him to Eg was waiting, sparkling white in the sun. He stepped over the sheets of ice with a sense of jubilation. He felt like singing, or playing the piano. The only thing that marred his pleasure was that neither Alma nor Ingemann had been there to see him, their only son, being sentenced.

III.

HOW IN FACT had it all started?

In Lauvslandsmoen School loft when I found the photograph of myself? In the square in Mantua where all the dead had assembled to listen to me? Or was it long before that?

I sit with Lake Livannet before me, putting the pieces together. It rains for four successive days. Then the frost returns like the last throe of winter. April comes. The nights are mild and light. The scent of spring is in the air. Then one day the lake thaws. I flick through Grandma's diaries. After the year of sorrow when Grandad died the diaries become less and less emotional, except when Pappa sickens and dies ten years later. Towards the end there are only simple, mundane comments about odds and ends, people she meets, work in the house and garden. There is a regular flow of dry facts that can appear fairly inconsequential. Yet to me she feels quite close, precisely because of this scant communication.

Both she and Grandad feel closer. Their lives rise out of Grandma's neat handwriting.

During the last year of Grandad's life he got himself a summer job. In fact he was a pensioner, but a vacancy arose for a driver on City Train, the small tourist train that criss-crossed Kvadraturen, Kristiansand town centre, from the market square with the cathedral through Kongens gate, past old St Joseph's Hospital, where I was born, past Aladdin Cinema, then to the left by the theatre, along the esplanade, past sights such as King Christian's round fortress and back to the market square. They were looking for an experienced driver. And that was Grandad. He had been driving since before the war. He had had a Nash Ambassador, and had even driven it to Oslo and back.

He applied and got the job. And Grandma documents the news in May of 1987. It came to my ears through Pappa, who informed me with a wry smile. I didn't quite know whether to be proud or embarrassed. Surely no one else had a grandfather who was the driver of City Train? On the other hand, there were very few people who had a grandfather who wore an all-white uniform and a large, white chauffeur's cap. I was proud and embarrassed. These feelings would not let each other go, in the end they belonged together, or they clung to each other.

Grandad was in a picture postcard of Kristiansand. He was standing beside City Train in his handsome white uniform. In the background was the towering cathedral, and the sea of flowers and vegetables on the stalls in the square, and further back the top of the courthouse, where he fell down dead a few months later. I saw this postcard on the small stand in Kaddeberg's shop, the one by the till, which made a deep creaking sound whenever you rotated it. There were long rows of them, and they were mounted next to other, similar cards with pictures of elk and trolls, idyllic small Sørland towns with wooden fishing smacks chugging towards the wharf. The postcards with Grandad stayed on display even after he was gone. I remember it well because by then the pride and embarrassment had let go of each other and inside me there was a silent candle that hurt. City Train also wound its way round Kvadraturen the following summer but with a different driver in Grandad's white uniform. The driver was different, but Grandad was still driving on the postcard. For several years, I think. Whenever I was in Kaddeberg's the postcards were there as a constant reminder that he had passed on. I wished they would disappear, I wished someone would buy them one by one, send their best wishes and post them. But no one did. No one ever came to buy them. The cards were there, and Grandad was as erect as ever, the train as shining white. Once I did think of buying them all myself. Instead of having my piggy bank opened at the bank in the community centre, I could do it myself, smash it and place the money on Kaddeberg's counter. The only problem was that I had no one to whom I could send the cards. I couldn't write to any of my friends, that would be too strange, no one sent cards without a reason, and besides we lived so close to one other. All I could do was send them to people I didn't know. I could consult the telephone directory, pick a name I liked, someone I felt was bound to be nice and in need of a few words. I could send my regards and post it. I imagined people receiving the card and staring at the picture; they would see the man with the erect back that was my grandfather, and read what I had written, and their faces would light up in a smile.

In the diaries there are several photographs I haven't seen before, wedged firmly between the pages as if they are of particular significance. In one, Grandad is standing on the underwater part of the cliff, more or less in the middle of Lake Homevannet. To know exactly where it is you have to have swum out there. It protrudes perhaps thirty metres from the shore, and all of a sudden you can stand up. In the second picture, Grandma is standing in exactly the same place. First of all he swam out alone and stood on the rock while she stayed on land to take the photograph, then she swam out and he swam back. Or could it have been vice versa? He is already completely white-haired, lean and bony against the dark forest in the background; she is wearing the black swimming costume from my memory of her. They must have had great fun making this discovery, and must have looked forward to seeing the pictures after they had been developed. They would have been in their mid-sixties, in which case it was probably around 1980. They both loved swimming.

I read my way through time, through the spring, summer and autumn of 1998, and two days after Pappa's funeral she writes: *Rain and strong winds. Gaute was here this evening. It was so wonderful.*

That was all. It was the evening I told her I was going to be a writer.

Further on, towards the end of her life. The last entry she ever made. Tuesday, 28 October 2003: *I was given an injection. Nice weather, mild.*

I sit with the black, still Lake Livannet before me, remembering the final days and weeks. I was in Prague at that time. It was one evening towards the end of January 2004, and I was sitting in a church in the city centre. I don't recall its name. I had happened to be strolling past and saw a little notice advertising a concert. On the spur of the moment I had decided to buy a ticket through a little hatch by the entrance, then gone in and found myself a seat. It was early evening. Outside, people were pulling coats tight around themselves; it was around minus fifteen degrees and lightly drifting snow filled the floodlit sky above the market square and the old town and the towering city hall with the astronomical clock, which I had just walked past. The organist was playing a fantasy based on *Ave Maria*. Perhaps it was Gounod's version, the same one that Teresa and Bjarne Sløgedal presented in Finsland Church on the first day of peace in 1945? I don't know. It was, at any rate, music that filled me with a special silence.

Back in Norway, Grandma had been admitted to Sørland Hospital. A few hours before, a light metal instrument known as a punch forceps was inserted into her trachea to take a tissue sample from her lungs. It was supposed to be a standard intervention. Previously a bulge in one bronchus had been located, which was diagnosed as a change in tissue. Instead it turned out to be the main artery.

Her lungs filled with blood in seconds.

I had never anticipated that she would die. Not at that time. Not while I was in Prague and the entire church was filled with pure music and pure silence, and freezing cold. She couldn't die.

And I was proved right.

A passage was freed to the second bronchus so that she could get air. She woke up, and she told the doctor leaning over her where she had been: on a sandy beach by a large lake. When I heard this story I at once thought it had to be Lake Homevannet. It seemed obvious. Standing on the beach by the Kristiansand Automobilklub cabin, where the public bathing resort was, looking towards the underwater cliff.

Where you could suddenly rise out of the water. She had been standing there with an indescribable desire to start swimming, but then something had prevented her, and she had woken.

She asked the doctor to be allowed to return. He smiled and said they weren't permitted to offer that kind of help in hospitals.

It was as if the music that evening in Prague gave her a few more days. My sitting there and listening.

A few more. A few more. A few more.

Then there was another haemorrhage.

That was 4 February 2004.

But the greatest of these is love. This was the sentence from Paul's First Letter to the Corinthians that she wanted on the gravestone when Grandad died. I can clearly remember her saying what she wanted, even though I was only ten years old at the time. I happened to be in her kitchen when she told Pappa, and it must have left quite an impression because I can still remember it. I pretended I didn't understand what they were talking about. But I did. It was her opinion that *this* was the only fitting inscription for the gravestone; the sentence was the only one that could describe what she felt. And it is the one that was engraved beneath her name too.

She wrote that in her diary as well. Suddenly, on 15 December 1988, a good month after he died. More snow came in the night, and then it cleared and it was numbingly cold.

But the greatest of these is love.

Epilogue

THE FOLLOWING HAPPENED one Sunday in August 2005. I was at home in Finsland for a short period to finish a large writing project, a novel about Friedrich Jürgenson, the man who tried to interpret the voices of the dead.

On that particular Sunday afternoon I decided to go for a long walk to clear my head. I was alone at Kleveland, I let myself out and walked down the road. I continued as far as the main road and down towards the school. Passing Aasta's house, I saw a helicopter flying low over the pinelands behind the school. It made a wide arc, descended with circumspection and landed in the middle of the grass pitch in Lauvslandsmoen. I had been so preoccupied with my writing that I hadn't taken on board that this Sunday it would be possible to fly over our region in a helicopter. The flights were in connection with the Finsland Days, which every alternate year brought together many thousands of people for a selection of cattle shows, flea markets and fairs, and above all this hovered a helicopter. As I approached the pitch I had already made up my mind. There stood the helicopter like a big, slightly sad insect with its rotor blades still and bent over. I was somewhat taken aback because there was no queue as I had expected. The helicopter stood there, strangely alone; the pilot had clambered out and was speaking to a second man, also alone. It transpired that this was the last trip for the day and there had to be at least two passengers for it to take place. With my arrival we were quorate. I got into the front, and the man sat at the back. I noticed that he was wearing a red jacket that crackled as he twisted to find a comfortable position in his cramped seat, and I felt his knees push into the back of my own seat. Then I put on the headset and the door was closed securely from outside by an assistant on the ground. I fastened the belt across my chest, then the engine started. There was a sudden intense smell of fuel and I glanced over at the pilot with a little concern. Straightaway I heard his reassuring voice in the headset, the blades rotated faster and faster above us, the engine roared, the pilot gently eased the joystick, and then the helicopter started moving. It cautiously shook itself free of the ground, and we climbed into the air, as easy as anything. It had all happened so quickly; from sitting at home engrossed in my writing until I decided to go out, then spotting the helicopter, and now, racing forwards, forty, sixty, eighty metres above the ground, at first above the old school building where a few years later I was to find the photograph of myself, above the library where the road divided into four, above cars and people, above Aasta's house, and in the end above tall trees with long, frozen shadows. I was twenty-seven years old, and it was the first time I had seen everything from the air. I was sitting in a glass ball, the ground was down below, beneath my shoes, there was a terrible racket around me, but in the headset the pilot's voice was soft and pleasant. He asked me where I wanted to go, and I pointed towards Kleveland. We banked and for a moment I was hanging in the seat belt, weightless, we shot over the school again, over the main road, and suddenly we were over the house, my home, which I both recognised and had never seen before. We climbed even higher and I saw for kilometres around me. We were over Mandalselva River and I saw Lake Manflåvannet to the north and Lake Øydnavannet in the north-west; as we pitched around once again I hung in my seat belt and my heart was in my mouth. Then we were over Laudal. I saw the church under my right shoe. Down there are buried my great-grandparents, Danjell and Ingeborg, from whom I have nothing except for a handful of pictures, among them a hunting photograph where Danjell is holding up a dead hare by its rear legs as though it were poised for an enormous leap. Then we swung east, and soon we were over Lake Hessvannet and Hundershei, and somewhere down there Pappa shot the elk. Then we were over Lauvsland, and the top of the ski-jumping tower in Stubrokka, off which Pappa launched himself some time in the sixties. We flew directly above Olga Dynestøl's house and barn, now long occupied by people I didn't know. We arced northwards and at once I saw the church down to the left. I saw the two cemeteries, one like a diadem around the church, where Grandma and Grandad and several of the others who appeared in Mantua four years later are buried. Some distance from the church is the other churchyard, which was strictly rectangular, and where Kåre and Pappa lay, even though at that point I only knew about one of them.

It was about then that I craned my neck and caught a glimpse of the man sitting behind me. It took me a few seconds. And then:

That's him, isn't it?

We soared up again. I saw the forest and all the lakes scattered around and about. A rainbow was cast far into the land like gauzy yarn. I saw Lakes Gardvannet, Kvedansvannet, as shiny as liquid pewter. I saw lakes Stomnevannet, Sognevannet. I saw lakes Livannet, Trælevannet, Homevannet, where the sky was reflected between the pine-clad headlands, and all the time my mind was saying: That's him. That's the pyromaniac. We banked over Dynestøl in a deep curve and I felt as if I were lying outstretched on my side in the air. Finally we were over Lake Bordvannet and descending towards the grass pitch. And then at last I had terra firma beneath my feet, and could feel the weight of my own body.

He had sat behind me without saying a single word, and I watched him walk across the pitch, past all the parked cars. He had moved back to the region after he was released from Eg, and lived there for large parts of my childhood. Naturally, everyone knew who the pyromaniac was, even I. I simply hadn't recognised him at once.

That was the closest I ever came to him. That was the helicopter trip, and there was the letter to Alfred, which read as follows:

Kristiansand, 12 June 1978

Dear Alfred,

This may be the first letter you have received from a pyromaniac. You will have to make up your own mind about whether or not to regard me as a scoundrel. I hope you don't. Anyway, I will probably have to reckon on a fair stretch in prison. I am hoping the fact that I came clean to the police, that I haven't got a record and that I cooperated during the interviews will help to commute the sentence. I can't remember everything from the final night. It is like a fog. But you know all that, of course. I heard you were considering visiting me, and I would really appreciate it if you did. I may not be lonely exactly, but time drags when you don't have anyone else to talk to apart from yourself. Hope you will drop me a line anyway, but don't forget to write your address on the envelope. Take care, say hello to everyone I know and tell them I am well, considering the circumstances.

He had tried to return to life. During his confinement he trained as a nurse. That made sense; after all, he had always been good-natured. He served his period of detention and moved back to the house at Skinnsnes, but in his home district he noticed that people were afraid of him. He applied for job after job, but was never accepted; he tried to flee from himself and his past, travelling back to northern Norway, where he married and lived for some years. But it didn't work. The marriage broke up. He returned to the house at Skinnsnes. Alma was ill. It was said that she had smoker's legs, and it had got so bad that in the end she had to have both legs amputated. *Had them cut off*, as they say. She was in a wheelchair for the rest of her life. Alma died ten years to the day of the Dynestøl blaze, when Olga's house and barn went up in smoke. Dag tried to get his life back on track. He sat upstairs in his room listening to music while Ingemann sat alone in the living room. During the Winter Olympics in Lillehammer they watched the broadcasts together without speaking. They never spoke about what had happened almost sixteen years ago. In 1995, in the spring, Ingemann suddenly collapsed in his workshop. Dag was there and tried mouth-to-mouth resuscitation; he was, after all, a trained nurse. But it didn't help. His father died in the workshop with Dag kneeling beside him. When he realised what had happened Dag strode to the post, wound the handle and the alarm went off like a torrent from the heavens.

He stayed on in the house at Skinnsnes, alone, in the middle of the magic circle. Eventually he got himself a permanent job, as a council refuse collector. He started at the crack of dawn, drove round the village in a blue council pickup and threw the black bin bags on the back. It was work he enjoyed. He was made for this kind of work. He had a fixed route, and he began to time himself. No one could do the job as fast as he did, and he always managed to knock off a few seconds. He jumped out of the pickup, ran up the drive, slung the refuse on the back, jumped in and moved off. He collected the rubbish from my house at Kleveland, and from my grandmother at Heivollen. I remember it, I remember someone drawing my attention to the fact that it was him. I remember a certain expectant scepticism among people. *Who was it driving up at the crack of dawn? Wasn't that the pyromaniac? The boy who had rocked the region. The boy who reduced eight buildings to ashes and almost took the lives of four elderly people nigh on twenty years ago. Wasn't that him?* Now he was driving round and collecting people's rubbish. And he did it faster than anyone else. After a while there started to be complaints. He drove so fast that the bags slid off the back and were left lying in the road. I found a bag in a roadside ditch in Vollan once when I was walking away from the bus. But I wasn't aware of the connection. He was doing the route faster and faster, and was dropping even more rubbish. He screeched into the drive, jumped out, ran to collect the bag, slung it up, leaped behind the wheel, shot down the road. On. On. Next house. And the next. Faster. Ever faster in a frenetic spiral. Again he was the best, by some distance.

In the end he was given the boot. He sat at home in his large, empty house. Then one day he sold it and moved, but even though new people occupied the white house at Skinnsnes, it was still *the pyromaniac's house.* Now he was in free fall. He had nothing and no one. He who had been so wanted and so loved. He who had been so good-natured and so well liked by everyone. He who had been such a good boy. He who had had his whole life before him. What did he have now?

He was taking a first and last helicopter trip over the area he had loved so much and to which he had such an attachment, the region where it had become impossible for him to be. He sat staring down at the major and minor roads that wound through the forests. All these roads he knew so well, which had enabled him to make a quick getaway time after time during that summer twenty-seven years ago. He saw the white houses and the red barns. He saw the fire station almost hidden between the trees, he saw Sløgedal's house,

Teresa's house and Alfred and Else's house, he saw the community centre and the old chapel in Brandsvoll, which was no longer a chapel but a storehouse. And he saw the house at Skinnsnes, which in fact stood all on its own. He saw everything. But he didn't see any people.

He died almost two years later, in the spring of 2007, twenty-nine years after the fires. He was in bed alone and the main artery in his stomach burst. Blood seeped all through his body like ink. It must have been quite painless, almost like falling asleep, gliding into the beyond, going. Night, sleep came, and it came as a friend.

I am sitting on the first floor of the disused bank surveying Lake Livannet. I have moved the desk a bit, so that I can see only the sky and the lake beneath me, and it gives me the feeling of being on a ship's bridge. I see the clouds drifting in from the sea; the birch tree outside sways in the wind and the shadows wander up the wall as before. It is spring. I will soon have finished; there is no more to write. I get up, walk to the window and lay my hand against the glass.

And so.

Teresa writes about an incident that took place during the last summer Alma was alive. They were still neighbours and from the kitchen window she could see Ingemann wheeling Alma onto the veranda and into the morning sun. There she sat the entire morning, as a rule all alone, until the shadow of the house finally caught up with her, and then he wheeled her back inside. One day, however, Teresa had spotted Alma being pushed along the road on the flat. She was being pushed by a young man; it was only when they came closer that she could see who it was. He was walking behind her. At that time she had no idea that he had even been released from Eg. It was the last time she saw them together. They didn't seem to be saying anything, both had their gazes fixed intently ahead of them, and they cast two amorphous shadows that soon merged into one. The whole incident is written in the form of a letter. It is dated 23 May 1988. Ten days later, Alma died and was laid in her coffin without her legs. I don't know who Teresa was writing to, but the letter was never sent. It was neatly folded in an unaddressed envelope. It starts as follows: *My dear, Let me put this into words before I burn.*

A Note on the Author

Gaute Heivoll made his debut in 2002 with the prose collection *Liten dansende gutt* [*Small Dancing Boy*], and since then has written poetry, children's books, short stories and novels. Heivoll was recipient of the 2003 Tiden-prisen Prize. In 2006 he was the Norwegian representative to the Literary Festival Project Scritture Giovanni and his short-story 'Dr Gordeau' was translated into English, German and Italian.